# INTIMATE ENEMIES

'They're a bit startling, aren't they, sir? said Fielding, with a wry look.

'Yes,' Anderson admitted, looking slowly around. All the pictures were equally strong. As photographs, they would not have been to his taste. But they were art, fine art; beautifully drawn, imaginatively composed, indecently seductive. He could have gazed all day, but there was something obscene about this alluring material disposed around a corpse. He gave Fielding his full attention. 'Now, Pat.'

'Yes, sir. We found the body just as you see it. Footprints outside the door, and some in the hall, and the dead woman's bicycle propped up outside. Nothing else. Nick and I have looked everywhere in here, everywhere we could look without upsetting stuff that Forensics will need. Nothing. No weapon, no substances, nothing.'

A MOMENT OF MADNESS
A Fairfax and Vallance mystery

DEADLY AFFAIRS
A John Anderson mystery

INTIMATE ENEMIES
A John Anderson mystery

# INTIMATE ENEMIES

by
Juliet Hastings
A John Anderson mystery

**CRIME & PASSION**

First published in Great Britain in 1997 by
Crime & Passion
an imprint of Virgin Publishing Ltd
332 Ladbroke Grove
London W10 5AH

Crime & Passion series editor: Pan Pantziarka

ISBN 0 7535 0155 4

Typeset by Avon Dataset Ltd, Bidford on Avon, B50 4JH
Printed and bound in Great Britain by
Mackays of Chatham PLC, Chatham, Kent

Was it a friend or foe that spread these lies?
. . . 'Twas one of my most intimate enemies.

Dante Gabriel Rossetti, *Fragment*

# ONE
## Wednesday 7.30 p.m.

Andrew was fractious, and even after Chris had read his favourite story twice through he didn't calm down. Chris thought of letting him whimper, but then he would be bound to wake Jessica and all his work in getting her to sleep would be wasted. In the end he picked Andrew up and walked around the room with him, pointing out the animals on the wallpaper until the little boy stopped grizzling and began to droop. Then he put him to bed, careful not to wake him up. Andrew had his thumb in his mouth again and Chris gently detached it and kissed the rumpled hair. Three-year-olds smelt sweeter than any woman's perfume.

Was Andrew's skin hot? Chris frowned as he turned off the light. He trotted down the stairs and pushed open the door to the living room. 'Franny. Franny?'

'In here,' said his wife's voice from the study.

'Franny, I think Andrew's got a temperature.' He squeezed his way into the study past the stacks of pictures which almost blocked the door. Francesca was standing by her desk, riffling through piles of paper. She didn't turn as he came in. 'Franny?'

'What?' She glanced briefly over her shoulder and raked her hand through her long auburn hair. The light from the desk lamp caught in its heavy waves and shone. He felt the familiar wring at his heart. He had never felt differently about her, never since the day they met. Even now, when she seemed

1

hardly to care about her children, never mind him, even now he wanted her.

'I think Andrew's got a temperature,' he said, with more patience than he felt.

She rolled her eyes. 'Oh, God. That's all we need.' She didn't stop searching through the papers, and her expression was anxious and abstracted. 'Well, keep an eye on him, darling. It's probably just a bug, but you never know, it could be meningitis or God knows what. Pop up and check on him in a couple of hours, hmm?'

Since he lost his job she had often seemed to treat him more as a servant than a husband, but this was too much. 'What about you?' he demanded angrily. 'What the hell are you going to be doing all evening? Sitting in front of the telly with a glass of wine?'

She sighed and turned to face him. 'Chris, I've got things to do. I have to go back to the gallery tonight.'

Her eyes met his, half wary, half defiant. He stared at her, feeling sick. He knew what that expression meant. His knuckles whitened and he could hardly make his taut lips move. 'You're going to meet him, aren't you?' he said thickly.

'Oh, for God's sake.' Francesca grabbed up a handful of papers, stuffed them into her briefcase and pushed past him into the hall. 'Him, him, him. How often do I have to tell you, Chris, there is no *him*. I've just got work to do.'

How could she do this? He went after her and caught hold of her elbow. She turned to face him, eyes wide, lips tense. 'Don't lie to me,' he insisted, pulling her close. 'You've been different ever since I lost my job, Franny. I know there's someone else. Who is he? Some still-high-flying executive you sold a dirty picture to?'

'Chris!' She flung up her hands, shaking herself free. 'Just stop it, will you?'

He knew every line of her closed, shielded face. He had seen it gasping in the act of love and tormented with the pain of childbirth. Now it showed that she loved someone else, and it was more than he could bear. 'Don't go,' he begged her.

She turned her head away. 'I have to. I'm – busy.'

'What with?' She didn't reply. 'Franny, don't go. Stay here. Franny, I love you.'

At that she looked at him with an expression almost of pity. Pity! It was the final straw. He caught hold of her and pulled her towards him and plunged his mouth onto hers, kissing her with the ferocity of utter desperation.

For a moment she resisted, her limbs tensed stiffly against his. But he knew her body almost as well as he knew his own, and when he thrust his tongue into her mouth and pushed his hand between them to fondle her breast she gave a sudden startled gasp and softened. He wrapped his arm around her waist and half pulled her, half guided her into the living room, never lifting his lips from hers. She responded hungrily now, arching against him as they fell together onto the sofa. That was a quick change, bloody quick, too bloody quick. She'd probably been thinking about the man who was waiting for her at the gallery. She was probably all fired up with imagining what they would do together. He slid his hand up under her heavy skirt and wasn't surprised to feel the crotch of her panties already wet. No, not for him, for that faceless bastard who wanted to take her from him.

'Chris,' Francesca gasped, pulling free, 'what's got into you?'

He didn't answer, just tugged the panties down and kissed her again. As his tongue entered her mouth his fingers found her sex and slipped inside her. She was so wet it was easy. He wanted to sob with the shame of finding his wife aroused by the thought of her lover. But then she would pity him even more for the jobless wimp he was. Instead he pulled his fingers out of her and fumbled for his fly and dragged it open. His cock was stiff and eager. Without a word he rolled on top of her and thrust blindly, the hot head of his penis searching for the warm haven of her body. After a moment he found the place and slid up into her, crying out with familiar ecstasy.

'Oh God,' Franny moaned. She pulled at the buttons on her blouse, tugging it open so that she could bare her breasts to him. He made a sound like a sob and fastened his lips to her nipple, sucking so hard that she gasped. Her hips lifted towards him and he responded with a sharp desperate thrust and then he was out of control, clutching at her as he lunged

3

feraciously into her, his mind spinning with tormented desire and a half-formed hope that he could screw her into loving him again.

It couldn't last. She cried out and writhed as he plunged and suddenly he felt his orgasm coming, the seed pulsing and burning as it jetted out of him. He wasn't ready, he hadn't meant it. He buried his head in Franny's shining hair and moaned, 'No, no.'

Then everything was quiet except for the pounding of blood in his ears. He shut his eyes tightly, fighting tears. In a smothered voice he said, 'Franny, I love you.'

'Oh, Chris.' Her fingers stroked his hair and the back of his neck. Was that a new note in her voice? He lifted his head quickly, scalded with hope.

But all he saw in her flushed face was pity, and as if she had slapped him he pulled away from her and sat on the edge of the sofa, legs spread, elbows on knees, hands pressed to his forehead. For a moment Francesca didn't move. Then she got up and restored herself to decency. He could sense her lifting her breasts back into the cups of her bra, fastening the buttons on her blouse, tucking herself in. But he wouldn't look at her. He couldn't.

Soon she was tidy. She stroked her hand across her hair a couple of times, then said diffidently, 'Chris, I'm going now.'

'Goodbye,' he said, without looking up.

'I won't be late back,' she said. 'At least I hope not. If I'm delayed I'll phone.'

Delayed! What did that mean? That she'd be late back if her lover managed to get it up more than once? Still staring at the carpet, he said, 'All right.'

'You'll keep an eye on Andrew, won't you,' she said from the door.

He lifted his head, knowing that his face showed what he felt at her betrayal. She recoiled slightly, then without another word turned away from him and went out into the hall. He stared after her, and as he heard the back door close his hands clenched tightly, as if he was crushing something.

# TWO
## Thursday 12.15 a.m.

There was no point in trying to park in Mill Lane, it was hopelessly narrow and always nose to tail with residents' cars. Detective Chief Inspector John Anderson turned his BMW into one of the white-painted spaces on the empty marketplace and sat for a few minutes with his headlights on and the wipers sweeping the drizzle from the windscreen at eight-second intervals.

What he could see of Wressingham village looked depressing with its twee attractions soaked by September rain. The street lamps reflected palely from the damp tarmac and cobbles and the only other light was provided by a few half-illuminated windows. From every shop hung baskets of flowers, drooping and heavy in the wet. The red and yellow blooms looked black by the light of the helium lamps. Altogether it was much as he remembered it. He had avoided the place for two years, since it had been the site of the terminal disagreement between him and his then wife, Sarah.

There was work to do, and he opened the car door and stepped out into the cold drizzle, turning up the collar of his raincoat. But as he walked across the square he found his eyes drawn to the front of the building opposite the pub. It was a boutique now, but then it had been a restaurant, a very pleasant place, one of their favourite haunts. He had wanted to apologise to Sarah for some offence or other, something so trivial that now he couldn't even remember it. He had suggested a meal, and they had driven out to Wressingham in carefully polite conversation, and there was the restaurant, dark and shuttered, with a notice on the front announcing that it had gone into liquidation.

He'd never understood why it had been the last straw, but Sarah had snatched the car keys from him and driven away, and from that moment his marriage had also been in liquidation. He had nurtured an unreasonable hatred against the place ever since, and was obscurely content that his dislike was finally justified. Wressingham deserved murder.

His footsteps echoed as he crossed the cobbles. Normally the residents of a respectable Surrey village would be fast asleep by this time, but now his eye was caught by movement and sudden splinters of light above him as people pulled back their curtains to examine the new arrival. Things were not normal tonight.

Around the corner in Mill Lane the congestion was as bad as he had expected. About a hundred yards from the corner of the marketplace a cluster of vehicles was pulled up outside a small half-timbered shop front; a marked police car, two unmarked cars which he recognised as belonging to CID, and an ambulance. The interior lights of the ambulance were on, and there were two uniformed officers sitting in the marked car. As he approached, one of them got out and shone a torch on his face, then said, 'Sorry, sir,' hastily switched the torch off and got back into the car.

A small, slight figure in a heavy jacket appeared in the doorway of the shop and bolted over to one of the unmarked cars. Anderson walked faster. After a few moments the figure emerged and straightened, revealing a pale face framed by wisps of damp hair and eyes which in the harsh light from the shop window looked as dark as pits. Detective Sergeant Patricia Fielding turned as she heard him coming and her strained tense face showed relief. 'Sir,' she said, 'I'm glad you got here so quickly.'

He pushed his hands deep into the pockets of his trenchcoat and looked up at the shop front. It was a smart, white-painted window, empty except for four large easels. The writing above it read LYONS GALLERY: FINE ART. Beside the sign was a security alarm, silent. It had not done its job. He looked speculatively at the alarm for a moment while the drizzle drifted into his face, then met Fielding's eyes. She looked anxious, but this should be nothing new to her. 'What's the story, Pat?'

'Come inside,' she said. 'It's miserable out here. I've just been trying to find out where the hell Forensics are.'

'Asleep again,' he said. He had been asleep too, but he woke up fast. It had taken him no more than forty minutes from the time he received the call to arriving in Wressingham.

He let Fielding lead the way through the open door of the gallery. Inside the ceiling was low and beamed. The walls were covered with pictures, good ones, mostly in oils but with a few watercolours. At another time he would have liked to inspect them. Instead he looked down at the floor. 'No tape?' he asked sharply.

'Whoever did it came in through the back door, sir.' Fielding sounded calmer than she looked. 'Into the gallery office. It's through this, ah, room.'

Surely he couldn't have heard a laugh in her voice. But he was sure that he had. For a moment he was angry, because murder was never funny. He went through the narrow doorway. The gallery was medieval, one low room after another. This one, too, was lined with pictures. He glanced at them and at once understood Fielding's odd tone.

The subject matter was far from the anodyne landscapes and still lifes of the front of the gallery. These walls pulsed with bare flesh, male and female nudes singly and in groups. Nothing really explicit, but not the sort of thing you would hang in the drawing room, either.

'If you think these are good, sir,' said Fielding, 'wait until you see the ones at the scene.'

There wasn't time to look, but even with just a glance he could see that some of the pictures were in fact very good: well composed and excellently realised. One by the door caught his eye, a pen and ink study of a naked woman stretching which positively shone with life. Apart from her face, she looked startlingly like Catherine: small breasts, narrow waist, splendid rounded haunches. Even the tumble

7

of shoulder-length hair was right. He had not seen Catherine for months. The picture reminded him sharply how much he wanted to.

The sudden glare of the photographer's flashgun called him back to himself. He went on into a narrow corridor leading from the room towards the back of the building. Plastic sheeting was laid over the stone flags. 'There are footprints here,' Fielding said as the flashgun flared again. 'That's the scene, sir, on the left.'

'Who's here with you?'

'Nick Parker, sir. The uniforms in the marked car are the ones who found the body. I've debriefed them, but I thought you might want to talk to them as well.'

'Nick Parker.' The new boy. 'Is he all right?'

'He's a bit shaken, sir. First time at a murder; you know what it's like.'

He knew what it had been like for him. He remembered his first murder as clearly as everyone did. An everyday killing, but to him extraordinary. He had felt revulsion, but not at the blood and the horror of violent death. What had revolted him was the chaos, the injustice. He had stood looking down at the body, filled with absolute certainty that he had the power to do what should be done.

It didn't sound as if Parker felt the same way. 'What's he doing?' Anderson asked.

'There are all sorts of prints and stuff outside the back door. The rain'll wash them away if we don't do something about it. I've got him rigging up a shelter.'

'Good.' That was a sensible thing to give a new boy to do. Fielding was very dependable. He took the pair of disposable gloves that she handed him and pulled them on. 'Let's go, then.'

The photographer nodded to him as he entered. 'I've finished, sir.' He withdrew, clutching his apparatus, leaving the room to Anderson and Fielding.

It was not a big room, and his peripheral vision told him that its walls were crowded with pictures. But he didn't look at them, because the tableau before him demanded his total attention.

There was a desk below the window, strewn with papers, and a big leather swivel chair under the desk. Beside the desk, next to a battered velvet chaise longue, a woman was kneeling. She was dressed in a smart blouse and a long skirt. Her thick, glossy auburn hair was caught in a loose ponytail behind her bowed head, and her hands were tied in her lap.

For a moment he could hardly believe that she was dead. Only her total stillness showed that he was looking at a body, not a living woman. He took a few steps towards her and dropped to one knee on the cold stone flags, breathing shallowly as he bent his head to examine her face.

She was an attractive woman in her middle thirties. Her eyes were open and already slightly glazed. Her skin was pale, even her lips. There were no marks, no signs of violence. He leant closer, wondering if the smell of some substance might linger on her mouth, but there was nothing. The absence of breath was sharply poignant. He pushed himself to his feet and looked down at her again. The kneeling posture, the bowed head, the bound hands, made her look as if she was waiting for execution.

He looked up quickly at Fielding. 'What have you found, Pat? Any weapon?'

She shook her head. 'Nothing, sir. Absolutely nothing. And look at her! If she hadn't been left like that, would you have thought it was murder?'

They stood side by side, looking down at the kneeling woman. Fielding suddenly gave a convulsive shiver and he glanced at her in surprise. 'I'm sorry, sir,' she said, 'but it's really horrible. I mean, it's not even violent, it's like some awful ceremony. Didn't she fight? Didn't she want to live?'

Typical Fielding, empathising instantly. What was the point of speculating before it was even clear how the woman had died? He said coldly, 'Tell me what you know so far, Pat.'

Fielding stiffened; his tone was not lost on her. 'Yes, sir,' she said, putting back her head. 'The dead woman is Francesca Lyons. Age thirty-six.'

'Who identified her?'

'PC Watkins, in the squad car, sir. He advised her last year when she was having the security system fitted.' Fielding jerked her chin at the security sensor in the corner of the room. 'This is her gallery. She lives about half a mile away, down Hobkettle Lane on the other side of the village. At 11.10 this evening her husband Chris called the station and said he was anxious because she was late home. She had called earlier to say that she was expecting to be back before eleven. The squad car outside was in the vicinity so they stopped by. They arrived at about 11.20 and saw a light on at the back, so they went around to the back door. The door was slightly open and they called out and went in. They found Mrs Lyons just as you see and radioed for CID. Nick and I got here at 11.35 and called you straight away.'

He frowned. 'When did she telephone her husband?'

'He said at about 10 p.m. sir.'

'And he called the police because she was late? Why didn't he just come and look for her?'

'Apparently they've got children, sir, and he couldn't leave them.'

He rested his chin on his hand, looking narrowly at the corpse. There was no need to ask about time of death, with a phone call neatly establishing that the dead woman had been alive not much more than two hours ago. 'What did you find when you got here?'

Fielding began to reply, but as she spoke he lifted his eyes to look around the room and saw the pictures on the walls. He forgot to listen to what Fielding was saying. These pictures were not just tastefully arousing, they were graphic. Nearest to him was a graceful pencil drawing of a woman straddling a man. Her buttocks were the centre of the picture, and the man's hands were clasping them, pulling them further apart as if offering her to the viewer. He swallowed and tore his eyes away. 'You'd better run that past me again.'

'They're a bit startling, aren't they, sir?' said Fielding, with a wry look.

'Yes,' he admitted, looking slowly around. All the pictures were equally strong. As photographs, they would not have been to his taste. But they were art, fine art; beautifully drawn, imaginatively composed, indecently seductive. He could have gazed all day, but there was something obscene about this alluring material disposed around a corpse. He gave Fielding his full attention. 'Now, Pat.'

'Yes, sir. We found the body just as you see it. Footprints outside the door, and some in the hall, and the dead woman's bicycle propped up outside. Nothing else. Nick and I have looked everywhere in here, everywhere we could look without upsetting stuff that Forensics will need. Nothing. No weapon, no substances, nothing.'

'Nothing.' He looked again at the body and noticed that whoever had tied Francesca Lyons' hands had done so in a most unusual manner. Her wrists were not crossed, as he would have expected, but held so that her palms were pressed together, her fingers laced in an attitude almost of prayer. The binding was a fine silk scarf, gauzy chiffon stretched until it was quite opaque. 'Did we get a picture of this?'

'Yes, sir.' Fielding's lips drew slightly back from her teeth. 'The position of the hands, and the knot, sir. Odd, isn't it?'

He nodded. 'Yes.'

Footsteps sounded in the hall and they both looked up. DC Nick Parker appeared in the doorway. He had only been in CID six weeks, and he still looked unused to plain clothes. The lapels of his cheap blue suit were crinkled with rain and his red hair stood up in spikes as if he had received an electric shock. Fielding ought to tell him that appearances mattered, even after midnight. Parker gave the body a hunted glance, then saw Anderson and jumped. 'Oh, er, evening, sir.'

'Nick.' Anderson nodded evenly.

'How are you doing, Nick?' Fielding asked.

Parker's eyes strayed to the corpse and he swallowed hard. 'I've got a piece of polythene sheet strung up,' he said, his voice harsh with bravado. 'Bit of a bugger to do without treading on the ground. I've done my best, Sarge.'

'Did you find anything?'

'Not a sausage. It's pitch black out there.' He jerked his head towards the front of the building. 'Think I heard a car, though. Must be Forensics, or the surgeon.'

Fielding glanced at Anderson. 'Do you want to brief them, sir?'

He shook his head. 'You do it, Pat. I'll go and have a word

with PC Watkins. Then we'll need to go and talk to the husband, what was his name? Chris?'

'Chris Lyons, sir,' she confirmed.

His eyes wanted to return to the pictures on the walls, but he wasn't going to show his interest with Parker standing in the doorway. He looked again at the corpse of Francesca Lyons, fixing every detail in his mind. Who had killed this woman, so softly as to leave no mark, and then left her in this strange ritual position so that anybody finding her must know that she was murdered?

As he turned to leave the room something caught his eye. It was the flashing light of the answering machine on the desk beside the telephone. He turned back and went over to look at it. Aloud he said, 'There are messages recorded on this machine.'

Fielding swung around. 'Messages?' She hurried over to stand beside him.

'I thought you said you checked this room, Pat.'

She flung a scalding glance at Parker, whose dead-white face slowly flushed dark red. 'I thought we had checked it, sir. I'm sorry.'

He raised his eyebrows and then extended one finger and pressed the button marked MESSAGES. The machine whirred briefly as it rewound, then clicked forward into PLAY mode.

A bleep was followed by a male voice. 'Fran, pick up the phone, it's me. Fran? –' The message was cut off as someone, presumably Francesca, lifted the receiver.

Another bleep. Anderson met Fielding's eyes. Her face was pale and bright and she was breathing shallowly.

'I'm surprised you're not there,' said a different voice. 'I'm coming anyway.'

There was a click, and silence.

Just after 1 a.m. Fielding tucked the unmarked police car into the side of Hobkettle Lane and turned off the engine. Anderson unfastened his seat belt and opened the passenger door. The lights of number 70 gleamed through the high wet holly hedge.

'I hate this part,' said Fielding.

'We all do. You go first, Pat. I'll watch his face. Let's see if this is news to him.'

Fielding nodded and set off up the gravel drive towards the house, a handsome Victorian villa covered in Virginia creeper. He followed her, a few yards back. There was movement behind the stained glass windows of the hall, and before Fielding reached the door it opened.

A tall man stood silhouetted in the doorway, running his hand over and over again through his hair. 'Franny?' The voice was trembling.

'Chris Lyons?' asked Fielding.

'Yes.' The outside light came on, revealing a face that would have been handsome if it hadn't been so white and strained. 'Where's Franny?'

Franny, not Fran. So who had left that message on Francesca's answering machine? Not her husband, it seemed. Fielding said, 'I'm Detective Sergeant Patricia Fielding, from Surrey Police. This is Detective Chief Inspector Anderson. May we come in?'

Chris stood back from the door, holding it open. His knuckles were white. As he entered, Anderson caught the whiff of alcohol on the man's breath. Chris glanced at him once, then returned his attention to Fielding. She gently put her hand to the door to close it, and Chris let go as if he had been bitten.

'Mr Lyons,' said Fielding gently, 'I'm afraid that your wife is dead.'

For a moment Chris stood completely still, not even trembling. Then, slowly and jerkily, he lifted his hand to his throat and clutched at it as if he couldn't breathe. Without a word he turned away from them and walked unsteadily across the black and white tiles to an open door at the back of the hall. Fielding glanced at Anderson and he nodded. They followed Chris through the door and into a big, comfortable living room, open plan to a limewashed kitchen. The floor was scattered with toys. Chris sat down with a grunt on a faded overstuffed sofa and reached for the bottle of whisky on the side table. His hand shook as he poured a good inch into a crystal tumbler.

13

It was so hard to tell whether this was genuine or staged. People reacted very differently to shock and grief. Perhaps Chris was utterly surprised; perhaps not. Anderson sat down beside him on the sofa and watched without comment as Chris lifted the glass unsteadily to his lips. 'Mr Lyons.'

The whisky vanished in one gulp. Chris gasped, retched and reached for the bottle again. Anderson glanced at Fielding and she gently but firmly took the glass from Chris. He didn't protest, just folded his hands in his lap and stared at the carpet. 'Mr Lyons,' Anderson said, 'I'm sorry we have to bother you, but please understand. We believe that your wife was murdered. I need to ask you some questions.'

Chris's shoulders began to shake. He covered his face with his hands and his breathing racked him. Anderson looked up at Fielding and she raised one shoulder in an infinitesimal shrug. She obviously wasn't convinced, either.

'Mr Lyons,' Anderson said again.

Chris jerked up his head. His lips folded tightly together and he drew in a long sharp breath through his nostrils. 'Yes.'

'Tell us what happened this evening. Why did you call the police?'

After a little silence, Chris said, 'I loved her.'

Moving slowly, Fielding sat down in a chair opposite the sofa. Anderson caught her eye, then returned his attention to Chris. The man was more than half drunk. There was no need to say anything, he would soon go on without prompting.

'I loved her,' Chris repeated thickly, knotting his fingers together. 'But it didn't make any difference, did it? Not after I lost my job.'

Fielding stirred uncomfortably on her chair. She was often impatient at this point. Perhaps she still didn't really believe that people would reveal more if you let them go about it in their own way. Anderson nodded at Chris and said quietly, 'So tell me what happened.'

'I lost my job,' said Chris again. 'Wasn't my fault, was it? Takeovers – downsizing – it happens all the time. Francesca started coming home from the gallery later and later. It used to be her hobby, know what I mean? Just something for her to do while I was away, I was away a lot. But now it was important. It paid the mortgage. God help me.' He was talking as if to himself, staring into mid-air, quite still except for those wringing hands. Sometimes people confessed in this state. It was just as well that Fielding was there too.

There was a silence. Chris's head slowly drooped forward and he let out a smothered sob. Anderson frowned, then said, 'And tonight, Chris. What happened tonight?'

'Same as usual, wasn't it,' said Chris. His voice was slurred and bitter. 'Back off to the gallery after dinner. She said she had work to do. I knew better.'

Out of the corner of his eye, Anderson saw Fielding sit up straighter in her chair, her tired face brightening. 'So if it wasn't work, Chris,' he asked, 'what was it?'

Chris lifted his head and at last looked Anderson straight in the eye. His mouth was slack with the whisky and his pupils were small pinpricks of rage. 'What do you think?' he demanded. 'She went to meet her lover, didn't she. That's who killed her. Rely on it.'

So, was this just a story to put the police off the scent? Probably not; Chris looked angry enough for it to be true. Just how angry was he? 'How long had you known that she had a lover?' Anderson asked evenly.

'Christ!' Chris jumped to his feet and began to pace around the room, his fists pounding at the air. Anderson and Fielding both got up too and watched him, wary of violence. 'She never told me,' Chris panted. 'She denied it. She lied to me, I knew she was lying. She said it was my imagination but I knew it wasn't.'

'So you didn't know who her lover was.'

'No!' Chris shouted. He stalked towards Anderson, his face tense and white. He looked ready to fight, and Anderson lifted his head and checked his footing. Chris stopped only a yard from him and said in a thick growl, 'Don't think I didn't wonder about catching them at it. I did. But I always had to look after the bloody kids, didn't I? I couldn't leave them to catch Franny screwing some –'

As if he had only just heard himself he stopped speaking and wiped his face with his hand. 'Franny,' he said. Tears filled his eyes and spilled over. 'Franny.'

There was a sound from above them. All three of them looked up at the ceiling. A child's voice whimpered, 'Mummy.'

'Oh God,' whispered Chris. Andrew. 'What'll I tell them?'

'Mummy,' called the child, more plaintively now. 'Mummy!'

'Don't tell them anything tonight,' Anderson said. Chris stared at him, trembling. 'Think about it in the morning. Let me call someone for you. Who would be able to come here and help you?'

'Help me,' Chris repeated, as if the words made no sense. For a moment it looked as if he couldn't reply. Then the child upstairs began to cry, a thin, scratchy whimpering. As if galvanised Chris said quickly, 'Call Sophie. Francesca's sister. Third button on the phone. Call her.' He flung out of the room and ran up the stairs and Anderson heard his voice in the room above, murmuring some meaningless comfort.

Fielding looked as if she had been sucking a lemon. 'Do you call the sister, sir, or shall I?'

'You told him,' he said, letting out a long breath. 'My turn.'

It was nearly 2 a.m. before they left the house. The rain had begun again. Fielding let Anderson into the car, then scrambled in behind the steering wheel. 'Do you want to do anything else tonight, sir?'

He shook his head. 'The rest can wait till the morning. Drop me at my car, will you, Pat?'

'I'll go back to the station,' Fielding volunteered. 'Get things sorted out for tomorrow. I'll do a first search on the computer, if you like.'

'Yes. The regional undetected crime index, for now.'

'It'll be on your desk in the morning, sir. Team briefing first thing, I expect.'

'Yes. Good.' He lapsed into silence as Fielding negotiated the narrow road in a neat U-turn. Then he asked, 'What did you make of Chris Lyons?'

The dashboard lights showed her brows contracting in thought. 'Don't know, sir, to be honest. He could be telling us the whole truth. Or this story about the lover is true, and he was angry enough to go to the gallery tonight and kill his wife. Or he's made up the lover altogether and there's something else going on. Perhaps it's to do with him having lost his job.' She glanced at him quickly, her face earnest. 'But when he said that he loved her, sir, he sounded as if he was telling the truth.'

'Yes, he did.' They were entering the village now. There was his car, gleaming with rain in the light of the street lamps. Fielding pulled up by the BMW's offside so that he could stay dry. 'But plenty of men have killed women they loved, Pat. See you in the morning.'

# THREE
## Thursday 8.15 a.m.

Anderson leant against the wall by his office door and folded his arms as he watched Fielding put back her shoulders and glance around the room. He was privately amused. She looked relaxed and competent and not as tired as she should have done after only a few hours' sleep. It was amazing what the prospect of promotion could do. With Inspector in her sights, she was throwing herself at every case as if it was her last. Well, good luck to her.

'Where's Nick?' Fielding asked.

'Gone for a slash, Sarge,' Gerry Hart volunteered.

'He hasn't cottoned on to bladder control as a factor for success in CID,' said Carrie Vickers. Gerry laughed, and something about his expression was significant. It was well known that he was bedding a WPC from the uniformed branch, but it looked as if he had managed to get his claws into Carrie as well. A reasonable choice. Carrie was very pretty, if you liked them blonde and buxom. From a purely spectator's viewpoint Anderson preferred Fielding, whose quick, dark, intelligent looks gave the impression that she might present a challenge.

'Want a coffee while you wait, Pat?' That was DS Bill McKie. He deferred to Fielding, and not just because she was senior to him. She had a good touch with the team; they respected and liked her. Anderson had always settled for respect.

Sometimes Fielding made him wonder if he could have done things differently.

'It's OK, Bill. Here comes Nick now.' Nick reappeared, sidling in as if he expected nobody to notice. Fielding said, 'All right, let's get started.' Silence fell. Everyone knew that there had been a murder last night, and from their expressions they relished the change from the everyday diet of car theft and burglary. The rest of the crime squad hunched over their desks and telephones, sulky and disgruntled. They would have to cope with extra work while their colleagues ran around trying to solve a murder. Anderson didn't sympathise. Nobody would manage the department for him so that he could immerse himself in the Lyons case.

The team didn't look so happy after they had seen the pictures. Carrie and Gerry glanced surreptitiously at Nick, wondering how he had coped with his first homicide. Bill McKie looked sombre and concerned. 'What's the cause of death, Pat?'

Fielding shook her head. 'Your guess is as good as mine. Nothing immediately apparent, anyway. The gov – The DCI's going to the post mortem this lunchtime.'

Most CID squads had some nickname for their chief, and Anderson knew what his people called him when he wasn't there to hear. At least it was just 'the governor' and not something unprintable. Some chiefs liked to be addressed by their nickname, but he wasn't one of them. It was unlike Fielding to let it slip.

Gerry volunteered cautiously, 'That'll put you right off your lunch, sir.'

'Actually,' Anderson said with a straight face, 'there's an excellent canteen at the morgue.'

Gerry looked puzzled, then his face twisted in distaste. Fielding caught Anderson's eye and her lips twitched, but she didn't smile either. 'Anyway,' she said, 'let's get this show on the road. The DCI's going to be involved in this case. Superintendent Parrish thinks there'll be a lot of Press interest, and I think he's right. I spoke to a reporter at 2.30 last night.'

'Vultures,' grumbled McKie.

'First stop is the crime scene,' Fielding said. 'Bill, you take

Nick over to the gallery today and as soon as Forensics have finished with something, see if it might be any help. You know the form. Gerry, Carrie, you do house to house in Wressingham.'

'House to house?' Gerry groaned. 'Sarge, it's pissing with rain. I did the last lot of house to house! Get Nick to do it.'

'No,' Fielding said bluntly. Quite right. Nick was new, and he didn't have the experience to carry out unsupervised house-to-house enquiries. 'You shouldn't be so good-looking, Gerry. You know all those lonely housewives love to talk to you.'

'Lonely housewives,' laughed Carrie. 'Au pairs, more like.'

There was a good example of Fielding's style. The joke and the flattery made it more palatable for Gerry to obey her order. Gerry grinned, not the least displeased. 'What about you and the chief?' he asked.

Anderson pushed himself up from the wall and joined Fielding at the front of the room. She moved aside a little and Gerry's face lost its grin. 'We've interrogated the RUCI and there's nothing there that looks helpful at this stage,' Anderson said. 'There's no incident suite available right now, so you'll be working here.'

'Typical,' Gerry muttered. 'Solve a murder from the corner of a filing cabinet.'

It was typical, but complaining wouldn't change matters. 'We've set up a Major Enquiry computer link, but I've already run the most obvious checks and I'm not sanguine about getting anything helpful. In any case, you heard the story so far. We have more than one possible suspect already, so basic methods will be enough for now. Francesca Lyons may have had a lover. Her husband doesn't know who he was, and Pat and I are going to try to find out. Bill, Nick, keep your eyes peeled at the gallery for anything that may be relevant; and you too, Gerry and Carrie, when you're doing the house to house. Pat and I will start with the husband. Then we'll come to the gallery and talk to whoever works there. As soon as you have someone who looks like a possible, report it and we'll do a trace, identify, eliminate.'

'Everyone clear?' Fielding asked. 'Bill?'

'Fine,' said McKie. 'What's the betting, though, Pat? Evens on the husband and three to one on on the lover?'

'Nah,' said Carrie, chuckling. 'Husband might have made the lover up, mightn't he? The lover has to be ten to one.'

Speculation at this stage was pointless, and it might put preconceptions in people's minds. 'If I were you,' Anderson said, 'I'd study the form before you start laying odds. Otherwise you might as well chuck money down the drain.'

As he had intended, this threw cold water on the conversation. Gerry and Carrie exchanged looks that suggested they would have little fun on this job with the governor along to blight the proceedings. McKie shuffled his feet, then said, 'All right, then, Nick, let's get down there.'

Andrea Maguire sometimes thought that the very best thing about running her own business was the chance it gave her to get up in the morning at her own pace. She generally opened the gallery at about 10 a.m., sometimes a little later, and that meant that she could get up slowly, make coffee and sit for an hour with the paper as she drank it, and only get in the car for her three-mile journey after all the morning rush-hour traffic had faded away.

But this morning she wasn't enjoying the leisure. James was being so bloody slow. There he was, bumping about in the bathroom. Why didn't he hurry up? He'd refused to talk last night about what had happened, and now her curiosity and anxiety were spoiling her breakfast.

At last he appeared, his hair still plastered wetly to his head, a towel wrapped around his waist. 'Coffee,' he growled.

She jumped up and hurried to put a brimming mug into his hand. He had the dark brooding look she had come to fear. Christ, did that mean that things had gone badly? Were they in trouble? She wanted to demand that he tell her, but it was a long time since she'd dared to demand anything of James.

He took the coffee from her and with his left hand grabbed her upper arm and held her while he took the first sip. His strong fingers gripped tightly, not quite at the point of pain. She knew better than to try to pull away. James was big, tall and broad-shouldered, and he was so much stronger than her that resistance was always useless. So she stood still, feeling the familiar sick grip of fear in the pit of her stomach. Please, she begged silently, don't let him hit me this morning.

Fortunately the coffee appeared to pass muster. James raised his heavy brows in surprise and approval and let her go. 'Good,' he said.

She returned to her seat at the kitchen table and unsteadily picked up her own mug, wishing that it had gin in it. James followed her over and sat down opposite her. A drop of water glittered among the dark hairs on his naked chest; another drop ran down from his wet hair, down the cords of his strong throat and into the hollow of his collar bone. If only he wasn't so gorgeous. If only she didn't love him. Then it would be easy. She ought not to stay with him. But he was gorgeous, and despite everything, she did love him.

He smiled at her, that dangerous smile that had melted her straight into his bed when they first met. 'You look good,' he said.

His approval was rare and so sweet. 'Thanks,' she said, blushing and hanging her head. 'I'm surprised. I mean, I didn't sleep well.'

'You wouldn't have slept at all if I'd told you what happened last night,' he said, burying his face in his coffee mug.

She lifted her head, cold with apprehension. 'God,' she whispered, 'what did happen? Has she called the police? Are we in trouble?'

'She didn't call anyone,' he said. He put down the mug and looked at her. His face was set and his bright brown eyes were quite unreadable. 'She won't be calling anyone, either.'

'You – you managed to convince her, then,' said Andrea. Was he just teasing her, trying to stoke up her fear? It wouldn't be the first time.

'No,' he said calmly. 'I killed her.'

Andrea forgot to breathe. She didn't believe what she had heard. After a long moment of horror she forced a laugh. 'James, that's in very bad taste for this time in the morning.'

'It's not a joke,' James said. 'She's dead. I killed her.'

Andrea's hands trembled so much that she folded them

together. The trembling spread relentlessly up her arms. 'James,' she whispered, 'please don't do this.'

Suddenly, without warning, James clenched his fist and crashed it down onto the table. The mugs leapt in the air and Andrea recoiled, her hands to her face, whimpering. 'Listen,' he hissed, 'you'd better believe that she's dead, because she is. And it's your fault just as much as mine.'

'My fault?' He must be joking. She pushed back her chair and retreated from the table, shaking her head. 'God almighty, James, it's nothing to do with me! You went round there to scare her, that's all, just to scare her.'

'I went round on your instructions,' James corrected her coldly. He got up and stalked towards her, his head a little on one side. 'You told me to make sure that she didn't tell anyone what she knew. Well, I did my best to persuade her, but she wasn't going to be persuaded. At one point she was about to ring the police. So –'

He paused. Andrea craned forward, horrified and fascinated. James eyed her for a moment, then smiled. 'I've got you hooked, haven't I? I grabbed her by the hair and shook her, but she still wouldn't see sense.'

Andrea wrapped her arms tightly around her, shuddering. God, how many times had he done that to her? She could imagine it, the fist in her hair, her head wrenched back, the room spinning around her. She would have seen sense straight away. She would have done whatever James wanted.

'There was a plastic bag in her bin,' James said. His eyes were glittering. 'I made her kneel down and fold her hands as if she was praying. I tied her wrists. Then I put the bag over her head and held her still until she died.'

Andrea fought down the sick horror that threatened to overwhelm her. There could be some advantage in this. James was a killer, a murderer. This might be her chance to get free. If she could manage to let the police know without in-criminating herself –

'Andrea,' James said softly.

She stared at him as he slowly came towards her. She was too frightened to move. He took hold of a handful of her hair and pulled back her head, looking down into her eyes.

'Andrea,' he said, 'I hope you're not thinking any disloyal thoughts. Because you know what happens when you do. You sent me there, remember? You told me to shut her up. I was acting on your orders.'

'But what will we do about the police?' Andrea whispered.

'Why should they find me? The only thing I touched was the plastic bag, and it's in a rubbish bin in the middle of Guildford.'

'You touched her.'

'Nobody ever got fingerprints from a person, did they? And nobody saw me arrive or leave, I'm sure of it. That village is as quiet as a morgue.' He laughed. 'Unfortunate choice of words, eh? But anyway, Andrea, if they do come –' His hand tightened in her hair '– then it's easy, isn't it. You just say that we were at home together all evening. It's an easy story. You were doing whatever it is you were really doing, and I was sketching.'

She tried to shake her head. 'James, no, I can't, I –'

Suddenly his grip was fierce. She gasped and put her hand to his. 'Listen,' he hissed. 'You have to do this, Andrea. You know you do. For a start, this whole thing is your fault. If it comes out that I killed the Lyons woman, it'll come out why. Your whole business will be bust. You'll be ruined, won't you? Nobody will ever buy from you again.' His words sank in. God help her, they were true. 'And as if that wasn't enough,' he went on, grinning into her face like a demon, 'I've killed one woman now. Do you want the second one to be you?'

'You don't have to threaten me,' she said in a very small voice. 'I know you're right.'

He looked startled and suspicious, as if he had expected more resistance. Then, gradually, his hand slackened in her hair. 'All right,' he said. 'I'm glad you see sense.'

She pulled carefully away from him and stepped back, smoothing her hair with her hand. Her heart was pounding. In a moment he would ask for sex, he always did when he had been violent. Normally she would let him, because it was always so damn good, but she couldn't, not this morning. Not with Francesca Lyons kneeling between them with a plastic bag over her head. She said unsteadily, 'I have to go to work.'

'Work can wait,' James said. 'I want to fuck you.' His voice was thick with lust and the towel around his waist was working loose as his penis swelled into erection.

Half of her wanted it. She knew what would happen. He would grab her and push her onto whatever piece of furniture was closest to hand, rip away her underwear and thrust himself straight into her, so hard and deep that she almost fainted. Then he would screw her with all that magnificent animal strength, and however much she hated him at the beginning, by the end she would be writhing and moaning and clutching him, because the way he took her proved that, whatever he did to her, he still loved her.

But she couldn't let him do it now, not now. 'I can't,' she said desperately, manoeuvring to get the table between them while she found her car keys. 'Not this morning, James. I've got someone coming in to see me at 10.30. 1 have to go.'

She darted for the door. He came after her, but outside it was pouring with rain. He stopped on the doorstep and yelled, 'I'll walk over at lunchtime. You'd better be ready for me then!'

Was it just the rain, or did the Lyons's house look as depressing as the *Psycho* mansion? Pat was reluctant to open the car door. Overreacting again.

Anderson noticed her hesitation, of course. 'Coming?' he asked, in that even tone of voice that didn't betray whether he was being sympathetic or critical.

For a moment she almost told him how she was feeling. Then she thought better of it. 'Sorry,' she said. 'Miles away.' She picked up the plastic bag that nestled by her feet and took a deep breath.

The gravel drive was studded with puddles. Anderson went in front of her with the collar of his olive-green trenchcoat turned up against the rain, and she walked carefully behind him. He always picked a path that would cause the minimum possible damage to his shoes, which was hardly surprising considering how much he must have paid for them. He could probably get caught in a riot and emerge as pristine as if he had stepped out of a fashion magazine.

The porch was a tight squeeze. Anderson rang the bell and then manoeuvred his way into a corner to make room for her. He ran one hand over his dark greying hair, sweeping off the drops of rain. It was so short that it hardly looked wet. Pat checked that her plait was tidy. It really might be a damn sight more convenient to have the whole bloody lot cut off. If a crop was good enough for a DCI it should be good enough for a would-be Inspector. Charlie had always wanted her to keep it long: why hadn't she had it cut after he chucked her? That would have been significant, a way of making the point that she was free and her own woman. But then again, she had been without Charlie for nearly two months and she hadn't found another bloke yet, had she? And sometimes it was useful to be able to look feminine.

The door opened and she brought herself back to the moment with a jolt. A woman was standing in the doorway, a tall thin woman with dark red hair. There were streaks under her green eyes, and she looked as if she had been crying. This must be Sophie Lessiter, the dead woman's sister. 'Are you the police?' she said, in a sharp, wary voice.

'That's right,' said Anderson. 'DCI Anderson, and Detective Sergeant Patricia Fielding. You're Mrs Lessiter?'

'That's right. Come in.' She stood back from the door, holding out her hand. 'Chris is in the living room. You can leave your coats here, on the hook.'

Pat took off her battered jacket and slung it up anyhow. Anderson shed his coat more carefully and straightened the collar before he hung it neatly from its chain loop. Sophie Lessiter said, 'I'll bring you some coffee, if you like.'

If Pat left it to her chief they wouldn't get any refreshments at all. He had a habit of refusing offers from people who might be under suspicion. It always amused Pat to catch him in a superstition, especially one she didn't share. She said quickly, 'I'd love a coffee, you're very kind.'

Sophie arched her brows at Anderson. He said, 'Thanks, but not for me,' and then as she turned away added without haste, 'Mrs Lessiter, it would be useful to talk to you as well; to find out if there's anything you know which might be relevant.'

For a moment Sophie looked at Anderson with wide, direct eyes. Then she said, 'Of course. But I doubt that I can help,' and went ahead of them across the hall.

What had Anderson seen in those eyes? It was so hard to tell what someone was thinking if they wouldn't look at you, and it could be very frustrating to do interviews with Anderson. Generally he liked to stay in charge, he called the shots, and so the suspect or witness always spoke directly to him. As a result Pat never quite got to grips with what was in the other person's mind. And Anderson was sparing in what he shared with her, too. Well, he was quite capable of doing interviews without her, she had to be thankful for small mercies.

In the living room Chris Lyons was sitting on the sofa, watching a little boy playing at his feet with a Playmobil Noah's ark. As they entered he looked up. It was obvious that he hadn't slept, his face was as white as a sheet and his eyes were sunken into blue shadows. He lifted his hand and Pat noticed with a shock that his nails were freshly bitten to the quick. He put his thumb to his mouth and tore at the side of the nail and said, 'Sophie, can you take Andrew somewhere else?'

'Do you want some coffee?' Sophie responded from the kitchen.

Chris shook his head. Sophie hesitated, then came forward and caught the little boy up into her arms with a grunt. She said apologetically to Pat, 'I'm sorry, I'm sure you understand,' and then to the child, 'Andrew, shall we go and feed the goldfish?'

Coffee would have been nice, but it wasn't the end of the world. Pat looked at Anderson, waiting for her cue. After a second his dark blue eyes met hers and then indicated a chair at an angle to Chris. She nodded very slightly and sat down, pulling her notebook out of the bag. The other thing in there could stay hidden for the moment. 'I'll be taking notes, Mr Lyons,' she said, in her most neutral voice.

Chris shot her one quick, hunted glance. His eyes were pale blue and rimmed with red. He looked as if he hated her, but she was used to that.

'Well,' said Anderson. He sat down opposite Chris. As often, he mirrored the body posture of the person he was talking to: leaning forward, elbows on his knees, hands loosely clasped. It looked natural, but most things that he did were carefully planned and acutely observed. 'Chris, how are you?'

For a moment Chris lifted his head and looked Anderson in the eyes. Then he slumped and covered his face with his hands. 'Just ask me whatever it is you want.'

'Tell me about your wife,' Anderson said. His voice was very gentle. As always, he sounded as if he really cared. Did he, or was he just exceptionally clever? Pat had worked with him several times, and she still didn't know him well enough to say.

'Franny,' Chris whispered. There was a silence. Then he said, 'What do you want to know?'

'Tell me how she was recently. How did she seem to you?'

Always such general questions. But he was right, of course, it was good practice. Specific questions get specific answers, and specific answers can be specifically unhelpful. Start broad, then narrow it down.

Chris was silent for some time, staring at the carpet. Then he said, 'She was worried.'

'Worried,' Anderson echoed.

'Recently. Not herself. I asked her about it, and she said it was something at the gallery, something she didn't want to tell me about.'

'Why shouldn't she want to tell you about it?'

Chris's lips thinned into a pale line. 'To start with I thought it was because – because of her lover. Something to do with him. It might have been. But then I wasn't sure. She went to London last week, something about a special trip to the Tate. She never went to the Tate, why should she? And she said it was about work. But –' His hands clenched tightly together as he rocked a little on the sofa '– but she would say that, wouldn't she? Maybe she went to meet him in London – maybe they went to Brighton, Christ knows, how should I know?'

'And when she went to London,' said Anderson after a little pause, 'did she look worried then?'

Slowly Chris lifted his head, his expression clearing slightly. 'Yes, she did. And I suppose that's why I believed that it wasn't anything to do with her lover. Because I didn't then, you see. But I thought she would have told me about it, and she didn't.'

'Did she normally tell you about problems at work?'

There was a long silence. Chris looked as though Anderson had slapped him in the face. Why? Pat narrowed her eyes and poised her pen, ready. At last Chris said very slowly, 'She – used to. But after I lost my job she – I –' He looked up as if for encouragement. Anderson's lean smooth face was neutral, sympathetic, betraying none of the interest that he must have been feeling. 'She said I was – interfering. That I ought to let her get on with it. And she, she stopped telling me about things. And then there was the lover –'

It was so easy to imagine. The unemployed executive stuck at home, self-esteem at rock bottom, grabbing at any chance to do the job he no longer had, interfering in his wife's business until she told him to leave it alone. He might have made the lover up entirely, a product of his lonely under-used imagination.

Anderson seemed to agree. 'Chris, what makes you so sure she had a lover?'

Another long silence. Chris tore again at his ragged thumbnail. It hurt to watch; the skin by the nail was spiky and bloody. His hands were trembling. At last he said, 'I just know.'

'How?' Anderson asked, his voice soft but persistent. 'How did you know?'

The torn fingers twisted and wrung together. At last Chris pushed himself to his feet and rubbed his hand fiercely over his face. His eyes were wide. 'I smelt him, all right? All right? We didn't – Franny didn't –' He stopped and said after a moment in a clotted voice, 'I can't.'

'Chris.' Anderson didn't get up, just filled his voice with empathy. 'I have to know. Tell me. It could be important.'

*I* have to know! Good old governor, thinking team as usual. Pat contained her irritation, because as usual the tactic had worked. Chris said, 'All right. All right.' He shut his eyes tightly and swallowed, then went on in a very precise voice, 'Franny

29

had a coil. An IUD. So we didn't need to – use anything. And one night I –'Two long breaths '– I could smell condoms on her. I could smell them.'

It wasn't possible to watch him suffering and not feel for him. But everything he said, every hesitation, every shudder of emotion made it more likely that he had killed his wife, not less likely.

Anderson said after a pause, 'You said you didn't know who he was, Chris. But who do you think he was?'

Chris slumped back down to the sofa, shaking his head. 'I don't know. I don't know. Some rich executive bastard who bought one of those bloody pornographic pictures off her.'

'You didn't like the pictures.'

'I didn't mean that. They are pornography, aren't they? They're there to turn people on. I didn't like her selling them. What would people think of her? But they made a lot of money. And she said they were art.' Chris hesitated, seeming to look inward. Then he added, 'She *believed* they were art. She wasn't a fraud.'

'And you think her lover was someone who bought one of those pictures.'

'It's likely, isn't it? They'd have got onto the subject pretty sharpish.'

That would make a nice collection of suspects, and a nice job going through all the gallery's records to find them. Pat hoped to God that someone could save them the trouble.

Anderson seemed ready to move on. 'Chris, tell me what happened last night.'

Chris also seemed to be ready for this question. 'Yes. I thought about it. She came home just after 5.30, when the gallery closed. We gave the children tea and then she played with them and they went to bed. Andrew had a bit of a temperature, I was worried. I thought we would have some dinner, but she didn't want to. She –' He hesitated. 'She said she was busy. She had to go back to the gallery; work to do, she said. She left about eight, I suppose, maybe a little before. At about ten she rang me and said she was still busy but she hoped to be home before eleven. And she always came back when she said, always.'

'At what time exactly did she call you?'

'Ten-ish. I don't know.'

'How do you know it was ten-ish?'

'I —' Chris looked puzzled for a moment. 'I was watching the telly and she called during the adverts. I turned on for *News at Ten*. So it was either the adverts just before or the ones in the middle. I can't remember.'

'All right.' Anderson paused for a moment, then asked, 'And what happened just before she left?' He hadn't missed that little hesitation.

'Nothing,' said Chris. 'She said she was busy and she had to go.'

He was looking into Anderson's face with appealing eyes, as if he was asking to be believed. Pat wanted to say, 'Come on, what really happened?'

Anderson said, 'How did you feel when she went back to work?'

Chris rubbed his hand over the nape of his neck as if his back ached. He didn't reply, but his eyes flickered.

'How did you feel?' Anderson repeated. His voice was still very gentle. He had the patience of a cat at a mousehole.

'I —' Chris turned his head away. 'I wasn't pleased, I suppose.'

'What did you say to her?'

'Look,' Chris burst out suddenly, 'leave it alone, will you? What has this got to do with anything?'

The more he fought, the more he dug a hole for himself. Anderson's face was very still. He looked dangerous. Christ, he looked as if he was about to caution Lyons. What had he seen that she had missed?

But Anderson said nothing. The silence drew out, and at last Chris said, 'All right. All right, we fought about it. We had a row. Is that what you wanted?'

'What sort of a row?' Anderson asked implacably.

'I — accused her of going to see her lover. She denied it. That sort of a row. And in the end she went.'

'What else?' Anderson asked. But Chris shook his head and looked at the carpet and didn't speak. Anderson drew in a long, thoughtful breath, then glanced at Pat. His dark blue eyes were sparkling with concentration. 'Pat, could I have —'

31

She got to her feet and silently passed him the bag. He reached into it, drew out a transparent plastic evidence envelope and held it out on the palms of his hands. 'Chris.'

Chris looked up and registered the bag. He didn't move. After a long moment he said, 'That's Franny's scarf.' His voice was choked.

'It's hers?'

'It's hers. I – bought it for her. Two Christmases ago. From Harrods.' He sounded as if he were fighting tears. 'There's a pulled thread at one corner. I –' His eyes lifted from the scarf. 'Can I keep it?'

'No,' said Anderson gently. 'I'm sorry, Chris. It's evidence.'

'Why?' Chris asked. He began to tremble. 'Why is it evidence?' He really didn't look as if he knew.

Anderson said steadily, 'Her hands were tied with it.'

Chris gave a little groan as if he had been hit in the stomach. 'Let me see her,' he said. 'I want to see her.'

'They're doing the post mortem at noon today. After that they'll let you see her at the hospital.' Anderson glanced around. 'Pat, will you explain to Chris how the system works? I'd like to have a word with Mrs Lessiter before we go to the gallery.'

Well, he couldn't have seen anything worthy of real suspicion. That was a relief, she hadn't either. She said, 'Yes, sir, of course.'

Anderson got up and said to Chris, 'Thank you very much for your help. Everything we can find out will be useful.' Then he turned and went out of the room, moving with quiet precision.

It would have been good to find out why he wanted to talk to Francesca's sister. Perhaps he would tell her later, but perhaps not. But Chris was gazing at her, and she sighed and made herself smile at him.

'What did Mrs Lessiter tell you, sir?' she asked as they got back into the BMW.

Anderson shook his head. 'Nothing. She hadn't spoken to Francesca for a couple of weeks, she said. She had no idea about the lover, not even any suspicion that there was one.' He hesitated, then added, 'That's what she told me, anyway.

But I wasn't sure whether to believe her.'

'What are they hiding?' Pat asked rhetorically. 'Chris wasn't being completely straight with us, either. What's going on?'

'Good question. Just don't try to guess the answer.' He swung the big car around the mini roundabout at the top of the market square by St Olave's church. 'Mrs Lessiter did suggest that if Francesca did have a lover, her best friend might know about him. I've got her name and address. Can you pick up that interview after we've finished at the gallery?'

'Yes, sir, of course.' Finding out the identity of the mysterious lover would be a major step forward. 'I'll take Nick with me. He takes good notes.'

'All right. I may go back to Mrs Lessiter. She was distracted, perhaps she didn't want to talk in front of the little boy.' He tucked the car neatly in by the side of the road in front of the gallery. The sign on the door said CLOSED and the lights were off, but there were people moving to and fro inside.

'So, sir, we get a handle on the Forensics, then interview the staff?'

'Exactly.'

A uniformed PC let them in. Anderson walked through the first two rooms without a glance at the pictures. Was he controlling himself this time? His reaction to the erotica had surprised her. For some reason she had thought he would disapprove, and he hadn't seemed to. In fact he had looked as if he would like to take a couple of them home with him. But then he was a bit of a ladies' man, in a private, low-profile sort of way, and why shouldn't he enjoy a bit of titillation? Especially when it came so persuasively packaged. The governor was a culture vulture, one of the few people in CID who could distinguish between classical composers, and he seemed to relish his reputation as an intellectual snob. So the combination of art and sex must be highly attractive to him. And yet –

They made their way down the corridor and into the room where Francesca had died. Pat followed Anderson, watching him. He glanced at a picture beside the desk and hesitated while his eyes darkened. Then he saw her look and

33

turned at once to the Forensics expert. 'Morning, Dave. How's it going?'

What about the picture that caught his attention? She took a step closer. A pencil drawing, fluid and accurate. A woman stretched out on a bed, her eyes closed, her throat tense. You could practically hear her crying out. A man knelt over her, his hands cupping the swell of her breasts, his face hidden in her belly. Pleasure glowed from her arched spine and parted thighs. A beautiful picture. But one thing made Pat uncomfortable. The woman's hands were tied above her head to the iron bedframe, her fingers stiff and spread as if her hands, at least, were struggling.

Dave was talking and Pat pulled herself back to business. What was her chief's taste in dirty pictures to do with her, anyway? 'Not so good,' Dave said. 'Lots of hairs, prints and stuff, sir, but you'd expect that from a public place like a gallery. There's absolutely no chance of isolating anything except on the telephone. That has only the dead woman's prints and her assistant's; I've done a naked-eye match. Obviously the exact results will have to wait for the computer, but it's pretty clear all the same. He's waiting in the kitchen for you, by the way, the assistant, name's Daniel Gough. Bill McKie's with him. Nick Parker's gone back to the station to get some stuff for me.'

'OK. What about the footprints?'

'We've got pictures of the ones in the hall and we've tried for casts of the ones outside, but it's difficult, the ground's so squashy. Gough says he had the same shoes on yesterday and we've matched the dead woman's shoes. There are at least two other sets of prints.'

'Two?' repeated Pat.

'At least two.'

'Two messages on the answering machine as well,' she said to Anderson. 'Looks as if Francesca may have had several visitors last night.'

'When you've finished here,' Anderson said to Dave, 'go along to the Lyons's house and get a set of prints from the shoes her husband had on last night. When we arrived he was wearing –' He broke off and glanced across. 'Pat?'

She had absolutely no idea. For a moment she stood open-mouthed, then shook her head. Her cheeks prickled with a blush and she set her jaw angrily. 'Sorry, sir,' she said, more carelessly than she felt. 'I didn't notice.'

'He was wearing Timberlands,' Anderson told Dave. 'Tan nubuck Timberland lace-ups. They had mud on them.'

Was there ever an occasion on which he missed anything? And Christ, why hadn't she noticed? She had known about the footprints and she had assumed that Chris was a suspect. She was angry with herself, and with Anderson too for showing up her omission.

'The back door opens on to gravel, not mud,' said Dave. 'But I'll check it out, sir. I should be finished here in ten minutes or so, then Bill and Nick can come in and go through the books and so on, whatever you want.'

'Good. Now, where's the kitchen?'

Anderson walked ahead of Pat all the way to the kitchen, so she didn't get a chance to ask him why he'd shown her up in front of Dave. Not that a bloody Forensics grunt mattered, but even so her cheeks were still burning. As they entered the kitchen she lowered her head and took a deep breath, making herself calm.

The kitchen, almost opposite the office, was a reassuringly ordinary place, done in battered white Formica and without any pictures at all. A young blond man in a collarless shirt with deckchair blue and white stripes was sitting at the table. He looked up when they came in, revealing an aristocratic-looking face with a long sharp nose and grey eyes under heavy eyelids. Bill McKie, beside him, said, 'Mr Gough, this is Detective Chief Inspector Anderson, in charge of the investigation, and Detective Sergeant Pat Fielding. Sir, this is Daniel Gough, Mrs Lyons's assistant.'

'Pleased to meet you,' said Gough, getting to his feet. He was not very tall and compact, with a strong slender body. In fact he was very nice-looking. He had a really classy voice, too. Upper-crust men like him always left Pat feeling vaguely dissatisfied and wistful, as if she spent her life surrounded by laddish macho coppers and there was more somewhere else if only she could find it.

'In fact,' Anderson said to Gough, 'I'm just involved in the investigation. DS Fielding is in charge.' And he stepped slightly aside to let her come forward.

What was he trying to do, make it up to her for having shown her up? Well, he didn't need to, but since Gough was tasty she was very chuffed that he had. 'Mr Gough.' For some reason she couldn't keep a smile off her face.

'I've just had a cup of coffee with Mr Gough,' said Bill.

'Please,' said Gough, 'call me Daniel. My surname makes me think of school.'

God, he really was the business, wasn't he? Nobody at Pat's school had been called by their surname, not even the teachers. Bill went on, 'Daniel was saying that he was in the pub last night with some friends, from nine until closing time.'

'So I think I have an alibi,' said Daniel, with a sort of rueful grin.

'It certainly sounds like it,' said Pat. She kept wanting to smile at him, and she didn't know why. But he was looking at her in that particular sort of way that made her feel that a smile would be – well, appropriate. Helpful. Even if it wasn't particularly relevant to the investigation. 'Bill, Dave's just about finished at the scene. If you could get hold of the books and start seeing if you can track down anything about what Mrs Lyons was doing here last night?'

'Sure.' Bill got up from the table and squeezed out.

'If there's anything I can do to help,' said Daniel, opening his big hands. 'Please sit down. Do you want a coffee?'

'Yes, please,' said Anderson and Pat simultaneously. That told Pat that, like her, Anderson had believed Daniel's alibi.

Daniel got up and began to mess around with a kettle and coffee cups. He appeared very disorganised. He had to pick up and put down one teaspoon three times before the coffee was made. Anderson watched him with an expression almost of disbelief, but this vague unconcern for organisation just made Pat want to grin. For a while she didn't say anything, but Anderson had introduced her as the officer in charge, so it was her turn to ask the questions. 'This must have been a shock for you, Daniel.'

He turned and looked at her with a lopsided, glinting

smile. She felt a lurch of sudden startled lust. Christ, he was gorgeous! But she couldn't get interested. For a start, even if he wasn't a suspect he was almost certainly a witness and, therefore, off limits. Plenty of people broke that rule, but not people with a nose for promotion. Anyway, he probably wasn't free. And if he was, that probably meant that he was gay.

'It's a hell of a shock,' he said, handing her a cup of coffee. 'I didn't know Francesca that well, I've only worked here a couple of months, but even so, good heavens! Arrive at work and find a policeman on the doorstep telling you your boss has been murdered? It's not something that happens every day.'

'What effect will it have on you?' asked Anderson.

'Oh,' Daniel sat down and examined the little granules of instant coffee floating unmelted on the top of his drink, 'well, it'll depend on what Chris decides to do with the gallery. But he'll probably want to keep it open, for the time being at least. You know he's out of a job, he needs the gallery. And he can't run it, he doesn't know the business. So I'll keep it going as long as he wants.'

'Altruism?' asked Anderson, his dark brows raised.

'Hardly.' Daniel looked up, not at Anderson, but at Pat. Why was he smiling at her? Surely an upper-crust art dealer couldn't be interested in a police sergeant? But it was to her that he said, 'It won't hurt me at all to run the gallery for a while. Looks good on the old CV, if you take my meaning.'

She would have liked to ask him much more personal questions, such as, What are you doing after work? But she had a job to do. 'Daniel,' she said, 'you said you didn't know Francesca that well. But can you think of anything – since you met her – that was suspicious? That might have suggested that things weren't as they should be?'

He frowned. His eyebrows were fair and elegantly arched, and when they drew together his forehead made tiny little folds between them, a study in concentration. He sipped his coffee, still thinking. He hadn't shaved that morning, there was golden stubble on his cheeks and chin. Was it at the soft stage, or still bristly? She felt an urge to reach out and touch him.

37

She did no such thing. After a moment he said, 'I'd like to help, but it's very hard to say. Recently, I mean in the last couple of weeks, I think there was – something not right, something going on. But she –' He broke off and looked into Pat's eyes as if wondering whether she could be trusted. What he saw seemed to reassure him, because he went on, 'Maybe you know that she wasn't terribly happy at home, I mean, since Chris lost his job. She didn't tell me about it, but one knows when that sort of thing is happening. So, if I thought anything, I imagine that I put it down to that. But now you ask, you see, I'm thinking, and perhaps I wonder if it might be something to do with the gallery. With the, ah, private art.'

'Private art?' It was pretty obvious what he meant, but if you weren't certain it was always best to check.

'The erotica. She'd spent a lot of time in here, in the office I mean, on the phone. I thought it was to one of the suppliers, and then last week she went up to the Tate for some reason. She didn't confide in me, though. So really I have no idea.'

He was obviously doing his best, but it was disappointing that he could add so little. Pat thought for a moment, then said, 'Chris believes that she had a lover.'

'Oh, I'm sure she had.' Daniel's voice and demeanour were totally relaxed, as if adultery was the done thing in his circle. Who knows, perhaps it was! 'No idea who, but I could have found out if I had been curious. Maybe it was someone in the trade.'

Pat caught Anderson's eye for a moment. Daniel was almost too carefree to be true. 'Daniel,' she said earnestly, 'do you *know* she had a lover?'

'What, do you mean, could I prove it? Oh no. I just wouldn't be surprised, that's all.'

She couldn't restrain a smile. 'I'm afraid you're very suggestible.'

He grinned back at her, unabashed. 'Oh, absolutely. Imagination's my strong point. I'll believe anything.'

'In that case,' Anderson interjected coolly, 'perhaps you would be especially careful to keep to things you know to be facts, for now.'

Daniel looked startled, then bridled slightly. 'If you insist.'

'So,' Pat summarised, hoping not to lose his goodwill, 'you didn't notice anything in particular in the run-up to Francesca's death.'

'No, well, I did a bit. She was, what would you say, preoccupied. But that's all.'

'And today. Have you seen the office?'

'Yes, I had a look.'

'Did you notice anything about it?'

'Like what?' He looked puzzled and slightly suspicious, as if he thought she was laying a trap for him.

'I don't know. Was there anything unusual about it, or anything changed from the way it was before?'

He pursed his lips thoughtfully and shook his head. 'Not that I recall. But –' He sipped his coffee. 'Might I go and have another look? Would that be OK?'

'Yes. Of course.'

She got up to follow him to the door. Anderson came behind them. As they crossed the corridor she smelt Daniel's cologne, an old-fashioned, floral fragrance, as classy as the rest of him. His blond hair was floppy on top and cut short on the back of his neck, like a schoolboy's, and there were little fine golden hairs on either side of his nape.

'Let's see,' he said, standing in the doorway. Bill McKie was in a corner by an open filing cabinet, but Daniel just gave him a vague smile and went on looking around. He was silent for several minutes. Pat was so taken by his absorbed, concentrated expression, that she forgot to check whether Anderson was looking at the same picture. Eventually Daniel said, 'Well –'

He needed encouragement. 'What do you think?'

The grey eyes narrowed quizzically. 'I'm not sure. I could have sworn there was another picture on the wall there.' He gestured at the space over Bill's head. 'A smallish picture, pen and ink. But I could be wrong.'

'Could it have been sold yesterday?' Anderson asked.

Daniel shook his head. 'Not that I recall. I mean, I didn't see it in the book. No, I thought – But it's really hard to keep track of them all. I mean, these ones were Francesca's special area. She didn't really ask me to know much about them.'

'But you think one is missing,' said Pat.

'I think so. Perhaps.' He glanced at her and gave a self-deprecating laugh. 'I'm not being an awful lot of help, am I.'

They went back to their coffee. Pat drained her cup and said, 'I understand that you haven't worked here long, Daniel, but can you think of anyone else who might have had a grudge against Francesca, anyone who might have been angry with her?'

'Well, gosh,' he said. Gosh! He sounded like the *Boy's Own Paper*. He was charming. 'I mean, that's a bit tough, isn't it. If I knew of anyone, you'd be after them, wouldn't you.'

'Yes,' she replied honestly. 'We would.'

He frowned. Then he said, 'Well, there was someone, I can't deny it. The chap who worked here before me, Paul Johnson. She sacked him, you know, and the circumstances were somewhat – murky. I didn't know the details. But there was him.'

'Where will we find his address?' asked Anderson.

'Oh, in the book.'

For some reason Pat found her mind turning to her surprise at Anderson's reaction to the pictures. She had expected him to disapprove. Aloud she said, 'Daniel, what did people think of the art Francesca sold?'

'What do you mean?' He looked confused.

'Did people disapprove? Did anyone get offended by it?'

He boggled slightly. 'Well, they didn't have to come in here, did they?'

'But I mean, did she ever get letters from people who thought she should stop selling this stuff, or angry comments in the local paper, anything like that.'

'Oh, I see. Well, once or twice people were a bit sniffy, and the local rag would have snide remarks from time to time about lowering the tone, you know the sort of thing. But for God's sake, it's art. Some people are always Philistines.'

That was perhaps more interesting than Daniel knew. She would have liked to have gone on talking to him, but she couldn't think of anything else to ask. She glanced at Anderson, who gave a little shake of the head. 'Well, Daniel, that's it for the moment.'

He nodded. 'Tell me, Sergeant –'

'Fielding. Patricia Fielding.'

'Sergeant Fielding, will I be able to open the gallery today?'

'I doubt it. I'm sorry.'

'Oh, it's no bother,' he said, with that boy's grin. 'I'll just take the day off. Perhaps I'll go up to town and knock about the National a bit.'

He got up. She said regretfully, 'If you think of anything else, Daniel, you will call me, won't you?'

For a moment he looked at her thoughtfully. Then he said, 'I'd jump at the opportunity of calling you,' and grinned again before he left the room.

Suppressing the urge to leap up and down shrieking in triumph, she looked across at Anderson and said nothing.

'He makes the worst coffee I have ever drunk,' said Anderson.

This was true, but why on earth should he make that comment? Perhaps he had spotted the chemistry between her and Daniel, and was – irritated, jealous, something. She wanted to preen.

'Not much information, either,' Anderson went on. 'Pat, what were you getting at when you asked about public reaction to the art?'

Now was the moment of truth. It wasn't often that she beat him to a possibility. 'Well, sir, I was wondering if this murder could have been committed by someone trying to eradicate what they see as pornography.'

There was a silence. Anderson's dark blue eyes were shadowed and utterly steady. 'A mission killer?'

'Yes, sir.'

The stillness of his face showed that he wasn't keen. Sod him, why did he always pour cold water on ideas that weren't his? 'Pat,' he said after a moment, 'That's absurd. Premature and unnecessary. We haven't even ruled out the husband or tracked down the woman's lover yet! I'm glad you didn't suggest it when Gough was here.'

She was shaken, but she wasn't about to drop it that easily. 'Sir, we have to consider all possibilities. What if it wasn't Chris or this unknown lover? What if it was some sort of psychopath?' His scathing expression just made her more earnest. 'Sir, I know it's unlikely, but just because it's unlikely doesn't mean it's impossible.'

'I realise that it's not impossible.' His voice was icily disapproving, and she was suddenly very glad that they were alone. She'd hate Bill to hear this. 'But as you say, it's unlikely. It's very unlikely. Rule out the probable before you try the improbable, Pat.'

'Sir –'

'Suppose a picture is missing. Why should a killer trying to eradicate pornography steal an erotic picture? Use some common sense.'

He was using all his chilly authority to try to change her mind. But he'd said that she was in charge of the investigation, and she was bloody well going to keep her theories, whatever he thought. She set her jaw and didn't reply.

Anderson got to his feet. 'Come on,' he said, 'we've wasted enough time with Gough. Let's get things going out there. What's the next step?'

And after all this he wanted to make her trot out investigative procedures, as if she was a probationer! She would have loved to tell him to get stuffed. But instead she replied very correctly, 'Check the records of erotic pictures sold in case one of the buyers was Francesca's lover. Match records of erotic pictures purchased against erotic pictures sold to determine whether a picture is missing. Follow up Paul Johnson.'

He looked at her for a moment in silence, then said, 'Good. I'll see you after the post mortem, then.'

When he had gone she took a few minutes to calm down. Was he deliberately trying to wind her up, or what? Well, she would hang on to her hunches. This could be a mission killer. Stranger things had happened.

As she crossed the corridor to brief Bill and call the team she gave a sudden uncontrollable shiver. If this was a mission killer, then they wouldn't have seen the last of him. Sooner or later, he would kill again.

# FOUR
## Thursday 11.45 a.m.

The studio faced north, like all good studios, and it was just as James liked it. He thrived on chaos. Only sterile, anally retentive people without a single creative impulse preferred orderliness.

He swept a handful of sketches off his stool and sat down on it, then lit a cigarette and took a long lungful of smoke. From beneath the pile of God knew what on the table he extracted a framed drawing and sat contemplating it.

It was signed *Mario Tauzin*, but Tauzin had been dead for years and this picture had been drawn not three months ago. James had drawn it. He contemplated it with satisfaction and anger. It was a bloody good drawing, beautiful, in fact: a graphic, poetic view of a couple making love. The woman sprawled beneath her man, her eyes closed and her hair spread out like tentacles, and he had shown with deft, economical lines how complex her pussy was, how it was stretched by the man's invading cock, how it was dripping with juice.

Christ, he had drawn the bloody thing and looking at it made him want to fuck. Where was Andrea when he wanted her? Busy, of course, and in any case he couldn't let her see this picture. She had sold it to Francesca Lyons with the pedigree of a real Tauzin and if she knew that he had retrieved it she would go apeshit. She would be right, too. He had been stupid to take it back. He ought to burn it.

But it was a good picture, one of his best. Who cared if it was drawn in another man's style? The stupid buying public didn't like his own style, oh no, they preferred art drawn by dead people. Any bastard's pictures, as long as he was dead. Talent meant nothing to them.

Damn. Why the hell had he taken it? With violent movements he cracked the frame and removed the glass. He held the picture up and flicked his lighter.

But he couldn't do it. It was one of his best. He'd hide it, just until things had calmed down. They could sell it again. Why get paid for a picture once when you could get paid twice? He chuckled as he looked around for a suitable hiding place.

PC Watkins was waiting in the lobby. He looked slightly green. 'Sir,' he said, the moment Anderson appeared, 'I won't have to watch, will I?'

'No, of course not. I'm going to stay, but you just have to identify the corpse as the woman you found. That's it. You can go as soon as you want.'

'I hate hospitals,' said Watkins. 'I hate the smell. It makes me feel sick.'

Anderson's stomach was accustomed to the smell of hospitals, and he didn't fear the brutal invasiveness of post mortems. He was always too interested in what might be revealed to be queasy about what he was seeing. When he said, 'Don't worry, you'll be out of here in five minutes,' his sympathy sounded distant and unconvincing even to his own ears.

The door of the post mortem room swung open and Dr Reid appeared, a small, squat figure in a white coat. Why in God's name did the man wear a beard? It made him look like an ape. But he was the best. If there was anything to be found out about the way Francesca Lyons died, Malcolm Reid would find it.

'Are you ready for me, Chief Inspector,' said Reid. It wasn't a question, and the pathologist's jocular tone grated. But Anderson just nodded to Reid and said to the miserable PC Watkins, 'Come on.'

In rather less than the promised five minutes PC Watkins had made a grateful escape, leaving Anderson, Reid and Reid's mousy male assistant with the white-shrouded body of Francesca Lyons.

'Interesting case, this,' said Reid, spreading out the police photographer's work on his table. He spoke with a Scottish burr and habitually gave strategically-placed r's an extra-long roll for effect. 'In fact, it's rrrrather nasty, isn't it?'

In more than ten years Anderson had never heard Reid describe a case as 'nasty'. He didn't bother to express his surprise and ask for clarification. Reid habitually chattered while he worked, and he never had to be questioned to say more.

As expected, Reid went on, 'No mutilation, no obvious cause of death, but such an unpleasant position to leave the poor woman in, kneeling like that. It looks calculated, and that's unpleasant. In fact, it reminds me of a military execution of a civilian. Wonder if whoever you're looking for has a military background? Have you called in the psychologists yet?'

Not Reid too! Fielding's theory had been unnecessary enough. 'No,' Anderson responded dryly. 'We have more than one suspect from the dead woman's friends and family. There's no need to look further afield at present.'

Reid glanced up at him with a grin. 'Mind your business, Dr Reid, you've been watching too much television. Eh, Anderson?'

Anderson didn't say anything, but he did allow himself a smile.

'Well, now.' Reid returned to the photographs. 'No immediate cause of death. No blood. Any blood anywhere?'

'No.'

Any weapon anywhere?'

'No.'

'Hmm.' Reid pulled on his surgical gloves and flexed his fingers. 'External examination, then. Always the most important in these cases. Mike, let's have her.'

Mike pulled back the sheet from Francesca Lyons's body without a word. She was as pale as wax. Her dark auburn hair pooled behind her and her eyes were closed. She had been lovely, and her body was still good, although her breasts and belly were marbled with stretchmarks. Anderson could not see a bruise or a wound anywhere on her blue-white skin. Deep down, below his professional detachment, he recognised a stirring of grief, no less strong because this dead woman was a stranger.

Reid stood back and inspected the body at long range, his head slightly on one side. After a moment he began to walk slowly around it, viewing it from every angle. 'Found within two hours of death,' he said. 'Is that right?'

'Yes, if you believe her husband's story. He says she rang home at between 10 and 10.15 p.m. and Watkins found her dead at 11.20 p.m. The body was warm and flaccid.'

'You're not anxious about time of death, then. I couldn't be much more accurate, in any case. Well, nothing stands out, does it? Now let's look at her.'

Reid examined the body with painstaking care, talking into a dictaphone as he did so. 'Slight bruising to the back of the head about three inches behind the left ear –'

'A blow?'

The dictaphone clicked off. 'I wouldn't say so. More as if someone pulled her hair, look at the tangles.' He grabbed at the air behind Francesca's head, showing how the hand might have been buried in the thick, glossy locks. 'Mmm?' Click. 'No marks on the throat at all, she wasn't strangled with a ligature. No facial lividity or bruising around the mouth. Even the lips are pale. No classical signs of asphyxia.'

Anderson frowned. 'Not choked, not strangled. How did she die, then?'

'There's no sign of struggling. Was there anything at the scene? It didn't look like it.'

'No, nothing.'

'It's hard to say in these cases, but she could have been killed with a plastic bag. Unless it's some sort of a poison, and that's very unlikely. Obviously I'll check when I examine the internal organs. But a plastic bag would explain it.'

A plastic bag. Of course. He should have thought of it for himself. 'It's a quick death, isn't it?'

'Much quicker than you can explain by anoxia. That's why the euthanasia groups recommend it. Nobody's quite sure why they die so quickly. Probably some sort of neurochemical cardiac inhibition. Not many signs to show it, either, unless the bag was tied around the neck, and it doesn't have to be. So not much for your case, I'm afraid. Nobody found a bag anywhere, did they?'

'I don't think so. I'll make sure the team checks, though.'

Reid moved on down the body. He had little fat hands, with fingers almost absurdly like bunches of pale pink chipolata sausages, and his touch was both deft and gentle. Was the pathologist's profession stranger and sadder than the detective's?

'Her hands were tied, of course,' said Reid as he lifted Francesca's left hand. She was still wearing her wedding and engagement rings. 'A soft ligature, by the marks. Was it a scarf?'

Anderson nodded. A scarf bought at Harrods, a present from a well-paid, happy executive to his wife. He didn't need to say anything. Reid had already moved on. 'So, let's see. The murderer tied her hands and made her kneel down, possibly with his hand in her hair. Then he killed her, we speculate with a plastic bag. Now–' Reid gently parted the stiff thighs, looked between them and frowned. 'Just a minute, Anderson. There were no signs that this might be a sex crime, were there?'

'No.' No, that is, apart from the erotic pictures all over the walls.

'That's verrry strange. Look here. Bruising. Not much, but some. And –' He lifted his head. 'Mike, swabs.' To Anderson he said, 'She's wet. There's something in her vagina.'

But it hadn't looked remotely like a sex crime. 'Semen?'

'Maybe.' Reid put aside the dictaphone and for some time he and the assistant were busy, huddled over the dead woman like a pair of vultures in white coats. You couldn't rush Forensics. Anderson didn't want to watch them, and he found his eyes drawn to the dead woman's pale, still face.

At last Reid straightened. 'Curiouser and curiouser. I'll need to do an analysis, of course, but there's definitely semen. Some light bruising. And I think there's some sort of spermicide, too, by the smell.'

'Spermicide?'

'Like the stuff on condoms. So she may have had sex with two people not long before she died.'

At once Anderson remembered Chris's words. 'I smelt him . . . she had an IUD, we didn't need to use anything.' So if a man with a condom had had sex with her before she died, who else had, and why?

'You said "had sex", Doctor. Would you say there was evidence of rape?'

Reid shook his head. 'No. Just a few wee bruises here and there. What you would expect after what I think they call enthusiastic consensual intercourse.'

This changed things. That there should be evidence of one lover was only to be expected, but two? It was both puzzling and disturbing. 'Dr Reid,' Anderson said, 'thanks very much. You'll excuse me if I don't stay for the rest of the examination. I'll send someone from Forensics to help you lift prints from the skin, if there are any.'

'As you wish,' said Reid, and as Anderson turned to the door he began to talk again into his dictaphone.

Anderson hadn't lied about the quality of the canteen, but he wasn't hungry. Outside the rain had begun again, and he turned up the collar of his suit jacket as he hurried to his car. Someone had stuck a note advertising a car boot sale under one of his windscreen wipers; he wrenched it free and screwed it into a ball.

Who were the men who had made love to Francesca? He tried to picture her last evening. An argument with her husband, a cycle ride to her gallery, a meeting there with some shadowy lover, and then what? Another unexpected visitor? Someone who knew her so well that he didn't have to wear a condom?

Speculation, speculation. But she had died in such a strange, passive way. Had someone she trusted made her kneel down and covered her face?

Well, he had to share this information with the team. Perhaps the thing that had killed her was still in a bin somewhere in the gallery. Perhaps they could find other traces of her lover's presence.

And after that he would go and speak again to her sister. She had known more than she had revealed, he was sure.

'Bloody Hell,' said Nick Parker as they turned into the sweeping gravel driveway. 'How the other half lives, eh, Sarge.'

Pat stopped the car beside the gleaming silver Renault Espace next to the front door, then considered the big house. It looked boring. Everything was too tidy, too arranged. It didn't have any character. 'D'you fancy it, then? I don't.'

'Are you kidding? It must have cost half a million quid.'

'Probably,' Pat agreed. 'But if I was going to spend half a million on a house, it wouldn't be this one. Come on, Nick, let's go and see Mrs Sargent.'

The woman who opened the door wasn't at all what Pat expected. She was small and blonde and dressed in overalls liberally daubed with paint. Her face was round and it should have looked cheerful, but it was pale and there were blue stains beneath her blue eyes. 'Yes, of course, the police. Do come in. I'm sorry to look such a mess, I needed something to do, I thought I'd sponge the conservatory furniture, it's needed it for ages.'

Somehow it was hard to imagine the woman who lived in this house washing furniture. Pat wondered if she was missing something. 'Sponge it?'

'It's a paint finish,' explained Clare Sargent. 'It takes ages, and you sort of have to concentrate –' She looked down at herself and waved her hands vaguely. 'Let's go and sit in the kitchen. I can't bear the conservatory now. It's raining and it just makes me think of –'

She turned away and walked rapidly through the house's big cream-painted hall to a kitchen that was presumably supposed to look Mediterranean, with terracotta tiles on the floor and lots of bunches of dried flowers hanging from the ceiling. 'What time is it,' said Clare, glancing at the clock. 'Good God, gone four already. Well, that's something. Don will be home soon. He promised he'd come back early. Now, let me make you a cup of tea.'

Nick looked taken aback by this flurry of words, but Pat had seen it before. Some people reacted that way to shock and grief, talking, talking, as if the moment they stopped they would remember what had happened. She indicated to Nick that he should sit down at the big scrubbed pine table in the middle of the kitchen. He got out his notebook and watched, brow furrowed, as Clare hurried to and fro, saying, 'God, I simply must get a new jug, this one's a disgrace – Tea, is Earl Grey all right? Water on, God, look at the limescale on that spout, the water round here is enough to fur up your arteries, never mind the pipes, do you take sugar?'

Pat had been listening and she smiled and shook her head. Nick jumped, startled. 'Yes, please, thanks.'

At last Clare sat down at the table and swallowed hard. 'Right then,' she said, 'let's go for it. How can I help you?'

Her voice was bright and brave, but it was easy to sense the brittleness and fragility of the surface. Pat said gently, 'You know we're investigating the death of Francesca Lyons.'

Clare swallowed again and nodded, as if she didn't trust her voice.

'We're treating her death as murder. So we have to speak to everyone who might know why she was killed. Her husband said you were her best friend, so obviously we wanted to talk to you as soon as possible.'

Another nod. Then Clare said, 'It was nice of them to send a woman. I was expecting some Dixon of Dock Green person.'

'I'm the officer in charge of the investigation,' Pat said. She always enjoyed saying it.

'Really? That's excellent, isn't it.' Clare looked genuinely pleased. 'It's good to see women making progress. I mean, it's not always easy.' Well, that was true, though Pat wasn't sure what Clare would know about it. Clare ran on, 'Look at Francesca and Chris. They adored each other, they were very happy. And then when Chris lost his job it all went to pot. It wasn't Francesca's fault, you know,' she added quickly, as if Pat and Nick might think badly of her friend. 'She never held it against him, never for a minute. But he just wasn't the same afterwards: moody, bad-tempered, awful. Except with the children, of course.'

'How long had you known her?' Pat asked.

'Oh, years, years. We met at ante-natal class for our first

babies, God, it's nearly seven years ago now. And we hit it off just brilliantly. And Chris and Don got on very well together, too, played golf and so on; though I have to admit that all fell apart a bit since Chris lost his job. But Fran and I went on seeing each other. I used to go into the gallery on quiet days and we'd just sit and chat for hours.'

'What did you think of the art she sold?'

'Oh, God, well, it's a bit fruity, isn't it? That stuff in the back room, I could hardly bear to look at some of it.' Clare's eyes flashed to Nick Parker, stolidly taking notes, and she began to blush. 'But she was frightfully daring, Fran was. Unshockable, really. She used to make a game of shocking me.' Suddenly Clare's eyes filled up and ran over. She gasped and grabbed for a piece of kitchen towel to blot them. 'Oh, I'm sorry. I'm so sorry.' Pat leant over and rested her hand on Clare's arm. 'But it's so horrible, horrible! Chris didn't tell me anything but I heard about it on the local news. Is it true she was just kneeling there, just kneeling on the floor?'

The blue eyes were wide with horror and curiosity. Pat wondered how a reporter had managed to find out the position of the body, but this wasn't the time to agonise over leaks. It also wouldn't be a good idea to confirm or deny. 'Clare,' she said gently, 'who do you think killed Fran?'

Clare shook her head helplessly. For a moment she sobbed into the kitchen towel, then she looked up. Her eyes were red. 'I don't know,' she said, between gasps. 'I just don't know. I can't think. I don't think anyone didn't like her. What was there not to like? She was lovely. And two children, oh God, poor little Andrew and Jessica, what will they do with no mother?'

Did nobody know anything concrete about Francesca? 'Well,' Pat went on steadily, 'how had she been recently? Was she perfectly all right? Was anything different?'

Clare sniffed hard and rubbed the back of her hand over her face. She held on to the bedraggled paper towel, twisting it between her hands. 'She did say that she had a couple of problems at work. I mean, first there was that assistant, that awful young man Johnson, Paul Johnson. You know she had to sack him? And she did tell me recently that he was being

– difficult. So she was a bit worried about it.'

'Her new assistant mentioned it to us.' The gorgeous Daniel, the grey eyes, the Henley voice. 'We've been trying to find him, but they don't know him at the address she had for him. I don't suppose you know where he lives?'

'That rat? No, I don't.'

'Why did she sack him?'

'He had his sticky fingers in the till, that's why.' Clare tossed her head, then gasped. And do you know, I may be able to help you find him. There's a pub in town he used to hang out in, full of young chaps all talking about art and smoking dope.'

'Would that be the Lamplighter?' Nick ventured. 'Down by the theatre?'

'Yes,' said Clare, and Pat nodded at Nick in approval. 'That's the place. Maybe you'd find him there.'

'That's very helpful,' Pat said. 'Thank you. Now, you mentioned that there might have been a couple of things bothering Fran.'

'Did I? Oh yes. Maybe there was something else, too, but I don't know what it was. She went up to London last week, something to do with the gallery. I hoped we could meet there, I wanted to treat her to a couple of sessions at the Sanctuary, poor thing, she hasn't been there for ages, but she said she was working, she wouldn't have the time.'

'And you don't know what it was about.' It was hard not to sound dispirited.

'No.' Clare shook her head. 'No. I'm sorry.'

She hadn't mentioned Francesca's lover. Would she, left to herself? 'Is there anything else that you can think of, anything at all?'

The big blue eyes filled up again. 'No.'

Feeling brutal, Pat said, 'What about Fran's lover, Clare?'

Clare's lips parted and she blushed scarlet and looked down. 'Oh. I didn't know that you knew.'

We didn't, but you've just confirmed it. 'Chris suspected.'

'Did he?' Clare looked up, horror-struck. 'God, and Fran said she'd been so careful!'

At least they had got onto the subject without having to

mention the post mortem findings. Pat didn't fancy telling Clare that at least two men had had sex with Francesca the night she died. 'Did you know her lover?'

'No. No, I never met him. Fran thought it was too risky. They met through work, you see, at an antiques fair, and he's local, and if once it got out everyone would know within an hour. So she wouldn't introduce us.' A shadow crossed Clare's sad face. 'She wouldn't even tell me who he was. It was very hurtful, actually. I mean, that she didn't trust me.'

Pat glanced at Nick, not even trying to conceal her disappointment. He rolled his eyes and she pinched the bridge of her nose between finger and thumb. 'You've no idea who he is.'

'No, none.' Clare's face suddenly tightened, as if the implications had only just struck her. 'Oh, God. Do you think he killed her?'

Pat said nothing, but Clare was off. 'My God! How awful! She said he was a wonderful man, she loved him to bits, she used to look forward to meeting him so much, and all the time he was just waiting to kill her! Oh my God, it's just like a film!'

'Who, do you think, would know who he was, Clare?'

Clare shook her head. 'Nobody. I'm absolutely sure. If she had told anyone, she would have told me.'

It was nearly 6 p.m. when Anderson left the office. As he got up to go his eye fell on the telephone and his hand reached out for it. He itched to call Catherine.

But he stopped himself. However much he wanted to see her, it made no sense to call. She was afraid of the intensity that their relationship had assumed after only three encounters, and if he seemed to be pursuing her he would only reinforce that fear. He had to wait. Three months had passed, but he still believed that one day she would be the one to call him.

It was better to work. Sophie Lessiter had agreed to meet him again, and it was time to go. She hadn't wanted to meet him at home. She had named a wine bar in the centre of Guildford, and she had sounded both wary and strangely resigned. He was tired, but he hardly noticed. His mind felt sharp and eager. He took his trenchcoat from its hanger and put it on. It would be easier to walk to the bar, despite the rain.

When he arrived the wine bar was crowded, but he couldn't see Sophie anywhere. He hung his wet coat on a hook where he could keep an eye on it, bought himself a Perrier and lurked until a table near the window became free, then sat down. He didn't like to wait, but there was nothing to be done except be patient. Outside it was still raining, and the plate glass was streaked with drops and fogged with condensation.

The people in the wine bar were a combination of elegantly dressed women with shopping bags and smart office workers in their late twenties and early thirties. He watched them laugh and flirt and drink their white wines and designer beers. Not far from him a young man and a girl sat at a corner table, engrossed in each other, holding hands. He looked down into his Perrier. Among the sparkling bubbles he saw Catherine's eyes, warm, brilliant, yearning.

'Hello,' said a voice.

He looked up quickly into Sophie Lessiter's cautious face. 'Good evening,' he said, getting up. 'Let me get you a drink.'

'Yes. White wine, please.' She sat down at the table and put her handbag in front of her like a shield. She was dressed casually, in jeans and a sloppy ribbed cotton sweater that suited her thin angular figure. She stared at her folded hands as he went to the bar. When he came back, carrying the drink, she didn't look up.

'Thank you for agreeing to talk to me,' he said as he put the drink in front of her.

Her eyes were a green flash in the dimness of the bar. 'If I hadn't,' she said, 'you'd have come to my house, wouldn't you. I've taken Andrew and Jessica home with me, and I don't want anyone there to remind them of what's going on.'

'How are they?'

She didn't reply. Her fingers tapped at the top of the bag. She had the preoccupied, miserable look of a reformed smoker. 'If you want a cigarette,' he said, 'go ahead.'

'I haven't smoked for months,' she said, her mouth twisting

wryly. 'Is it that obvious?' He smiled, and she shook her head. 'I won't,' she said. 'What's the point of giving up if you start again the moment the going gets tough?'

'How are the children?' he asked.

'No.' This time the shake of her head was not friendly. 'The children aren't relevant. Why did you want to talk to me again?'

'You didn't say much before. I thought that with Andrew there perhaps you were – constrained. I wondered if there was anything you wanted to add.'

'No.' She drank half the wine and took hold of her handbag again. She studied the clasp as if it fascinated her. 'No, nothing.'

'Who do you think killed your sister, Mrs Lessiter?'

'I have no idea. No idea at all.' Suddenly she looked up, her face set. 'I think you want to prove that Chris did it. If you do, you're a swine. Do you really think that that man would kill his own wife? His children's mother?'

'All I want,' he said very steadily, 'is to find out who did do it. Tell me who you think did it.'

'I don't know.' Her voice was equally steady. 'If I did, don't you think I would have told you?'

'I think you know something you haven't told me.' She looked into his eyes for a moment, then away. When she finished her drink, she didn't look hurried. He said quietly, 'Did you know that Francesca had a lover?'

Her expression didn't change. 'Why do you ask?'

'Chris believes she had a lover. Clare Sargent knows she did. Chris thought that she was going to meet her lover last night. There were messages on her answering machine and footprints in the hallway. Do you understand why we have to find out about this man, whoever he is?'

'If Clare Sargent knew,' said Sophie, 'ask her.'

'We have. She says that Francesca wouldn't tell her who he was.'

Sophie laughed. 'Well, that was sensible, anyway! Clare couldn't keep a secret if her life depended on it.'

'Mrs Lessiter, do you know who Francesca's lover was?'

She didn't speak. Her right hand hovered in the air before her face, then lifted to her mouth as if it held a cigarette. Her lips twitched in a memory of sucking in smoke. Then she seemed to realise what she was doing, and she folded her hands around the clasp of her bag.

'Mrs Lessiter.' She didn't look up. 'Sophie.' A green glance, then her eyes were shrouded again. She knew what he needed, he was sure. He had to get it from her somehow. After a moment he said slowly, 'I was at the post mortem today.'

Her face lifted, stiff and pale. She looked like her dead sister. 'You bastard,' she said in a whisper.

'Sophie, Francesca is dead. I don't know how you felt about her, but I do believe that you know more than you're telling me.'

She looked away. 'It's not your business. I promised her.'

'Sophie, she's dead. Before she died, two men made love to her.'

'What!' Sophie's voice was so loud that the couple at the nearby table glanced round. She noticed and shut her eyes for a moment, then said, 'What are you talking about? This is revolting! What are you expecting me to believe?'

He held her eyes. 'There was semen in her vagina, and there was also spermicide from a condom. What are we supposed to believe? Do you understand why I need to find out who her lover was? Sophie, you know who he was. Tell me.'

'I don't believe it.' Sophie closed her eyes against tears. 'They were made for each other. They were so happy. If it wasn't for the children she'd have left Chris for him. I told her not to, because of Andrew and Jessica. I promised not to tell. And now —'

She covered her face with her hands. The young couple were still staring, and the man gave Anderson a look of stinging rebuke. What did they believe he was doing to Sophie? He stretched out and put his hand on her arm. 'Sophie. Tell me who he is. You may be the only person who knows.'

Slowly she lowered her hands. 'I am the only person who knows. And I can't believe that he killed her.'

'And you can't believe that Chris killed her.'

'I don't believe that any man she loved would have killed her!'

He could have pointed out that this was contrary to most of his experience, but he didn't. 'Just tell me who he is, Sophie.'

She looked defeated. 'All right.' She pushed her hand through her hair and let out a long breath. 'His name is Richard Allen. I don't know where he lives. He has a gallery in Guildford. That's all. That's all I know.'

'Thank you.' He wrote down the name with quiet satisfaction. Now that he had the long-awaited information he could focus on his subject. She looked exhausted, and suddenly he was worried about her. 'Look, do you want me to drive you home?'

'No.' Her eyes were pinched with hatred. 'Just go away. Leave me alone.'

She would probably have another drink and then drive home over the limit. He wasn't happy, but he knew not to insist. 'All right.' He got up. Sophie put her hand to her brow as if to hide herself from him, and the young man at the nearby table leant across to his girlfriend and whispered angrily into her ear. Anderson ignored the disapproval radiating from them. 'Thank you for your help,' he said.

She lifted her head and stared at him. 'You're on the wrong track, Chief Inspector. Why are you assuming that it was someone she knew? Is it easier for you? It was some maniac who did this, some psychopath. Do some real investigation. Find out who it was, before he kills someone else.'

# FIVE
## Friday 8 a.m.

Fielding was already at her desk when he walked in. She was deeply engrossed in a sheaf of papers, and she didn't took up. 'Morning, Pat.'

'Oh! Morning, sir. Have you seen the local rag?'

'Yes.' A lurid front-page report, fortunately containing a few gross errors of fact. Where did those reporters get their information from? 'If I find out who leaked it, there'll be trouble.'

'I'll be right behind you, sir. At least it wasn't completely accurate.' She lifted the piece of paper she was holding. 'There's a report from Dr Reid here, anyway.'

'Yes? What's the picture?'

'He's got semen samples from Francesca's body and pubic hairs that were found mixed up with hers. And the prints man managed to lift two prints from her skin.'

He whistled. 'That's pretty impressive. Are they any good?'

'He says yes. He lifted them from her abdomen. Another couple of hours and they wouldn't have been there to find.'

'That should help us pin things down.'

'Yes, sir.' Fielding put down the report. 'How did you get on with Mrs Lessiter?'

'She gave me the lover's name.' Fielding's expression changed instantly from weariness to disbelief and excitement. 'She didn't know his home address, but I've got the address of the gallery he runs in town. We should go there first thing, in case she calls him to warn him.'

'Bloody hell! Right you are, sir. When d'you want to go?'

'We'd better be there at nine. Here's the name: I got the address out of the phone book. Run a computer search before we go, will you?'

'Yes, sir.' Fielding hesitated, then added, 'How did you persuade her to tell you, sir?'

There had been no magic about it, after all. 'Nothing complicated, Pat. She hadn't wanted to talk in front of the child. And she felt constrained by – what would you say – loyalty. That's all.'

'Last night,' Fielding said, 'after you left, a message came over from the Super. It's on your desk.' Her face showed that she had read the message and that she had liked the contents and thought that he wouldn't. He went into his office prepared to be irritated. Why couldn't Parrish just leave him to get on with things?

The message was short and to the point. Parrish had heard about Fielding's mission killer theory – and who had told him, anyway? – and thought that it shouldn't be left unexplored. He had arranged for Anderson to visit Ian Carroll, PhD, at the Surrey University Psychological Profiling Unit, at 11.30 on Friday to discuss the case and get Carroll's initial opinions.

Parrish! He was so concerned with covering his arse that he wouldn't make easy decisions, never mind hard ones. Why waste time and money on an academic at this stage? There were three possible suspects and enough forensic evidence to make an initial case. Simple solutions were always preferable to complex ones.

Fielding appeared at the office door. 'I'm doing that search, sir.'

She hadn't come to tell him that. He raised his eyebrows and folded his hands and waited. Fielding shuffled her feet, then said, 'Sir, if you don't feel like going to see Dr Carroll, I'll go. I don't mind.'

A police officer with a theory going to see a forensic psychologist? That was a recipe for escalation of psychobabble.

Better to keep control himself. 'It's all right, I'll go. I'll be interested to hear what he has to say.'

When Richard Allen went through to open up the gallery he noticed a couple waiting in the doorway. That was promising, first thing in the morning. Perhaps they had seen his advert in the local paper. As he busied himself with the locks he surveyed them out of the corner of his eye, wondering how much they would be likely to spend.

The man definitely looked like a prospect. He had his back to the door, and he was fairly tall, with greying dark hair cut very short and the slim, well proportioned body of someone who took care of himself. He was wearing a trench-coat in an olive-green fibre with a slight shimmer, an expensive, Italian-looking garment. The loosely fastened belt hung from anodised brass loops and the deep collar was turned up against the rain, revealing heavy hand-stitched underlining. The sort of man who didn't mind spending money on quality.

His companion, on the other hand, was less of a dead cert. She was perhaps in her early thirties, and also good looking, small and slim with dark glossy hair tied back in a loose plait, but although her clothes were unremarkable and smart they didn't inspire him with confidence in the way the man's did. Fawn trousers, an ivory roll-neck jumper and a dark, heavy jacket freckled with drizzle. No jewellery that he could see. Somehow the two of them looked ill-assorted. What was it, the way they were standing? The woman had her arms folded and the man's hands were thrust deep into his well-cut pockets. They weren't a couple. Brother and sister? Boss and secretary?

Well, there was an easy way to find out. Richard unfastened the final lock and pulled the door open. 'Morning. Another horrible one, eh? I do hope you haven't been waiting long.'

The man turned around, revealing a sharp, lean face with a pronounced widow's peak and disconcertingly dark blue eyes beneath strong brows. He didn't smile. 'Mr Richard Allen?'

Suddenly this didn't look like business at all. 'Yes.'

The man and woman came in and Richard shut the door after them, feeling apprehensive. 'Mr Allen,' said the man, 'I'm

DCI Anderson, from Surrey Police. This is Detective Sergeant Fielding.'

Police! What did they want this early in the morning? 'Pleased to meet you, Chief Inspector. Sergeant.' Well, he wasn't, but *toujours la politesse*.

'Mr Allen,' said the man, 'we're investigating the murder of Francesca Lyons.'

Richard blinked. For a moment he thought that he was going to faint. Christ, oh Christ, Fran dead! What would he do? And what were the police doing here? How had they found him?

'Mr Allen,' said the woman.

'I'm sorry.' He pulled himself together. He was going to have to think very fast indeed. 'I thought you said Francesca Lyons. I'm – shocked. What's happened?'

'She was killed at her gallery on Wednesday evening,' said Anderson. 'I thought you would have heard about it. It's been on the local news, and it's in the newspaper today.' The dark blue eyes were watching him very carefully. Murder! And if the police were here, that meant they suspected him. God almighty.

'I don't read newspapers.' He wanted to cry. He mustn't. He clenched his hands to stop them from shaking, and said, 'Look, I'm really – don't know what to say. I knew Francesca quite well. Could we just go to the back of the shop for a minute? I'd like a cup of coffee.'

He didn't wait for an answer, but turned the sign on the door back to CLOSED, threw the bolt and went to the kitchen. The police officers followed him in silence. All the way he was thinking at ferocious speed, working out a story that would hang together. He had to stay out of this. Any involvement would mean that Jill would find out, and that would be disastrous. He wasn't ready. He certainly wasn't ready if Fran was dead. *Sauve qui peut*; if his marriage was all that was left, he had to protect it.

As he put the kettle on Chief Inspector Anderson said, 'You said you knew Francesca quite well. How well?'

'Through business. We met a few years ago at a fair.' Stick to the truth as much as possible. 'We had some interests in common. I was intrigued by the erotica she sold, for example. We used to have a drink together sometimes.' He set up the cafetière and poured the boiling water, concentrating on keeping his hand steady.

'Francesca's sister says that you were her lover,' said the quiet voice behind him.

The water slopped over the brim of the cafetière. He put the kettle down and swung around, letting his face show his emotion. 'That's rubbish! Why should she say that? I'm married, I've got three children.'

'You weren't Francesca's lover?'

'No! As I said, we were friends, that's all.'

'Where were you on Wednesday night, Mr Allen?'

'Ask my wife,' he said. For once a lie could come in useful. 'She knows. I was here, at the gallery, until about 10 p.m. I was home before 10.30. Jill will tell you.'

'You weren't at the Lyons gallery?'

'No. Absolutely not.' What would they have found at the gallery? Had he touched things, left fingerprints? He added unhurriedly, 'I was there last week, looking at a few of her new acquisitions. But not since.'

The Chief Inspector's eyes hadn't wavered. They revealed nothing, but the female sergeant's face was overtly sceptical. He was definitely under suspicion. He wasn't surprised when Anderson said, 'Mr Allen, I'd like to ask you to come to the station with us. I want you to make a formal statement explaining what your relationship was with Francesca Lyons and where you were on Wednesday night.'

'Am I under arrest?'

'No. Not at this stage. I'm just asking for your cooperation.'

'I've got nothing to hide.' It was astonishingly easy to tell the lie. 'Of course I'll come. Now, this minute?'

'If you don't mind.'

'No, not at all. Let me just go to the loo and lock up.'

He turned away, but Anderson's voice stopped him. 'Mr Allen, when you're at the station I'm going to ask you to give fingerprints and footprints and what we call intimate samples. Do you know what that means?'

He thought he did, but he shook his head anyway. Anderson

said, 'Blood, semen and saliva. Do you understand?'

For a moment he couldn't speak. The horror of what might have happened to Francesca broke on him like an icy wave. At last he said, 'Was she – raped?'

'I can't disclose details to you,' said Anderson in a colourless voice.

He covered his mouth with his hand. 'My God. Poor Fran.' But what risk was there? He had been wearing a condom, so there wouldn't be anything inside Fran's body for them to match. And they'd flushed the condom afterwards, the way they always did, so there was no evidence there.

Suddenly the callousness of his own thoughts overwhelmed him. 'I've got to go to the loo,' he said. He dashed away to the little bathroom at the back of the shop and slammed the door, then sat down heavily on the closed seat. His legs felt like jelly and tears surged up in his eyes, scalding and hot as acid. Fran had removed the condom from his cock afterwards with her usual little flourish, waving it in the air like a trophy before she wrapped it in a twist of tissue paper to ease its passage down the loo. She used to joke about making a collection of used condoms, arranging them artistically like butterflies, and selling them to the Tate Gallery for hundreds of thousands of pounds. The Tate would probably have bought them, too. Fran, Fran. Dead.

For a moment he covered his face with his hands and pressed his fingers to his eyes to keep in the burning tears. Then he got up, flushed the unused loo and splashed his face with cold water. He looked at himself in the fuzzy mirror over the basin and schooled his face into a suitable expression. Fran was dead. Nothing he could do would bring her back. So the next best thing was for him to keep their secret.

'Fran,' said the tape recorder on Anderson's desk, 'pick up the phone, it's me.' A shriek of rewinding. 'Fran, pick up the phone, it's me. Fran –'

'It's him,' said Fielding, stabbing the rewind button again. 'I'd swear it.'

'The tape's poor quality,' Anderson said, shaking his head.

'It'd be hard to get a decent voiceprint off it, and harder to get it accepted in court.'

'But it's *him*,' Fielding repeated, gritting her teeth.

'I think it's him, too, Pat. But don't lay too much on it. Don't let him get away with anything in the interview, though.'

'Aren't you going to interview him, sir?'

'No.' He concealed his irritation. 'I have to go and talk to Dr Carroll. You do it, Pat. You handle the samples, too. Don't forget to tell Superintendent Parrish.'

Fielding looked both excited and anxious. 'Yes, sir.' For a moment he thought she was going to say something else, but she shook her head and turned quickly away.

Dr Carroll was at the opposite end of the spectrum from Dr Reid. He was young, certainly no more than thirty-five, and cultivated an air of almost comical severity. Probably trying to compensate for the woolly, soft-edged nature of his chosen specialism. His office was pristine, and a number of framed certificates were prominently displayed on the wall.

'Chief Inspector,' said Carroll, sitting down behind his bare desk, 'I know that my department doesn't have a good reputation with you.' His voice was clipped and exact. 'So I won't waste your time. Superintendent Parrish has sent me the papers. Would you like to hear my conclusions?'

Anderson assumed a composed, neutral posture. Carroll was a practising psychologist and as likely to try to manipulate him as any suspect. This crisp, factual delivery was no doubt chosen to be acceptable to him. Well, it was acceptable; but he was still aware of the manipulation. He said dryly, 'I'd be very interested.'

'Very well.' Carroll opened a drawer and drew out a file. It contained the police photographs, a copy of the forensic reports and various other pieces of information. 'Superintendent Parrish told me that one of your officers had suggested a mission killing. I understand that the body was found in a room containing pornographic pictures.'

Anderson felt inclined to correct this to 'erotic art', but he didn't intend to rise to any of Carroll's barbs. He said only, 'That's correct.'

'Well, the officer concerned was very perceptive. This murder has all the hallmarks of a classic mission killing. I'm sure you're aware of the literature on serial murder, Chief Inspector. You know that most serial murderers are not psychotic, and that mission killers, in particular, are typically highly organised and take great care in perpetration of the crime. There will be little evidence in the way of weapons or fingerprints. The offence is planned against a targeted, personalised victim, and the whole crime is highly controlled. The victim is often restrained and compelled to adopt a submissive role.' He drew out a photograph of Francesca's body, kneeling, head bowed, hands tied. 'I think you'll agree that this fits completely with what you found at this crime scene.'

Yes, it fitted completely. But why invent a psychopath, when there were real live suspects available? Why bother to imagine a hypothetical explanation for a given set of facts, rather than simply following the facts to the logical conclusion? 'Dr Carroll, I acknowledge that this crime has some of the features of a mission killing. But not all. There were no aggressive acts carried out on the body, for example, and it didn't appear to have been arranged after death.'

Carroll shrugged. 'People are individuals, Chief Inspector, even killers. You must expect variations between one crime scene and another.'

This condescension should have been infuriating, but since Carroll was wrong it was actually mildly amusing. 'In addition, Dr Carroll, the post mortem showed that the dead woman had sex with at least one man shortly before her death. I don't think that this fits with your ideal profile.' He couldn't keep the irony from his voice.

Carroll looked shocked. 'No. Absolutely not. I would be astonished if a mission killer had engaged in sexual intercourse with a victim. It wouldn't happen.'

'Well,' said Anderson, with some relish, 'it appears that the dead woman had two visitors on the night of her death and had sex with two people. So unless we choose to invent a third, psychopathic assailant, who entered after two others had left and left no clues at all for his visit, we are bound to come to the conclusion that she had sex with her killer.' Carroll's face was stiff. 'Do you have any thoughts on that, Doctor?'

'No,' said Carroll. 'I'd have to reconsider. If the forensic evidence is that clear – Perhaps if there was evidence of rape –'

'The post mortem results suggest that intercourse was consensual.' It was satisfying to see the confusion on Carroll's face. 'Please send me a written copy of your initial findings, Dr Carroll. But I'm sure that you'll understand if we don't ask you for further help at this point.'

'I'd like to see the post mortem report,' said Carroll quickly as Anderson got to his feet.

'By all means.'

'There may be another explanation. Shall I –'

'For the moment, Dr Carroll, we have plenty of suspects in the frame. I'll be in touch if we want to pursue your theories further.'

'Your theories,' said Carroll bitterly. 'Your officer's. Not mine.'

At last, at 3 p.m., the rain had stopped. The clouds were parting to show bright blue washed sky, and the tarmac outside the Lyons Gallery was steaming.

The front door of the gallery was locked. Pat walked down the gravel path at the side. The killer's feet would have crunched on this gravel, just as hers were crunching.

She knocked on the back door and stuck her head inside. 'Carrie? Gerry?'

Daniel Gough popped out of the kitchen door like a jack in the box. Pat jumped back, startled. 'Daniel! I didn't think you'd be here.'

He grinned at her, the same lopsided, heart-stopping grin. 'I hoped I might be able to open up today, the phone's been ringing non-stop, but your DCs haven't finished yet and they say I can't sell anything until they've gone over all the records.' He swiped his hand through his floppy hair. 'Honestly, though, can you believe people? They read about poor Francesca in the local paper and they're ringing up in their hundreds to find out about the "juicy pictures". Quite revolting, really.'

Gerry Hart appeared at the doorway of the office. 'Sarge, is that you?'

'Yes. Sorry,' she said to Daniel. 'How are you doing, Gerry?'

'Bloody hell,' said Gerry, rolling his eyes.

Pat smiled apologetically at Daniel and said, 'I'll come back to you later and let you know if you can open tomorrow.'

'I hope so. That's what I've been telling all the prurient punters.'

Daniel returned to the kitchen and sat down again at the Formica table. In front of him were a pot of taramasalata, a packet of potato crisps and a large, thick book. He grinned at Pat as she went down the corridor.

'Bloody hell, Sarge,' said Gerry again as she entered the office, 'these pictures, Christ, they're enough to stop a clock, aren't they? Right put me and Carrie off the job sometimes.'

'You mean they made you want to be on the job,' said Carrie from the desk. 'Sarge, we heard you got Francesca's lover. Any luck with him? Is he nicked?'

She shook her head. 'Sorry, Carrie, no. He insists they were just friends and he wasn't here on Wednesday night. I didn't believe him, but he cooperated fully, gave all the samples like a lamb. Maybe when the prints are matched we'll have a chance, but the lab's working ten to the dozen, they couldn't do it while we waited. They promised tomorrow. And until then –'

'You've had to let him go,' said Carrie, with the resignation of an experienced officer.

'You guessed it. And the governor's been to see the psychologists and blown bloody great holes in my mission killer theory.' She knew her voice revealed her anger, and she didn't care. 'So we're back to basic detecting. How are you two doing? Any signs of any missing pictures?'

'Well, there's a few we'd give a home to, eh, Carrie?' said Gerry. 'What d'you think of this one, Sarge?'

He held out an unframed, mounted picture. Pat took it from him and looked at it. She managed to keep her face straight, but she wanted to gasp with shock and arousal. The picture showed a pretty girl kneeling over her lover, mouthing his cock while he studied her open sex and pushed his fingers deep into her. Her face was suffused with an astonishing blend of voluptuous enjoyment of her mouthful and uncontrollable pleasure at what the man was doing. The man's face was hidden, but suddenly Pat's mind changed the girl's face for her own and made the hard supple body of the man into Daniel's body; the erect veined shaft of the penis that the girl so lovingly sucked, into Daniel's penis.

She hastily put the picture back into Gerry's hand. 'Yes, Gerry, I see what you mean.'

'Given us some ideas, though, hasn't it, Carrie?'

Carrie grinned, apparently not in the least embarrassed. Didn't she think it unprofessional to have Gerry flaunting their relationship in front of their sergeant? Apparently not. Anyway, it was time to get things back on track. 'Well,' Pat said, 'how many pictures are missing?'

Carrie made a face, as if she'd rather have gone on showing Pat the erotica. 'Well,' she said, holding out their notes, 'she didn't keep records separately for the different types of picture, so we've gone through everything. There are about a dozen unaccounted for, dating back more than a year. Here's the list. We've just about finished now.'

Pat looked at the list, nonplussed. 'Which of these are erotic?'

Gerry shrugged. 'Don't know, Sarge.'

'Well –' She shook her head. 'Tidy the things up. Daniel will need to open the gallery tomorrow. I'll ask him about these pictures. You get back to the office and see if the governor's got anything for you to do.'

Carrie said slyly, 'He's a bit of all right, isn't he, Sarge? Daniel, I mean?'

'Is he? I hadn't noticed.'

What a blatant lie. She went through to the kitchen. Daniel looked up from his book with a mouthful of taramasalata. There was a little blob of it at the corner of his upper lip. How wonderful it would be to lick it away. The image of the picture was burned on her mind, she couldn't shift it.

'How are things?' Daniel asked.

'We've just about finished looking at the records. You'll be able to open up tomorrow.'

'Excellent.' He dipped another crisp in the taramasalata and held it out to her. 'Fancy some?'

Yes, she fancied some, and straight away. But she couldn't. She would have liked to have fed from his fingers, but she couldn't do that either. 'I had lunch in the office,' she said, sitting down beside him.

'The office,' he said. 'I heard you say that before. Isn't it a police station, where you work?'

'Yes.' His curiosity made her smile. 'Uniformed officers call it the nick. But in CID we call it the office.'

He ate the crisp with its load of fish. 'If it's not frightfully improper of me,' he asked tentatively, 'could I ask you what it's like, being a detective? I mean, especially when you're a woman.'

She had to control this, or it would get out of hand. 'Daniel,' she said, looking into his innocent grey eyes, 'could you help me with this list of pictures? I don't know one artist from another, and I need to know which of these might have had an erotic subject; whether they could be the one you thought might have gone missing.'

He looked disappointed. He took the list from her hand, staining it with oil and fish roe. 'Well,' he said after a quick look, 'yes –' He looked around vaguely for a pencil and she handed him her pen. Their fingers touched and she felt a shock, but he didn't respond. He was left-handed, she noticed. He put a tick against three of the pictures and handed the list and the pen back to her. 'There you are,' he said. 'The Tauzin, the Gill and the Dodson. Dodson's my favourite, by the way.'

For a moment she didn't know what to say. She put the pen away. Daniel dipped another crisp, then looked up at her. 'Listen,' he said, 'I don't suppose, I wonder, I mean, would you, could you come out to dinner with me tonight?'

She couldn't believe that he had actually asked her. And she was going to have to refuse! For a moment she nearly said Yes, and bugger the consequences, bugger her promotion, bugger everything. But she couldn't. DI was too important to risk. 'Daniel, I'm very sorry. But I can't – see anyone who might have to give evidence in this case. Otherwise I'd love to. I hope you understand.'

He looked as if she had thrown water in his face. 'Well,' he said after a minute, 'I don't understand, not really. But if you say you can't, well, I just have to take your word for it.'

'I'm sorry,' she said again.

All the way down the gravel path she felt as if it should still be raining.


Anderson was half immersed in paperwork when Nick Parker appeared at the door, lurking tentatively. 'Sir,' he said, 'do you have a minute? Sergeant Fielding's not back from the gallery yet, and I –'

Anderson put his pen down and nodded. 'All right, Nick. Come in. What's up?'

Nick shut the door and bit his lip. 'I've been to the Lamplighter, sir, looking for Paul Johnson. There was someone there who told me where to find him.'

'Well done.' That was pretty good going, for a new detective constable. 'Was it easy?'

Slowly Nick's white skin flushed cherry red. 'Yes and no, sir. You know what sort of a place the Lamplighter is. I, I didn't say who I was, I just –'

He broke off and Anderson restrained a smile. The Lamp-lighter was a gay pub, and Nick must have let it be thought that he was looking for Johnson for personal reasons. That was beyond the call of duty. 'Good move, Nick. I bet you were glad you were on your own.'

'Yes. Don't tell Gerry, will you, sir? He'd never let me forget it. Anyway, I got his address and I tracked him down there. He was – busy. He was with his boyfriend.'

The blush was deepening and Anderson watched Nick with a certain amount of concern. It looked as if he might have found this whole thing quite difficult, and that could have affected his judgement. 'What did he tell you, Nick?'

'He said he hadn't seen Francesca since she sacked him. He said he was at home with his boyfriend on Wednesday night. So I suppose he's got an alibi, sir.'

'Did the boyfriend confirm it?'

'Not in so many words, sir. He wasn't there, he was in the bedroom. Johnson was, he was in a state of undress, sir.'

Poor young Nick, out on his first solo bit of detecting and confronted by a naked homosexual murder suspect. It shouldn't happen to a dog, but even so it was a pity. 'Look, Nick, you seem a bit shaken. How certain are you that Johnson was telling you the truth? You know that alibis from lovers can be unreliable.'

'I'm as sure as I can be, sir,' said Nick stolidly.

'All right. Write up the interview and tell Sergeant Fielding as soon as she reappears. And well done for following through, Nick.'

'Thanks, sir.' Nick nodded uncomfortably, then slithered out.

Ah well, it wasn't all a waste of time. Nick had found Johnson, after all, and that could be useful. He'd have to send Fielding along there; Fielding and Vickers, perhaps. If women did the interview, Johnson would be devoid of any sexual weapons to wield against them.

But he didn't have time for it today. His desk was covered in reports, forms and notes, all the usual paraphernalia of two days' local crime – theft, assault, even a suspected arson. People didn't stop misbehaving just because CID were investigating a murder, and he couldn't concentrate when he knew that things were piling up. He'd work at it tonight for as long as it took, read all the reports, sign everything he was supposed to sign, and tomorrow he'd be able to give his full attention to the Lyons case.

He got up and went to the door. Nick walked past on his way to the kitchen and said, 'Cup of tea, sir?'

'Yes,' he said. 'Good idea.' Then he closed the door and sat down at his desk with a long sigh.

# SIX
## Saturday 9 a.m.

'Jesus,' Pat said, shaking out the newspaper, 'don't the tabloid press love this stuff? "Beautiful Art Dealer Executed in Chilling Ordeal" shock horror probe. I think nobody should be allowed to be a journalist unless they've had a violent bereavement. That would teach them a thing or two.'

'Four confessions yesterday, apparently,' said Anderson dryly. 'Just as well not all the details got out. None of them know about how her hands were tied, so we can rule them out.'

Pat folded the newspaper and put it down. 'Sir, I've been thinking about my theory.' His face changed, becoming cold and remote. 'I want to run some more searches on the national computer. To widen the parameters. You know that serial killers often travel. And it must be time we set up a proper incident room.'

He shook his head. 'Pat, you know as well as I do how resource-intensive a computerised incident room is. Not just money, people. Where we can handle the case locally, especially with local suspects, it's not justifiable. Deal with the data you've got before you look for more. You're just hoping to find facts that fit your theory.'

What would it take for him to listen to her, another killing? She would bloody well do the searches anyway, and stuff him. He didn't have to know. She felt that her face might be showing her stubborn determination, so to throw him off the track she said, 'We got that phone printout, sir. A call was made to the Lyons's house from the gallery at two minutes to ten on Wednesday night. So if Francesca made it, we have her time of death pinned down to within an hour and twenty minutes.'

'And if Chris made it, he didn't leave fingerprints.'

'My money's on Richard Allen, sir. He wasn't telling us the truth. I wonder if –'

'We haven't got enough evidence for an arrest. What do you want to do, bring him in and grill him? Wait until the fingerprints are checked. If the ones from the body come out positive you can have him for as long as you want. And there's still Johnson. There were two messages on that answerphone and two sets of footprints.'

'You don't think Nick did much of a job on Johnson, sir.'

'No, I think he was thrown. It sounds as if Johnson's one of the upfront sort of gays. I think you should go back and reinterview him later.'

That made sense. 'All right, sir.' She shuffled her papers and pulled out the list of missing pictures, still stained with Daniel's taramasalata. 'Sir, this is the list of the pictures which Carrie and Gerry couldn't tie up. They may include the picture that Daniel thought was missing.' Her voice tried to go all soft and fuzzy when she said 'Daniel', but she kept it crisp. The last thing she wanted was to let her chief know that she was falling for a witness.

She pushed the paper over to Anderson. He looked at the oily stains with distaste. 'All right,' he said. 'What are the ticks?'

'Those are the erotic pictures, sir. I thought that we should concentrate on those, given what Daniel said about Francesca's state of mind – that he thought she was worried about the private art.'

'Good idea. Well, we need to know where she bought them, for a start. Then we can start looking for them.'

'I've got that somewhere.' She flicked quickly through the papers. 'Here you are, sir. Carrie made another list of the sources of all the missing pictures.'

He took the second list from her. 'Right.' There was a short silence while he compared the two. 'Hmm. Two of the erotic ones come from the same dealer. So only two to visit, on this first shortlist.'

'One other thing, sir. Gerry found the cash book entry relating to Francesca's trip to the Tate. It said "Checking provenances". I wasn't sure what a provenance was,' she admitted, looking up hopefully.

'It means a picture's history,' he said.

'Oh. Well, it didn't say which picture it related to.' She hesitated, then said, 'Sir, I was wondering whether we ought to contact the Yard. They've got an Art and Antiques unit, haven't they? They might be able to help us.'

'It's a fraud unit,' Anderson said. 'Fraud's not relevant here, we're investigating a murder. We're quite capable of tracing these pictures back through their dealers.'

She might have guessed that he would take the suggestion badly. He was very independent; in an ideal world he'd prefer to do everything himself, and he certainly didn't like asking people from outside the patch for help. He didn't like dealing with the Regional Crime Squad, let alone the over-resourced, over-paid and arrogant Met. It didn't matter, anyway, it was just a thought. She shrugged. 'I'm not bothered, sir.'

They looked at each other for a moment. He didn't seem to have any more comments to make, and there wasn't anything she wanted to add. 'Well,' she said at last, 'I'll go off and talk to Johnson, then. Sir, if you'd like to go to the art dealers, I'd be grateful. I'm sure you'll speak their language better than I would.'

That got a smile, anyway. She felt a twinge of relief. It was distinctly uncomfortable to be in his black books for any space of time. Anderson stretched and said, 'Well, it'll make a pleasant change.' He looked at her sidelong, then added, 'Though it occurs to me that you seem quite eager to make up for your lack of knowledge in that particular field.'

Damn! Was she so transparent? She couldn't think of anything to say in response, so she smiled awkwardly and got up to go before her blush made things worse.

Anderson had never noticed before quite how many art galleries there were. Now that he had an interest in them some roads seemed to be lined with one after another, all sadly similar in their good-taste minimalism of white shop fronts with plain black copperplate writing.

His first target was no different. It was a smallish frontage, labelled PHILIP FAIRFAX, FINE ART. One single picture, a rather fine eighteenth-century landscape *à la* Stubbs, stood in the window.

There was nobody in the gallery, and this on a Saturday, too. How did these people earn their livings? They must charge a swingeing margin when they did sell a picture.

A buzzer had sounded when he pushed open the door, and after only a few seconds a tall, grey-haired man appeared, eyebrows elegantly arched. 'Good morning,' said a voice that would have cut crystal, never mind glass. 'Can I help you?'

'Mr Fairfax? I'm Chief Inspector Anderson. We spoke on the telephone.'

'Oh yes. Of course.' Fairfax looked Anderson up and down as if he had expected something completely different. 'Do come through, Chief Inspector. I've looked out the papers relating to the Gill. A lovely little work. I was sorry to hear it has been stolen.'

'I don't know that it has been. It's possible, though.'

Fairfax led the way through to a little sitting-room at the back, furnished with a fine antique desk and leather overstuffed chairs. 'More seasonable weather now,' he commented. Anderson nodded amiably enough, but he didn't want to talk about the weather. After a second Fairfax said, 'Now, here are the records. I bought the picture – it was an etching, by the way, an original signed etching – from a London gallery at the end of last year. Francesca bought it from me about six months ago.' He handed the book over to Anderson. His face was lined beneath his perfectly-coiffed silver hair. 'I must say,' he said, 'I was so distressed to hear about her murder. How utterly appalling. If there's anything else I can do, of course, you only need to ask.'

Anderson copied the details of the picture from the heavy ledger. 'Actually,' he said after a short pause, 'there is a way you could help. I'm not familiar with your business, and it's just possible that whoever killed Francesca may have known about the art she sold. If you can give me any explanation of provenances, say, I would be grateful.'

'Well, of course. Shall I make us a cup of tea?'

Over beautifully-served Darjeeling Fairfax proceeded to explain. 'Provenances are frightfully important. They're the history of a picture. They show how it got to where it is, from museums, galleries, private collections. Mostly the picture carries labels on its back that show where it's been, and if you look in the Tate gallery under the painter you'll find details of each known work and what the Tate knows about that picture's travels.'

'Why are they so important?'

'Not just because they authenticate the picture, though that's essential, of course. It's because people will pay more for a picture with an illustrious history; one that belonged to somebody famous, for example. Take that one in my window. That used to belong to the Prince Regent, if you can believe it. He gave it to a servant as a present and I can trace it right the way through from there. People will pay a huge amount to be able to describe a picture's history with such accuracy.'

Wasn't the appearance of the picture the important thing? Well, never mind. 'And how would you make sure that a provenance was authentic?'

'Well, for a start, ask the person selling the picture for the documentation. Originals, preferably. And if you're concerned, call up the galleries who are supposed to have sold the picture to check with them. I get calls regularly. It's much better to help people out than end up associated with an un-authenticated picture. We have our reputations to think of.'

Anderson was surprised by the seriousness of Fairfax's tone. 'Is there a lot of fraud, then?'

'Well, there has been a fair amount in twentieth-century works recently. Like that Gill, by the way, though of course that had an impeccable history. A gang based in France has forged some very famous works – Corbusier, Giacometti, Magritte – and planted false documentation all over the place, including in the Tate. It created quite a stir. I haven't heard of anything in the erotica market, though. Fraudsters are generally greedy, they go for paintings worth hundreds of thousands of pounds. That little Gill sold to Francesca for £5,000, and she wouldn't have sold it on for more than £8,000.'

He hadn't been wrong about the mark-up. Deep in thought, he finished his tea. It was excellent to the last drop. When he set down the bone china cup Fairfax said, 'Well, that's all, Chief Inspector. I could talk for hours, of course, but I think that's a fair summary.'

'Thank you for your help, Mr Fairfax. May I come back to you if I need anything more?'

'Of course, of course.' Fairfax got up to accompany him to the door. And you do know that Scotland Yard have a special unit who deal with art fraud? I spoke to one of them once. A frightfully common chap, but he knew what he was talking about.'

'Thank you,' said Anderson dryly.

As they left the study he looked out into the street and almost stopped breathing. There, looking at the landscape in the window, was Catherine Marshall. He nodded to Fairfax, brushed at the lapels of his jacket and went quickly out of the door.

She was still looking at the picture, her brows knitted in a worried expression that softened his heart. For a moment he stood behind her, not speaking, just looking at the tousled waves of her shoulder-length brown hair and remembering how silky it was to touch. Her scent was a faint fresh fragrance that made his eyelids heavy with remembrance. It was strangely moving to be so close to her while she was unaware of his presence.

She was about to move on. He said softly, 'Catherine, hello.'

Her eyes met his in the glass of the window. Her lips parted. She said nothing, but he saw in her soft mouth and her dark pupils that she was not unhappy to see him. He smiled at her reflection. 'How are you?'

'Fine,' she said, her voice hardly more than a whisper.

'Are you thinking of buying a picture?'

'Oh –' She turned away from the glass and glanced up at him, face to face. God, her eyes were so gentle, her mouth was so lovely, he wanted to kiss her. Her throat was white and smooth. If he caught her by the arms and pulled her towards

77

him it would be revealed, prey for his predator's lips. But there was no rush, now that he had found her again. He would stalk her at his leisure.

'I was thinking of it,' she said after a moment. 'Not for me, it's for my brother, for a present.' She smiled, a little hesitant smile. He was standing close to her, but she didn't move back. He could almost feel her warmth. 'I know what you're doing,' she said. 'They mentioned you on the local news. You're investigating the murder of that art dealer. How horrible.'

He didn't want to talk to her about work. 'Catherine, you're right, I am working. I'd love to ask you for a cup of coffee, but I can't stop now. But I'm so glad we met. I've been thinking about you a lot.'

'Have you?' She looked as though she expected him to have been forgetting her.

'Yes. I've missed you.'

She turned away, her eyes cast down as if she wanted to hide her response. 'Catherine,' he said softly, 'Come to dinner with me tonight.'

There was a long pause. Then she turned around, meeting his eyes with sudden boldness. 'No,' she said. 'But I tell you what, John. I'll buy you dinner tonight.'

He smiled at the resolution in her face. She was a business-woman, after all. Was it only to him that she showed the fragility beneath the surface? 'What is this,' he enquired with a glint of laughter, 'some sort of a test to find out how Neanderthal I am?'

'No!' she protested, then her face softened. 'Well, yes, it is, a bit. It's important, John. I want to be independent. Before, you always –'

He didn't want her to think about before. 'I would be very happy to come to dinner with you,' he said, with smiling formality.

'You would?' She looked astonished.

'Yes.' He watched her face. It didn't look reassured. How could he get through to her? 'Now you're wondering if I've just agreed because I want to impress you.'

That hit home, but her reaction was not what he intended. She swung away from him, saying in a choked voice, 'God, John, don't read my mind –'

'Catherine.' He put all his sincerity into his voice. 'I've missed you. I want to see you very much. Even if my self-esteem depended on my always paying, I'd probably still let you pay. But it doesn't.'

There was a silence. Then she turned and looked up at him with her face set as if she had just accepted a challenge. 'All right,' she said. 'Well, if I'm paying, you should choose. Where would you like to go?'

'How about the Black Swan?' he suggested easily, and saw from her eyes that she had expected him to choose somewhere less expensive and was pleased that he hadn't. 'I can walk there from home,' he explained. 'It's a shame to have to drive to a place with such a good wine list.'

'The Black Swan would be excellent,' she agreed.

'8 p.m.?'

'That's fine. Yes.'

'I'm looking forward to it, Catherine. Very much.' Should he kiss her now? No. No, not now. Time enough for that later. He smiled at her. 'Good luck in finding a painting for your brother.'

'Thank you.' She looked down at her shoes, then up into his eyes. Her face was pale. 'See you tonight.'

'Tonight,' he echoed, and all the way to the car he was walking on air.

'Are you going to start off with a caution, Sarge?'

Pat slammed the door of the car and looked up at the block of flats. It was a rather ordinary place, not what she had come to expect from these artistic types, but it was a good deal nicer than an unemployed shop assistant should be able to afford. Perhaps Johnson's boyfriend had enough money for two. 'I ought to, strictly,' she admitted. 'But if he's clever he'll insist on a brief and God knows what. Not for the moment.'

Gerry shrugged. He was never excited by policies and procedures. 'You're the boss, Sarge.'

After a long wait the door opened to reveal a tall, thin, dark young man dressed from head to foot in black. His eyes flashed over Pat and moved straight on to Gerry, whose broad shoulders and curling hair were clearly much more interesting.

'Paul Johnson?' said Pat coldly.

'Yes.' He had a posh voice too, but unlike Daniel's it was lazy and sardonic. She didn't like it.

'I'm Detective Sergeant Fielding, Surrey Police. This is DC Hart. We'd like to talk to you.'

He stood with his hand on the door, scowling. 'I already spoke to one of your people. Red-haired chap.'

'We'd like to talk to you too.'

For a moment it looked as if he would refuse. Then he turned abruptly from the door. 'Come in.'

The lounge was painted cream and hung with prints in elaborate frames. Every chair was draped with rugs and throws in neutral colours. There was a big plant in the corner. The overall effect was rather like the sitting room of an old-fashioned boarding house. The furniture oozed the suspiciously sweet scent of marijuana. Gerry wrinkled his nose and looked sharply around. He said, 'Where d'you keep the stash, Paul?'

Johnson arched his brows superciliously. 'I don't know what you mean.'

Gerry shrugged, then went over to stand in the shadows by the window, folded his arms and leant against the wall.

'Your boyfriend in?' Pat asked.

Johnson had been staring at Gerry, but now he looked angrily at her. 'No. He works on Saturdays. Why, what's it to do with him?'

'We need to talk to him. I understand he's your alibi. Where does he work?'

'Look,' said Johnson, 'leave him alone.'

'But you said he was with you on Wednesday evening. We want to check on it.'

He bit the inside of his cheek. 'There's nothing to check. I don't know anything about what happened to Francesca.'

'But she did sack you, didn't she?'

He hesitated. 'Yes. That doesn't mean I wanted to kill her, though.'

'Why did she sack you?'

'It's not relevant.' Johnson shifted from foot to foot and glanced across at Gerry. His thin, sensual lips were quivering.

She could just imagine him sidling up to poor young Nick, threatening him sexually, putting him off. Well, it wouldn't work with her, and Gerry was too thick-skinned to mind.

'What do you mean, it's not relevant? Two months ago she gives you the big E, and nobody seems to know why.' There was no need to reveal what Clare had said about Johnson's sticky fingers. 'And now she's dead. I would have thought it was extremely relevant.'

'I didn't go near her,' Johnson insisted. 'I was with Hugh.'

'Nobody's spoken to Hugh. You didn't even let him out of the bedroom before. Where does he work?'

'Look, just leave Hugh alone, will you?' The pitch of his voice was rising as he lost control. He wasn't the best liar she had ever seen. Nick must have been really upset to have missed this.

'Sounds as if he doesn't trust his boyfriend to cover for him, Sarge,' commented Gerry from the window.

'I agree,' she said. 'Listen, Paul, you'd better tell us exactly what happened between you and Francesca. Then maybe we'll leave Hugh alone.' Johnson turned away, lacing his fingers. He didn't reply. After a moment she added, 'What did you do, eh? Did you nick something, or what?'

He spun around, his pale face rigid. 'What the hell do you know?'

'Educated guess.'

For a second she thought he was going to break, but he didn't. 'That's ridiculous. She just didn't like me, the cow.'

'How long had you worked there?'

'Two and a half years.' He leant against the fireplace and looked down his nose at her.

'Why didn't you sue her for wrongful dismissal, then?' He said nothing. Pat glanced at Gerry. 'Well, your problem, Paul. Gerry, I think we've got enough to arrest Mr Johnson at this point, don't you?'

'Absolutely, Sarge.'

Johnson lifted his head, looking horrified. 'The cells should be nice and full on a Saturday night,' Pat told him with a smile. 'I think we can promise you some very interesting company. What happened to the last gay bloke who got left in over a

Saturday night, Gerry? I heard he didn't sit down for a week.'

'This is absurd,' Johnson whispered. 'You're threatening me. You can't do this. You've got no evidence.'

He was absolutely right, but she felt brazenly confident. 'Just watch me. All I have to do is tell the desk sergeant your flat smelled of dope. He hates the stuff! Gerry, have you got the cuffs?'

Bluff, pure and simple, but it worked. As Gerry reached into his pocket Johnson lurched upright and said, 'All right. Look, hang on, OK?'

'Are you going to cooperate?'

'Yes.' His voice was sullen.

She smiled. 'All right, Gerry, stand down for now. Paul, let's start again. Why did Francesca sack you?'

'She said –' He hesitated, then jerked up his chin angrily. 'I took a couple of pictures.'

Now the truth was coming out. 'You stole them?'

'She hardly bloody paid me, stingy cow.'

'You stole them. What did you do with them?'

He looked unrepentant. 'Sold them.'

'And she found out?' A petulant shrug. 'Well, if she caught you, why didn't she prosecute you? Why not call the police? She didn't, we'd know if she did.' Silence. 'Paul, why didn't she prosecute you?'

At last he met her eyes. He didn't look so brazen now. 'I – knew something about her.'

Blackmail! That explained the lifestyle. It was easy to guess what he had known, but he might as well dig his own hole. 'What did you know?'

'That she had a lover.' Johnson's face was a mirror of old anger. 'I came back to the gallery one night, I'd left my jacket, and I found them at it. Fucking like minks on that old chaise longue in her office. And she had the gall to disapprove of my lifestyle! At least I wasn't cheating on a husband and two children.'

Vicious self-righteous bastard. 'How much did you get out of her?'

He wrinkled his nose. 'Not much. Mean cow. Moaning about her mortgage.'

God, poor Francesca! Supporting her husband and family, staying with them although she loved someone else, torn in two, and at the same time this little toe-rag Johnson extorting money from her. He might have killed her, too. He was callous enough. 'Right,' she said, fighting down her anger. 'That's enough. Johnson, you're coming to the station with us. I want a formal statement from you.'

'What?' He looked astonished. 'But you said –'

'A formal statement and intimate samples. Know what they are? Blood, semen and saliva.' She glanced across at Gerry. 'What have we got in the magazine line, Gerry? Anything that'll help Mr Johnson give us a semen sample? I shouldn't think *Penthouse* will do much for him.'

'Might have something in the confiscations lock-up,' Gerry said, straight-faced. 'Or maybe we ought to let him bring his own, so to speak.'

Johnson looked winded. Pat gave him her very best feral grin. 'Right, Paul. All ready?'

Stephanie considered herself in the mirror and was satisfied. She had spent half the morning getting ready, showering and perfuming herself, dressing carefully from the pretty under-wear outwards, applying a little subtle makeup, drying and brushing her long thick hair until it gleamed and tumbled. There was an advantage she had over Andrea, for a start. Andrea's hair was short and fine, like a child's; very gamine, very fetching, but not sexy like Stephanie's glossy mane. At least, she hoped that James would see it that way.

She had wanted James ever since she met him. He hadn't been the original reason that she had agreed to help Andrea, she had done that for the money. Nobody got rich from working at the Tate Gallery, and the prospect of several thousands of pounds on a regular basis, for not that much effort, was irresistible. But although she now had a tidy little reserve tucked away – offshore, of course – she didn't pull out of the game. And that was because she wanted James.

And today she was going to have him. Last time they met he had seemed to be dropping hints that all wasn't as it should be between him and Andrea. That meant a chance for her.

She didn't believe Andrea's protestations of friendship. This was all business. Andrea needed her because she could plant false records in the Tate's archives, and the day she stopped being useful Andrea would drop her.

For a moment Stephanie imagined Clive and felt guilty. Strictly speaking she should probably have chucked him before she tried to seduce James. But then if she failed she would be left with nothing. It was safer to adopt a belt and braces approach.

The doorbell! That would be James, late as usual. She ran to the door, smoothed her skirt and tossed back her hair, smiled and opened it. 'James. Hi.'

He was leaning against the doorpost, looking down at her with those glittering brown eyes. His tangle of curly dark hair tumbled over his forehead. God, he was gorgeous. The aura of danger that surrounded him made her weak at the knees. 'Stephanie. Hi.' His voice was rough and he always sounded as if he was mocking her.

'Come in. Come on in.' She gestured him through the door. 'Jane's away for the weekend, so we're all alone.'

As she had intended, he caught the significance of that remark. 'All alone?' He turned and looked at her. He didn't smile, he rarely smiled.

'Want some coffee?' she said brightly. She meant to get him into bed, but she wasn't going to hurl herself at him. He was an artist, after all, he would appreciate a bit of subtlety.

'Yes. Thanks.' He came and stood behind her in the kitchen, looming over her. Six foot two if he was an inch, and shoulders like a bodybuilder's. Wasted on Andrea, wasted. 'So,' he said, 'are you still happy with another Tauzin for the latest project?'

'Yes.' She arranged the coffee carefully in the little gadget she had brought back from Italy and set it on the heat. 'Yes, definitely. He's ideal. There are several well-attested pictures that are untraced, and where that's the case we can invent others with very little risk. And I've managed to find a supply of labels and invoices from the O'Hara Gallery in the West End. It closed down in 1990, nobody will be able to check anything, and it often carried erotica. It really did do a retrospective on Tauzin in the middle eighties. We could do two, if you like.' She turned around and looked up into his brooding face. 'Apart from anything else, James, you do do them so beautifully.'

He raised his heavy brows. 'Thanks.'

'Don't sound so cynical, I mean it. That last one you did was gorgeous. Really sexy.' She braced her arms against the counter top and leant back, allowing her breasts to protrude.

He didn't seem to notice, or if he did he didn't react. 'What's the likely value?'

'A couple of Tauzins sold at auction in Italy last month for more than 25 million lire each.'

He frowned. 'How much is that?'

'More than £10,000, darling.'

The dark brows arched again. 'Andrea will like that. She's been nagging me to get us into the five-figure bracket.'

'Well, we have to balance the risk against the return, don't we? Andrea just puts them on to the market. You and I are the ones that do all the work.'

The thin lips twisted slowly into one of his rare smiles. 'Maybe. But it was her idea originally, wasn't it.'

The coffee was simmering. She poured it into espresso cups and said, 'Let's go through to the sitting room. We can discuss subjects, if you like.'

She sat down on the sofa in a shaft of sunlight and crossed her legs. Her short skirt slid up her thighs, stopping just short of the tops of her stockings. She saw James look, and the concentrated expression on his face made her swallow. She took a sip of her coffee, trying not to show that she knew he was looking. 'Tauzin liked the idea of two girls together,' she said. 'Or one girl alone, come to that. There's a lovely one of a girl masturbating.'

'Yes,' said James. 'I know.' He put down his coffee cup and came and sat down next to her. There was a silence. She watched his face, and her breathing made her lips cold.

At last he said, 'Does Clive know about this, Stephanie?'

'About what?' she asked, her voice high-pitched with anxiety.

'That you're trying to seduce me.'

Now was the time to get cold feet. But she didn't want to

get cold feet. She wanted James. She said steadily, 'I hadn't intended to tell him.'

'And Andrea?'

'That's up to you,' she said.

He leant towards her. His mouth was no more than a foot from hers. Through his parted lips she could see his sharp white teeth. He was silent. Her breasts ached, she wanted him so much. 'James,' she said.

He put his hand on her thigh, just below the hem of her skirt. She jumped with shock. Still looking into her eyes, he tugged her knee sharply towards him so that her legs were parted. His fingers were very hard and strong and so rough that she felt a shudder of delicious fear. Without a word he slid his hand up the inside of her thigh. His fingers found the edge of her knickers and lifted it and slipped inside. She gasped as he pushed one finger into her, so deeply that it felt as if he had stabbed her. But she didn't protest or pull away. This was what she had wanted.

'You're wet,' he said in a voice thick with lust. 'Jesus.'

His finger moved to and fro, stirring inside her. He slid another finger in beside it and clutched at her, pressing both fingers hard against the front wall of her vagina. A sudden wave of pleasure made her reel. 'James,' she moaned.

'Shit,' he said, still thrusting and squeezing. 'How long have you been planning this, Stephanie?'

She made her eyes open. 'Since I met you.'

'Horny bitch.' He grabbed her hand and put it on his fly. Beneath the fabric his erection throbbed, already hard for her. She gasped and fumbled with the zip. He continued to fuck her with his fingers and with his other hand he pulled up her tight top to reveal her breasts and hauled one soft mound out of the cup of her bra. His fingers closed on her nipple and she gave a little sharp cry of pleasure.

At last his zip came undone and she pushed her hand inside, eager for her first feel of his cock. There it was, hot to the touch, silky and hard. She pulled it free and gasped with admiration. It was just what she had imagined, as splendid as his body, thick and strong and ridged with dark veins.

'Suck it,' he gasped. He grabbed her head and pushed it

down into his lap. She would have liked to have taken her time, to have licked the shaft and flicked her tongue delicately around the glossy head, but he was in a hurry. He thrust up towards her face, found her parted lips and pushed between them without hesitation. The thick shaft slid into her mouth so far she thought she would choke. She moaned in protest, but then his fingers slipped out of her wet vagina and began to tease and titillate her swollen clitoris and the pleasure was so wonderful that she slumped over his lap and let him fuck her mouth, gagging every time the head of his cock nudged against the back of her throat.

His hand clutched at her hair and he grunted as he thrust. Was he going to come in her mouth? No, she didn't want it, she wanted him to screw her. She began to struggle, trying to pull free, and at last he released her and tugged her head back to stare into her face with fierce eyes. 'What's the matter?'

He looked really dangerous now. She wriggled, vainly trying to get her hair free. 'I just –'

'Bitch.' He caught her by her arm and her knee and threw her backwards onto the sofa, so hard that the breath was bounced out of her. She tried to get up and he pushed her back with one hand and held her down, while with the other he forced up her skirt and grabbed at her panties.

'James,' she whimpered as he tugged at them, 'don't!' But it was too late, the fabric gave a protesting shriek and he flung the panties aside. Her only pair of La Perla! 'James, you bastard!'

Suddenly it wasn't just his hand holding her down, but his whole body. He was incredibly heavy, she could barely breathe. The head of his cock was hot between her legs. Half of her was frightened, and the other half had never been so excited. 'You're just getting what you wanted,' James hissed into her face. 'Don't call names.'

He began to nudge his way between her legs. Christ, he wasn't wearing a condom! What did he take her for? 'No,' she said, pushing at him with both hands and arching her back, 'no, James, don't, let me get a condom, there's some Durex in the bathroom –'

He caught hold of her wrists and pushed them down to the sofa. 'Forget it,' he said.

'But James, I'm not – James –'

Then his mouth came down on hers, smothering her, and the head of his cock found the soft wet opening of her body and his strong hips tensed and thrust and he penetrated her, the whole thick length of him sliding up inside her, so hot and hard and blissful that she couldn't protest, she couldn't struggle, she just moaned and heaved her loins up towards him, blindly seeking more, more, more.

He was magnificent. Nobody in her life had ever fucked her like him. He was so strong, so determined, he let go of her wrists and caught her hips in his hands and held her so that she was wide open to him, panting and gasping as he shafted her. For long moments she revelled in the sensation, not seeking a climax, not looking for consummation, just enjoying the feel of that big cock forcing its way into her over and over again. But then her body took over. She moaned and touched her breasts with her fingers and the shimmer of orgasm began to surround her.

'Come on,' James grunted, plunging into her with such ferocity that she screamed. 'Come on, Stephanie, come, come. Can't you feel my cock in you? Come on, I want you to come, I'm coming, I'm coming.'

'Yes!' she shrieked, clawing his shoulders as the torment of climax siezed her. 'Yes!'

He clutched her and gave one last desperate lunge and then he was still, trembling and groaning as his come pulsed into her.

For a long time they didn't move. He was hot and heavy and he crushed her, but she didn't care. When at last he drew back a little she reached up to touch his face and said, 'Oh well, that's what the morning-after pill was invented for.'

He pulled out of her with shocking suddenness, so that she whimpered. 'James?'

'Stay there.' He heaved himself off the sofa and picked up a pad of paper and a pencil from the table. He began to scribble on the pad, casting sharp glances at her as he did so. God, he was drawing her! She was horribly conscious of her position, breasts brimming out of her bra, skirt rucked up around her waist, legs flung wide, hair no doubt a rats' nest of tangles. But it was wildly flattering, too. She closed her eyes and immersed herself in blissful post-coital ache. His semen was leaking out of her, trickling slowly into the crease of her arse.

At last he said, 'Here.' She opened her eyes and sat up and he handed her the pad. The sketch was lovely, drawn in his own quivering linear style. He had signed it. 'Oh, James,' she said. 'Thank you.'

He sat down beside her and took hold of her wrist. 'Now listen,' he said. 'Not a word of this to Andrea, all right?'

She hadn't been thinking of telling Andrea, but he sounded so serious that she felt a frisson of jealousy. 'Why?' she asked, not bothering to restrain the pout.

'Because I say so.' His hand tightened on her wrist until it hurt.

She tried to pull away. 'James, let go. You're hurting me.'

He grinned at her. 'That's right.'

God, what did he mean to do? She twisted her arm and his fingers burned against the skin of her wrist. He was so strong! 'Let go,' she whimpered, 'let go.'

'You won't tell Andrea,' he hissed.

'No. No, of course not.'

'Promise.'

His hand was like a vice. 'I promise!' she wailed.

He let go. 'Good.' As if nothing had happened he got up and reached in his pocket for his cigarettes. He pulled one out, tapped it on the packet and lit it. She hated him smoking in the flat, but she didn't dare tell him to put it out. 'Now then. About the subjects for these Tauzins.'

She stared up at him in disbelief. What sort of a bastard was he? Her wrist was red and sore. Was he like this with Andrea?

What had she got herself into?

# SEVEN
## Saturday 12 p.m.

This place at least looked different from the others. No shop front, no pictures in the window, just a pair of small brass signs, one reading ANDREA MAGUIRE, FINE ART and the other JAMES MAGUIRE, PORTRAITS.

He rang the entryphone. After a moment a woman's voice said, 'Hello?'

'Mrs Maguire? DCI Anderson. We spoke on the telephone.'

'Of course. Come up. Top floor.' The door buzzed open.

He walked along a high-ceilinged corridor to a wide staircase. The building was a fine old Georgian house with big sash windows. He ran lightly up the stairs, still thinking of Catherine.

At the top of two flights of stairs the door was open. A petite woman with fine short dark hair was standing in the doorway, smiling at him. She appeared in her mid-thirties and was very attractive, with wide green eyes and pale skin. Her smile was warm and genuine. 'Hello,' she said. 'It's a long climb.'

He hadn't noticed it, but he smiled in return. She led him through into a big bright room, south-facing, with tall windows in the eaves. Every wall was covered with pictures, mostly portraits, and more pictures were stacked in piles against the walls. At one side was a desk with a couple of chairs and three battered filing cabinets. A comfortable damask three-piece suite occupied the rest of the floor space.

'Do have a seat,' she said. 'Now, how can I help? You mentioned wanting to check a couple of provenances?'

She really was very attractive. Her face was heart-shaped, with a pointed chin, and the close-cropped dark hair suited her perfectly. She made him think of a china kitten. It seemed a shame to talk to her about crime, but it had to be done. He sat on the sofa and took out his notebook. 'I'm trying to find out about two paintings which have gone missing recently. They're by Tauzin and Dodson, erotic pictures. I believe you sold them.'

A shocked, wary look appeared in her vivid eyes. 'Yes, I did,' she said, 'and I remember who I sold them to. It was Francesca Lyons. Are you investigating her murder?'

It was always easier when people guessed for themselves. 'That's right.'

'Oh, heavens. Well, of course I'll help in any way I can. I heard about it on the news. How awful. I mean, in a place like Wressingham!'

For a moment he almost told her what he thought of Wressingham, but his opinions were not relevant. 'It can happen anywhere,' he said. Anyway, we're following up anything we can. The pictures are missing, and it's possible that if they were stolen it could be related to the murder. So if you can tell me anything about the pictures, it would be very helpful.'

'Of course, of course.' She jumped to her feet and hurried over to the filing cabinet. 'Let me look. Honestly, all this paper. I'll computerise one day, but I can't stand the bloody machines.'

He sympathised, but all he did was smile. Andrea Maguire moved beautifully, as deftly as the cat she resembled, and it was a pleasure to watch her. She was wearing a tight black long-sleeved body, a floaty skirt and a matching scarf wrapped closely around her slender neck, and low elegant shoes. The overall effect was of a ballet dancer on her day off.

'I've known Francesca for some time,' she said as she worked. 'I've sold her a lot of pictures over the years, erotica particularly. Not many retailers carry that sort of thing, and when I found something at auction or came into it in a lot with other works it was good to know I had someone to pass it to. I was so shocked when I heard about her being killed.' She bent down to pull a file from a bottom drawer. 'James and I were at home on Wednesday night. I thought about it when I heard. We were just sitting at home, and she was being – murdered. Terrifying.'

Imaginative people loved to terrify themselves with patterns of their own devising. 'If you think about it,' he said, 'people are dying all the time, violently and naturally. It only surprises you when you know them.'

She straightened and shut the drawer with a jerk of her knee. Her pretty face was slightly flushed. 'I know. But still – ' She came and sat down beside him. 'Here you are, copies of the provenances for the Tauzin and the Dodson. There's photographs of both of them. I liked the Tauzin especially, a really lovely work. He was a genius. It's just called *Making Love*.'

It was a lovely work, and it reminded him strongly of what he intended to do to Catherine that night. He felt a stirring of arousal. Now was not the time, and he looked unhurriedly at the photograph and then put it behind the other papers. There were copies of bills of sale, catalogue entries, a photograph of the back of the work with the gallery labels, and so on. 'Some of this came with the picture,' Andrea offered helpfully. 'Some of it's from the Tate's records. There's all the same sort of thing for the Dodson.'

He glanced through the second collection of material. 'May I take these documents away and have them copied?'

'Yes, of course. But you will bring them back, won't you?'

'They'll be returned as soon as possible.'

'Let me get you an envelope or something.' She jumped to her feet and hurried over to the desk. He got up more slowly and went over to the door. A picture beside it had caught his attention, a portrait of Andrea. It was a very good portrait, it captured her quickness of movement and the brightness of her eyes, and yet it was harsh and unappealing.

'Oh,' she said, coming up behind him, 'that's by my husband. James.'

He nodded. The signature was a long scrawl, JM. 'He's

very good,' Andrea said sadly. 'I've always loved his work. But the trouble is, the public doesn't. I can't sell it.'

He could see why not, if James could make a woman as attractive and eager as his wife look somehow forbidding. But all he said was, 'I saw the plate on the door. What sort of commissions does he get?'

'None, really.' She glanced up into his face. She was no taller than his shoulder. 'Do you like art? Would you like to see some more of his stuff?'

He didn't particularly want to see more work of that type, but he was very happy for her to show him something she felt enthusiastic about. 'Yes. Thank you.'

'This way.' She handed him a couple of envelopes for the papers. 'Just over the corridor. A north-facing studio, of course.'

'Is it usual to have a studio in office premises?'

'Well, no, but I got such a great deal on this top floor, and our house is small. It's a bit of a pain, because we only have one car and unless James comes with me in the morning he has to walk here, but I suppose it keeps him fit.' She unlocked the opposite door and kicked a wedge under it. '*Voilà!*'

The first thing that struck him was chaos. The room smelled strongly of smoke, and there was a brimming ashtray on the table. Paintings and equipment were piled up apparently at random, heaped on flat surfaces, hung over easels, stuck up anyhow on the walls. Then he saw that James Maguire was not just a portraitist. Among the pictures of faces and people were erotic drawings.

They took his breath away. They were formidably well drawn, but pervaded by the same sense of oppressive harshness that filled the portraits. He found himself staring at one of them in which a tall, well-muscled, dark-haired man grasped a small slender woman by the nape of her neck and bent her forward so that he could penetrate her from behind like a beast. The woman's head was thrown back, her lips parted in helpless ecstasy. The face was Andrea's.

'Oh, that one,' said Andrea, in a small voice. She tugged uncomfortably at the scarf around her throat as if she was hot. 'It's – a self-portrait.'

He looked down at her. She was gazing at the painting

with an expression of mingled fear and desire. Her fingers fiddled with the scarf, and it came loose and fell away.

Beneath it were four dark blue marks, small bruised circles. Fingermarks. She saw him looking and replaced the scarf with a gasp, but he knew what he had seen.

Some people believed that upper-middle-class men didn't abuse their wives. That certainly wasn't true. What never ceased to amaze him was that the women put up with it. This woman, Andrea, so intelligent and attractive, why should she stay with a man who hurt her?

She turned away from him as if she would leave the room. He said, 'Wait,' and caught her arm to hold her back. She didn't fight, just looked up at him with big sad eyes as if she was ashamed, as if it was her fault.

He pushed back her sleeve. As he had expected, her white forearm was marked with a circle of blue bruises and her wrist was red and swollen. 'What happened to you?' he asked gently.

'Nothing,' she said, as she was bound to. 'It's just – I – I was lifting some suitcases onto the wardrobe at home and they slipped, the strap caught around my arm.'

'That's a new one,' he said kindly.

For a moment he thought that she was about to confide in him. But then her eyes opened wide and she pulled her arm free of his hand, and as he turned he knew who he would see.

A big, dark man in jeans and a denim shirt stood in the doorway, glowering. The original of the picture, James Maguire.

'What the fuck is going on here?' James exclaimed. He strode across the room, grabbed Andrea's arm and tugged her towards him. 'What the hell are you doing?'

'Don't do that,' Anderson said in a careful monotone.

James didn't let go of his wife's arm. Andrea stood in trembling silence, obviously not daring even to struggle. 'And who are you?' James demanded.

It was easy to see why Andrea might have fallen for him. He was a handsome devil, with the sort of saturnine face that attracts women. But he was wrong if he thought he could bully Anderson. 'I'm Detective Chief Inspector John Anderson,

Surrey Police.' He kept his voice steady and even.

'He came about the pictures I sold Francesca Lyons,' Andrea offered timidly.

James didn't let go.

'Mr Maguire,' Anderson said, 'you're hurting your wife.'

'Am I hurting you, sweetheart?' James asked Andrea in mock concern.

Her great eyes flickered to Anderson's and then away, and she shook her head.

What a bastard. Anderson despised him, and he had an opportunity to make him uncomfortable. 'Where were you on Wednesday night, Mr Maguire?'

'I was at home with my wife,' said James, jerking Andrea's arm. 'Andrea?'

'I told him,' Andrea said. 'I was reading, and you were sketching. It was a horrid evening, we didn't want to go out. I talked to my mother on the telephone.'

If James had had any involvement with Francesca's death then there was no reason to believe an alibi given by his wife. The records were full of battered wives who lied to protect their husbands. But the question really didn't arise, because there was no reason whatever to connect James to the murder. Anderson knew he was indulging himself not because there were any grounds for suspicion, but because he wanted an excuse to save Andrea from her husband. She deserved better. Why didn't she ask him for help? One word and he would deal with James.

Without it he had no right to interfere, and he had what he needed. He said reluctantly, 'Mrs Maguire, thank you very much. It's been a pleasure meeting you.'

She didn't say the word, just nodded perfunctorily. Her face showed fear. Anderson said as coldly as he could, 'Goodbye, Mr Maguire,' and walked away.

As the policeman's footsteps faded James stood very still. Andrea watched him, shivering with fear. Eventually, when they heard the door downstairs closing, he let her go. He stalked over to the door and slammed it, then turned on her. 'You bitch!'

She was terrified. Anderson had been touching her, actually touching her arm! James would kill her. She shrank back, raising her hands as if she could hold him off.

'I just said what we agreed,' she said urgently. 'That's all, that's all!'

He lifted his fist, about to strike. 'Don't touch me!' she said. 'I'll call him, I swear it. I'll tell him everything. Don't hit me!'

For a moment she thought he would hit her anyway, but at last his face twisted in frustration and he cursed and grabbed her arm. She tried to pull away, but he wrestled her over to the door. 'Get out,' he panted. 'Go home. I'm going to work.'

The door slammed in her face. 'Bastard!' she shouted. Tears of shock were coming now. 'Bastard!'

But she had got off lightly. After finding her like that he might have skinned her alive. With any luck he was so angry that he wouldn't come home.

There were men in the world like Chief Inspector Anderson, men who spoke softly and touched her with gentle fingers, as if they really cared. For a moment she'd seen the possibilities of a different sort of relationship.

But Francesca Lyons was dead, and now she would never get away from James.

There was no reason at all for Pat to visit the gallery, but somehow she found her feet carrying her towards it. The door was locked and the CLOSED sign was up. What was going on? It was barely 5 p.m.

For a moment she stood before the door, coming to terms with her own disappointment. Then she saw that the light was on at the back of the gallery.

She hurried down the gravel path and glanced through the kitchen window. Her heart jumped with sudden fear. Daniel was slumped at the kitchen table, his head buried in his arms, motionless.

Christ, what had happened? She tapped on the window and called, 'Daniel!'

He gave a huge start, sat up and looked over his shoulder, then smiled. Her pounding heart began to slow. His lips said, 'Hi,' and he pointed towards the back door.

'What's the matter?' she asked when he opened it.

'Nothing.' His grin was broad and welcoming. 'Did I scare you? I was just knackered. It's been a madhouse in here all day. I couldn't take any more.'

They stood on the step looking at each other like a pair of fools. At last Daniel said with a start, 'Sorry. I should have said, Come in. Have some tea.'

'I shouldn't. I only came out here to go and talk to the landlord at the Lamb.' But she was already walking in.

Daniel went ahead of her into the kitchen and put the kettle on. He leant against the work surface by the stove and folded his arms. He looked tired, and she wanted to stroke his hair. 'I don't suppose,' he said after a moment, 'that you've had second thoughts about that dinner. Or do you have to work Saturdays?'

'It varies. On an enquiry like this I often have to. But Daniel, I can't. You're a witness. Can you imagine how it would look if you were giving evidence in court and the defence counsel asked you whether it was true that you were – seeing a member of the investigation team?'

He looked stubborn. 'Not if it wasn't relevant to the investigation.'

She sighed. 'I know. Maybe I could. But –' She hardly knew him, but she wanted to tell him the truth. 'Look, Daniel, it's like this. I'm trying to get promoted. I've passed the exams and all the boards, I ought to be an Inspector now. But last time there was a vacancy I didn't get it. Another one might come up any time. I can't afford to put a foot wrong.'

'Detective Inspector,' he said, looking at her as if she came from another planet. 'I just can't connect what I see with the job you do.' His smile was so warm that she could feel herself melting. 'I'd love to get to know you better.'

A surge of physical longing gripped her, so strong that for a moment she could hardly see. She took a step towards him. She couldn't help it. He said, 'Oh,' and came to her and caught her arms in his hands and looked down into her face.

His lips were hovering over hers. She wanted to kiss him, she wanted to pull down the blind and make love to him, then and there, on the kitchen table if they had to. But she couldn't. As his mouth moved slowly towards hers she pulled away from him and burst out, 'I can't, I can't, I mustn't. I'm so sorry. I shouldn't have come.'

She shouldered blindly through the door, but before she could escape he ran after her and caught her arm. 'Look, I – I don't even know what to call you.'

Slowly she turned and faced him. 'Pat.'

'Pat, please don't go. Come home with me. Please.'

For a moment she covered her face with her hands, gathering her strength. 'I can't. I've got work to do. Daniel, I'm really sorry. I won't do this again.'

He let go of her. He looked stricken. She closed her eyes and sighed, then turned away.

She pushed her way grimly into the Lamb and eased through to the bar. It was already crowded with Saturday-night drinkers. Perhaps Daniel would come here later.

She shook herself and said to the landlord, 'Hello, Phil.'

He nodded to her. 'Evening. Want a drink?'

'Not on duty, thanks.'

'You came because of my call, did you?'

'Yes. Thank you for taking the trouble. What's up?'

'It's just that Giles came in this evening,' said Phil, jerking his head at a table in the corner. 'He's a regular but he's not been in for a few days, he's had a cold. But he was here on Wednesday night. I thought you might have missed him on your house-to-house enquiries. He said he thought he saw someone leaving the gallery Wednesday evening. Giles!'

A middle-aged man wearing a cap looked up from his pint of Guinness. Phil called, 'Here's the detective sergeant, Giles. Come and tell her what you told me.'

As the man came over to the bar she could see from his expression that he was going to be a trial. Before he opened his mouth she knew what he was going to say. 'So you're a detective sergeant, eh? My goodness, you're far too pretty for such a tough job.'

'Phil tells me you may have some information which could help us in our investigation of the Lyons murder,' she replied, as if he hadn't spoken.

'Well, I don't know. He thought you might be interested.'

'Tell me about it, Mr —'

'Friedland. Giles Friedland. I live down Mill Lane, at number 25, one of the old almshouses.'

'Thank you, Mr Friedland.' She got out her notebook. 'Now, please tell me what you saw.'

'Well, it wasn't much. It's just that when I was on my way home I saw a man leave the gallery. I was surprised, because it was so late and it wasn't Chris Lyons. He walked past me on the other side of the road and got into a car on the marketplace.'

'What time was that, Mr Friedland?'

'Oh, I don't know. When do I go home, Phil? Some time before ten, anyway.'

'Can you describe the man you saw?'

'It was dark, you know. He was fairly tall, a bit bigger than me, I suppose. Short hair. Balding, I think. Sorry it's not a better description. I'd remember you, love.'

She was too excited even to give him a withering glance. Richard Allen! He was so thin on top it was hardly there. She kept her face calm. 'Did you notice the car?'

'Yes. It was one of those nice old MGs, a little sports car. Bit difficult to see the colour, but it was dark. Green, maybe, you know, British Racing Green.'

She itched to get to the car and call this through. 'Mr Friedland, thank you very much. Is there anything else you noticed?'

'Well, when I walked past the gallery on my way home the lights were on at the back.'

She made another note. 'Thank you very much indeed, Mr Friedland. I may need to send one of my team around for a formal statement. Will you be at home?'

'Yes, I'm usually in. I'm in the book, if you want to call me first.'

She thanked him and the landlord again, then ran out to the car. This was what she needed to take her mind off Daniel: a good, old fashioned, down to earth clue. She pulled her car out of the parking space and told Control to check the car out.

Within a few moments the radio beeped. That was quick! 'Fielding.'

'Pat, it's Anderson. Good work on the car. It's the icing on the cake.'

'You've got the fingerprint match!'

'Yes. It's not 100 per cent secure, prints lifted from skin deteriorate quickly. But it's good enough.'

'So he was at the Lyons gallery and he did make love to Francesca.'

'Looks like it. We should go to his house. Shall I meet you there?'

'Yes, sir. Give me the address. I can be there in twenty minutes.'

'It's the other side of Guildford.'

'I'll drive fast. Tell the traffic boys to stay off my tail.'

Allen lived in a street of ordinary smart 1920s houses with big front gardens. Pat saw Anderson's car parked a few doors away from the house and she pulled in behind it.

He emerged at once. 'You were quick.'

'Yes, sir.' He didn't look himself, his face was even more emotionless than usual. Why, when they were on the point of an arrest? 'Something wrong, sir?'

He gave her a sharp glance, as if he hadn't expected her to notice anything. 'No.'

He couldn't have had something planned for Saturday night, could he? That was news. He'd been a puzzle for months, apparently not seeing anyone, but not on the market either. Plenty of women at the Guildford nick fancied him, but he was hard to catch. WPC Kim Baines had recently decided that the time was ripe for a shot. She'd made a pretty obvious play, and he'd turned her down, firmly but politely. What was going on?

She didn't dare to ask, but she did try an oblique, 'Looks like a busy evening for us, sir.'

'Yes,' he said icily. She was right! He'd had a date. Poor sod.

As if wanting to prevent further enquiries, Anderson said, 'You go and ring. Let's keep this low-profile if we can. If you need me, I'm here.'

'OK.' She walked up the path between well-trimmed rose bushes, conscious of the burden of shock that she was carrying towards the Allen household. What would this do to his wife and three children?

She rang the bell. After a few seconds it was opened by a self-possessed girl of six or seven. 'Yes?' said the child.

'Hello,' said Pat. 'I'm looking for Richard Allen. Your father.'

'He's not in,' said the girl.

A harrassed-looking woman appeared in the hall. 'Gemma, who is it?'

'It's a lady,' said Gemma, standing reluctantly back from the door.

'Mrs Allen? Hello. I'm Patricia Fielding. Is your husband in?'

The woman looked at her with utter hatred. Oh God, she suspected that Richard had a lover and she thought that Pat was the scarlet woman! But there wasn't anything to be done. If Mrs Allen knew that the police wanted her husband, she might warn him, hide him, anything.

Mrs Allen said with vitriolic satisfaction, 'He's not here.'

'Oh. I'm sorry. Where is he?'

'He's at some antiques fair in the west country. Lyme Regis. Not back till tomorrow evening.'

'Do you happen to know where he's staying?'

'No,' hissed Mrs Allen.

She was going to slam the door, but Pat put out her hand to hold it open. 'Mrs Allen, please. I really need to find him.'

'I'm sure you do,' snapped Mrs Allen. 'I'm sure you'd love to. Well, I don't know where he is, and if I did know I wouldn't tell you. Drive to Lyme Regis, if you want him that badly.'

This time Pat let her close the door. She walked back to where Anderson stood waiting, tall and slender and precise. 'He's not there. His wife thinks he's at an antiques fair in Lyme Regis.' She smiled. 'I think she thought I was his lover.'

He didn't look amused. 'What d'you think, Pat? Has he tried to cut and run?'

'Don't know, sir. I'd be surprised.' They walked back and stood by Anderson's car. 'Sir, I'll go back to the office and put out a description of him for the ports authorities just in case

101

he's decided to run over to the Continent. And I'll drive down to Lyme Regis first thing tomorrow and pick him up, if he's there.' She looked into Anderson's impenetrable navy-blue eyes and grinned. 'There's no need for you to come back to the office, sir.'

He wasn't convinced. 'You're sure you can handle it?'

'I'm sure, sir.'

He looked at her steadily, then nodded. 'OK, Pat. It's all yours.'

Without another word he opened the door of the BMW, ducked inside and drove off. Pat watched him go, shaking her head. She'd just saved his evening. He might have said thank you.

After all the rain earlier in the week it was a beautiful evening, warm and clear and rustling with moist autumnal scents. Anderson walked quickly down the towpath towards the Black Swan, enjoying the last caresses of dappled golden sunshine.

He shouldn't have been so stiff with Fielding earlier. But he had hardly been able to bear the thought that Allen's arrest would rob him of his long-anticipated reunion with Catherine, and he'd had to try so hard to keep his disappointment under control that he had overcompensated. Oh well, she had been eager to pull Allen in, anyway. Had she succumbed to that beautiful boy Daniel yet? It was only a matter of time.

The Black Swan appeared before him, its lights a welcoming glitter in the darkening twilight. He straightened his tie and ran his hand over his hair, then brushed at his immaculate jacket. It was his current favourite, very simply cut to show off the fabric, a beautiful rough-textured silk in subtle shades of green and chestnut. He felt good in it, secure and confident. What would Catherine be wearing? One of her simple dresses, perhaps, or perhaps the snug white body which showed off her small high breasts so beautifully. She didn't really need to wear a bra, but he was glad that she did.

On the doorstep of the Black Swan he stopped, noticing his own feelings. His pulse was faster than it should be and there was a knot in his stomach as if he was a teenager. What was this, love at forty-two?

He was exactly on time, but Catherine was already sitting at the bar with a glass of wine in her hand. She was wearing a dress he hadn't seen before, an elegant, simple shirtdress in rust-red sueded silk that outlined her slender waist and draped flatteringly over her full hips. She was looking into her wine glass, and she didn't see him approaching. He stood behind her and closed his eyes, drawing in her scent. Then he gently drew her tousled brown hair away from her neck and set his lips to her nape.

She didn't jump, but she drew in a long, quivering breath. When he drew back she turned and looked up at him. Her eyes were dark and her lips were parted. He smiled at her and said softly, 'Hello,' then leant slowly forward and kissed her mouth.

Her lips trembled under his. She stayed perfectly still. He didn't touch her, but he could sense her body shivering. At last he stood up and she stared up at him, breathing quickly. Her nipples were tight and hard beneath the soft fabric of her dress.

There was a short silence. Then she managed a smile. 'If you're trying to suggest that we can do without dinner, forget it. I'm buying, remember.'

'I wouldn't dream of it. I'm starving.'

'Let's go in, then.'

He followed her through to the dining room. The waiter held her chair for her and Anderson seated himself and watched with affectionate admiration as she signalled, with a commanding flourish of the menu, that she was in charge.

Ordering took a little time. Catherine was studiedly composed, but she did not look relaxed. When he kissed her she had wanted him, he was certain, but now her defences were up. Sometimes her eyes met his and then fled away, as if she was afraid of him. They talked about what they had done in the summer – a week in the Highlands for him, a trip to the Dordogne with her brother and his family for her. The first course came and went, delicious, but he hardly noticed it. A few words about work, nothing significant. She was keeping him at a distance. Why?

He wanted to break through the barrier between them.

Perhaps he needed to offer something of himself. He hadn't exactly been secretive with her in the past, but she had wanted to talk and he had wanted to listen and so she didn't really know that much about him. After another uncomfortable little pause he said, 'After we met today I felt as if I was walking on air.'

She smiled, but she didn't look happy. 'You said you'd missed me. But –'

Was that it? Was she wondering what had happened in between times? Well, that was easy. 'There hasn't been anyone else.'

Now her eyes met his and didn't try to escape. He wasn't sure that she believed him. She bit her lip. The main course arrived and for a moment they were engaged in being served, in selecting vegetables, refilling wine. He had ordered calf's liver, and he tried a bite. It was perfect: succulent, sweet, pink in the middle.

Abruptly Catherine said, 'John, have you slept with many women?'

He didn't laugh, but he smiled. 'That depends. What's "many" in your book?'

'God, I don't know!' She looked embarrassed.

'Well, you're the accountant.'

'Oh, God, I don't know. Ten?'

'Ten is many?'

'Yes.' She set her jaw resolutely.

He didn't have to count. 'Then no. I haven't slept with many women.'

She frowned at him. 'I thought you would have done.'

He took another bite of the liver, assembling what he wanted to say. After a sip of wine he said slowly, 'I've never exactly slept around, Catherine. And I was married for ten years, and Sarah and I were engaged before that.'

'I didn't mean –' she began.

'It's all right. But I'm, well, cautious. I don't rush things. I don't rush anything.' He smiled into her eyes. 'I know we slept together on the first date, Catherine, but that's probably as rare for me as it is for you.'

She seemed to be absorbing this. After a moment she said,

'I hardly know you. We've never talked about your work, and I suppose I don't want to. But it's very important to you, isn't it.'

'Yes,' he said simply. 'It is.'

She ate a bite of her dish, a lattice of salmon and turbot. Then she said, 'When did you become a policeman? Did you join straight from school?'

'No. I went to work in an office. My father thought I ought to do something respectable, something with prospects. I'd suggested the police before, but he didn't like the idea. Too rough.'

'Why did you change your mind?'

It was harder to tell her about this than he had imagined, but it was necessary. She needed him to open up to her. Her face was intent, completely engaged, and more relaxed than he had seen it all evening. He drew a deep breath and carried on. 'It was after my father died. I realised I – didn't have to do things for him any more. So I joined the force. I was, what, twenty-five, I suppose.'

'Why?' she asked after a little pause. 'Why the police?'

'Well –' He drank some more wine, thinking. 'Partly I was excited by the idea of being a detective. But mostly I think it was because most people see that things are wrong and they don't do anything about it. I wanted to do something about it. I wanted to make a difference.'

It was absolutely true, but had he sounded quite ridiculous? Perhaps not. Her eyes were very bright. 'You're an idealist,' she whispered. 'You still want to make a difference, don't you.'

'Don't tell anyone at CID. All I'm supposed to care about these days is resource management.'

She shook her head, looking suddenly anxious. 'How can you be so certain that you know what's right and wrong? All I know about it is that everything's too bloody complicated to be certain.'

Her mind was making odd leaps. He didn't know what would come next, but he could answer her questions. She wanted to know him. 'I'm good at my job,' he said. It was true, but would it sound insufferably arrogant?

'We all make mistakes,' she said softly.

'We all do,' he agreed. 'But I make as few of them as possible. And there's something else, Catherine. I don't decide who's guilty, a jury does that. And I don't punish.' Her sad, tense eyes were fastened on his face. 'You look as if you expect all policemen to be like Attila the Hun and want to bring back hanging.'

'Well,' she challenged him quickly, 'do you?'

'No.' He shook his head. 'As you pointed out, we make too many mistakes.'

There was a long silence. She looked as if she was about to cry. At last she put down her knife and fork and lifted her hand. He reached out and caught it, lifted it to his lips and kissed it. Her mouth tightened. Then she said, 'Thank you.'

For what? For telling her about himself? Whatever it was, he was glad to have pleased her. 'It's a pleasure.'

Over dessert and coffee they were almost silent. She must be feeling it too, the growth of tension, the increasing heat of desire. As the meal drew to its close, they were both thinking about the night to come.

She paid the bill. There was no fuss. Then he said, 'As you've bought me dinner, I think you ought to walk me home.'

She laughed, and she didn't say no.

They walked back along the towpath, hand in hand. The lights of the Black Swan faded behind them. They were silent, listening to the sounds of the river flowing past them. Brilliant light from a full moon glittered from the water's surface.

About a quarter of a mile from his apartment they stopped under a huge spreading willow tree. The ground beneath it was quite dry, protected from the rain by the long sweeping branches. She tipped her head back and looked up at the stars through the canopy of leaves. Her pale skin looked blue in the moonlight. 'What a beautiful night.'

He gently pulled her into his arms. She didn't stop looking up at the sky. He murmured, 'I can see the stars in your eyes.'

She smiled up at him. 'I can't believe that a tough detective says romantic things like that.'

'It's true,' he said, and kissed her.

To begin with the kiss was gentle, tender. Her body was

warm and pliable in his arms. She sighed and relaxed against him. But he knew what pleased her, and it wasn't always gentleness. She needed to be shown the force of her own desire. He buried his hands in her soft hair and slowly bent her head back and pressed his lips to her arched white throat.

She moaned helplessly. 'John. John.' Her head was heavy in his hands. He wanted to hear her crying out as he touched her. But his cock was hard, aching, burning inside his trousers. Its insistent urging would spoil his concentration. Before he could serve her as she desired, she would have to serve him.

He bit her neck softly and her spine tensed, pressing her hips against him. With one hand he found the peak of her breast, standing up below the silk, and he cupped it and chafed the nipple. She gasped and her breathing became heavy and irregular.

His hand tightened in her hair and he pressed her downwards. Her eyes opened and she made a little sound of protest. He leant forward and kissed her mouth, then said softly, 'Kneel down.'

She tried to shake her head, but he held her firmly. 'Kneel down.'

'Why,' she whispered, though she was not fighting him.

'Do it, Catherine.'

She leant her head against his hand. Her rapt face was beautiful. He wanted to enfold her, to overpower her so completely that she would have nothing left except pleasure. Gradually she sank to her knees, and he kept his hands in her hair. She looked up at him, her lips loose and soft, her eyes shining. He pressed her head forward until her lips brushed against his groin. His penis leapt towards the touch, surging with eagerness. He said steadily, 'Take it out. Suck it.'

She shuddered and let out a gasp. 'Not here. Someone will see.'

'There's no one. Do it.'

Slowly her fingers reached for his zip. Her hands were trembling. Very gently she freed his cock from its cloth prison. She hesitated and licked her lips and he could sense that her whole body was shaking with longing. She would serve him now, and later he would repay her.

Her mouth closed very gently over the head of his cock. He groaned with pure pleasure and tightened his fingers in her hair, thrusting gently. Already he could feel the pressure rising, building up, waiting for release. Soon, soon –

Catherine moaned, a smothered, ecstatic sound. He opened his eyes and looked down at her kneeling in the dappled moonlight, hands loose at her sides, her soft lips framing his shining cock. He held her head still and slowly tensed his hips and thrust into her mouth and she moaned again. He was deep in her, touching the back of her throat, but she didn't fight him or pull away. The knowledge of her trust filled him with a sudden surge of emotion and then he was coming, crying out helplessly as his cock pulsed in her mouth. She swallowed obediently, over and over again, then gently licked the last drops from the tip of his glans.

He caught her by her shoulders and pulled her up to kiss her. She put her arms around his neck and relaxed completely against him. Her face was ecstatic. He stroked her shoulders, cupped the swell of her full buttocks in his hands, ran his fingers down her spine.

'Let's go home,' he whispered to her. 'It's your turn.'

Her turn! Catherine was trembling so much when the lift stopped that she thought she would hardly be able to walk to the door.

Why had she convinced herself that he was the wrong man for her? What had he done? All she had seen at dinner was gentleness and an openness that had really surprised her. And then on the towpath a deep shuddering thrill had filled her as he spoke in that soft, commanding voice. And when he had pushed his cock into her mouth she had thought for a moment that she was going to come just from feeling him between her lips.

She had said, 'How can you be so certain?' But when it came to making love she was very glad that he was so certain. It was blissful to have all the responsibility taken out of her hands, to trust him absolutely with the task of her pleasure.

Now she wasn't even going to try to guess what would happen. She followed him into the flat and stood in the living room, remembering its size and brightness. He said, 'Would you like a drink?'

She shook her head. The wine she had drunk over dinner was already spinning in her brain.

He stood and looked at her as if he was sizing her up. His brilliant dark blue eyes passed up and down her body and she felt them as if they were physically touching her. Between her legs she was moist and sticky, and her nipples ached. She was dying for him. But she didn't have to say anything.

After a moment he smiled. 'I'm going to get myself a whisky. Go into the bedroom and take your clothes off. Sit on the bed and wait for me.'

He turned away. She opened her mouth to protest. Who did he think she was? And then, somehow, she didn't. She left her handbag on the floor and went through to the bedroom.

As she unbuttoned her dress she saw that her hands were shaking. It felt so strange. She had undressed for him before with him watching, removing each garment at his order, and now she didn't understand why he didn't want to watch. But how strange and how arousing, to know that she would be sitting on the bed, naked, vulnerable, waiting for him to come to her.

She had bought new underwear especially for the evening. He wouldn't see it now. She frowned with disappointment. But she took off the lacy bra and the high-cut panties and hung them neatly over the chair.

Naked, she sat down on the edge of the bed. How did he want her to sit? It felt odd, wicked, to be perched there with her breasts bare, just waiting. She sat very upright, her thighs pressed together, her hands in her lap. What would he do to her?

John appeared in the doorway, a glass of whisky in one hand, his jacket slung over his shoulder by the other. He looked her up and down and nodded. 'Good.'

He strolled over to the chair where she had put her clothes and hung his jacket over the back of it. He picked up the panties and examined them. 'Very pretty. Are they new?'

'Yes.' She was hideously conscious of her nakedness.

For a moment he held her gaze. Then he lifted the panties

to his face and drew in their scent. His eyes crinkled with a smile and his muffled voice said, 'Well, someone's been excited.'

She looked away, a blush scalding her cheeks. He put the panties back down on the chair and came towards her, loosening his tie with one hand. 'Lie down.'

Slowly, hesitantly, she wriggled her way onto the broad bed and lay back. It was incredibly arousing to be displayed before him like this, naked, helpless. But he was so cool, so controlled. Couldn't he feel that she was shuddering with wanting him?

As if he read her mind, his face softened. He said softly, 'You look beautiful. You're lovely, Catherine.'

He sat down on the edge of the bed, still unfastening his tie. With the other hand he traced the line of her jaw, trickled his finger down her throat, across the white skin between her breasts. She closed her eyes, feeling her nipples harden. 'John,' she whispered.

'Put your hands above your head. I like the way it makes your breasts lift.'

With a sigh of delight she obeyed him. What a wanton pose this was, her hands raised, stretching out her body as if inviting assault. Her fingers brushed against the cold wrought iron of the bed head. His hand cupped her breast and stroked against her nipple. A shaft of sudden pleasure lanced through her, making her gasp.

'That's lovely,' he said softly. 'Let's keep you like that.'

Then his hands were on her wrists. Her eyes flew open and she saw him leaning over her, his expression concentrated, deftly tying her wrists together with his silk tie. 'John,' she said anxiously.

'It'll be fine,' he said. 'Trust me.' He kissed her. His tongue slipped between her lips, tasting of whisky. She moaned with pleasure and didn't try to resist as he very gently tied her hands to one of the uprights of the bed head. When he sat back she tried to move and realised that she couldn't. Suddenly she was afraid, but the fear aroused her. She clenched her fists and arched her back and she was a prisoner, trapped in Bluebeard's castle, waiting for a fate worse than death.

John sat over her and stroked his hand down her body. She

shivered and moaned. 'Do you remember last time?' he asked her. 'Do you remember what I made you do?'

He had ordered her to masturbate for him and she had obeyed, and since then whenever she had masturbated that had been what she thought of, her body writhing as she stroked herself and John's blue eyes watching every movement, every touch of her finger, every shift of her limbs. 'Yes,' she whispered. 'I remember.'

He caressed her breast, circling her taut nipple with his index finger. Bliss! She whimpered, and he licked his finger and did it again. The cold wetness made her nipple pucker even more tightly, made the pleasure even more intense. 'This time,' he said, 'I want you to tell me what you think about when you masturbate.'

'What?' She opened her eyes and stared at him.

He continued to fondle her nipple. Her eyes slid shut as his other hand touched her too, running down her rib cage, stroking her flank, her loins, the inside of her thigh. His gentle voice said, 'Tell me a fantasy.'

She couldn't reply. She let her legs fall apart and his hand slipped between them, touching her where she ached to be touched. 'Tell me,' he said, as she moaned.

'I can't.'

'You must.' His finger was inside her now, filling her, and his other hand was slowly, regularly pinching her nipple, so hard that she whimpered. She tensed her hands against the bonds and couldn't move, and the sense of delicious help-lessness overwhelmed her. 'Tell me,' he said. 'Or I'll stop.'

'Don't stop. Please don't stop.' But what could she say? She couldn't tell him that since they met he had been her fantasy. What had it been, before then? What had worked?

At least she didn't have to look at him. She thought back, projecting images. At last she said, 'It's nothing special.'

'Tell me,' he whispered. His finger slipped out of her and moved to her clitoris, pressed it, flicked against it, teasing her.

'There's a man and a girl,' she began, searching for the words. 'They're on the sofa, they're kissing. He's got his hand inside her blouse, squeezing her breast.' It was months since she had thought of this, but as she spoke its old power began

111

to return. 'She's putty in his hands, she can't prevent herself reacting. She doesn't want to let him but she can't help herself. He pushes up her skirt and begins to – to finger her.'

Punctuating the fantasy, John's hands were touching her, squeezing her breasts, easing into her sex. Her head rolled helplessly. 'Why does this turn me on? Why? I don't know. He – he pulls off her panties and makes her spread her legs, there on the sofa, and he puts his – his cock inside her and – ' She couldn't say any more. John was stroking the lips of her sex, caressing her clitoris, making her moan. 'John, that's so good, don't stop, don't stop.'

'What then?' he whispered. 'What then?'

'Don't. I can't.' She tugged against the silk fastening her wrists to the bed.

He put his lips to her nipple and sucked hard. It was as if ice and fire were flowing through her. His warm mouth moved down her body, his shirt rustled between her legs. She tensed her hips, lifting herself towards him, seeking for his lips. She had dreamed of his tongue touching her.

His breath was warm against her. 'What then?'

'John –'

'What?' He blew on her, cold on warm wet flesh, making her squeal. 'Tell me.'

'He –' She swallowed and gasped. 'He – does it to her until she comes. She's moaning, she's crying out. She looks like a slut with her breasts showing and her skirt around her waist. But he doesn't come.'

'Good,' he whispered, and then he licked her. She gave a great sigh of relief as she felt his strong tongue on her. 'Good. What then?'

He was sucking her, worming into the most secret parts of her. She writhed, half trying to escape, half trying to push herself against him. 'He – turns her over. He wants to – No, I can't. I can't.'

Oh God, his hands were between her thighs, underneath her, cupping her buttocks, pulling them apart. Reading her mind, he was reading her mind, and she couldn't escape him! 'No,' she cried, shrill with panic. 'Don't, don't.'

'Don't what?' he whispered, and then he drew her clitoris

into his mouth and sucked it and his fingers stroked the crease of her backside and she couldn't escape. She was coming, helpless heaving spasms, her body twisting and writhing, her head beating on the pillow.

As the racking pulses of pleasure faded she heard the rustle of a condom. She opened her eyes and saw him kneeling beside her, still dressed, his fly open to reveal his proud sheathed cock. He reached up to her wrists and pulled them free of the bed head, but didn't loosen them. 'On your knees,' he said.

'No.' She was afraid of what he meant to do to her. But he caught hold of her and rolled her over, her bound wrists on the pillow. He slid his hands down her haunches and lifted them into the air and she felt the tip of his cock between her legs, gliding over the slipperiness of her desire, and then he lunged into her, one deliberate surging thrust that took him right up to the hilt. His warm hands caressed her, moving along her shoulders, down her arms to touch her wrists, then back to stroke her spine. He reached beneath her, found her dangling breasts, tugged at her swollen nipples.

'I can't,' she moaned. She couldn't come again, there was no more pleasure left in her, she was an empty shell filled by his cock. But he would not be denied. His hands moved, finding her clitoris, stroking it, and his cock slid to and fro inside her with deep steady strokes, and after a few stunned minutes she felt herself filling up with ecstasy, gasping as he plunged into her, moaning as he withdrew, lifting inexorably towards another climax. He was crying out too, calling her name, and when at last she came he lurched forward and clung to her, his face against her spine, his eyelashes brushing her shoulder, his voice whispering that she was beautiful.

Then he reached forward and unfastened her hands and gathered her into his arms. She rested her head against his throat and closed her eyes. His pulse beat steadily against her cheek and his fingers stirred in her hair. So warm, so secure. The echoes of pleasure rippled through her. She gave a single helpless shudder. His hands tightened around her, and as she fell asleep she knew that she was safe.

# EIGHT
## Sunday 9.30 a.m.

For a moment she didn't know where she was. Then she remembered.

She opened her eyes. Pale sun was streaming in through the big window. There was nobody beside her in the bed, but there was a rose on the dented pillow.

Faint noises came from beyond the door, the sound of John preparing breakfast. Catherine sat up and covered her face with her hands.

She must have been drunk. Drunk, and manipulated. How else could she explain what had happened? This time it was supposed to have been on her terms. She had wanted him, all right, desperately, but this time she had wanted to be in control. And here she was again, in his flat, in his bed.

Putty in his hands – Oh God, what had she told him? What had she done? Could it possibly have been worse?

It couldn't have been better, a little voice reminded her. She shook her head, denying the memory. She had to get out. Hastily she got up and began to pull on her clothes, making a face as she saw the pretty brand-new underwear. As she dressed she muttered, 'I've got to go. I'm sorry, John, but I've got to go,' as if the words could stop her mind from filling with the images of last night: his hands, his mouth, his soft commands; her wrists fastened together above her head, her voice mumbling filthiness, her bound wrists lying on the pillow where the rose lay now.

There were stains on the front of her dress. She knew where they came from; from kneeling on the ground to suck John's cock. She brushed at them frantically.

As she shoved her feet into her shoes the bedroom door opened. She raked her hand through her hair and looked up.

John was wearing a white dressing gown and carrying a tray. There was a bottle of champagne on it, two glasses, a pot of coffee and a basket with croissants in it. He was smiling, but when he saw her dressed the smile turned into a frown. He put the tray down beside the door. 'Catherine, what's wrong?'

'I've got to go,' she said. It wasn't any easier for the practice.

She wanted to go past him, but she didn't dare to touch him. His face was still. 'What's the matter?' he asked in that velvety voice. 'There's no rush.'

'I've got to go. I'm sorry.' She looked from side to side. 'Where's my bag?'

'It's in the living room.' He stood a little aside to let her go through the door, then followed her. 'Catherine, don't go. We should have all day.'

She didn't answer, just shook her head as she picked the bag up.

'Look, I don't understand.'

There was tension in his voice now. Good! She couldn't bear it that he could stay so bloody cool when she was so upset.

'You didn't have to come here last night. I didn't make you do anything you didn't want to do.'

You did, you did. You made me do all kinds of things and now I wish I hadn't.

'Catherine, why did you come?'

Logic wouldn't get rid of him. He was bright, he could pick holes in anything she said. What else might work? She slung her bag over her shoulder and tossed her head, trying to look callous. 'When I saw you I – remembered how much I wanted to go to bed with you.'

His face changed. That had hit home! She wasn't sure why,

but it had worked. 'Was that all?' he asked softly.

It wasn't, of course it wasn't. She could remember every word he had said over dinner. But now she was frightened and it was him that was frightening her and she wanted to make him go away, any way that would work. So she said, 'That was all.'

He lifted his head with a little jerk and his jaw tensed. Before he spoke his mouth twitched, as if he was thinking of words to say and discarding them. Then he said, 'I don't like to be used, Catherine.'

An argument would do just fine! End with a fight, and she could write the whole thing off. 'You got what you wanted, didn't you? Didn't you!'

'Didn't you?' he retorted, so quickly that she flinched.

Yes, her body told her. But she said, 'No!' and ran for the door.

As she touched the handle he caught her arm. His fingers were strong and very gentle.

'Catherine.'

No anger in his voice now, only tenderness. God help her, couldn't she even fight with him?

'Catherine, don't go. Stay with me.'

It was the same voice, quiet, authoritative. She shuddered and blurted, 'Don't give me orders! I'm not your – slave!'

He took a deep breath. His dark blue eyes mesmerised her. Very softly he said, 'Can't you feel that we're falling in love?'

'No. Not love.' She shook her head desperately. 'It's not love for you, is it, John? It's – possession.'

He let go of her arm and stepped back, shaking his head. For a moment she couldn't move. His eyes held her as tightly as the bonds on her wrists. But at last she pulled free and hauled the door open and ran for the lift. As the doors closed behind her she pressed her hands against the mirrored glass and stared at her feet, and her tears fell into the empty air.

Andrea slammed the door of the car and half ran to the stairs. She had steeled herself during the drive and now she had to tell James before she lost her nerve.

As she leapt up, two steps at a time, she thought of the

policeman who had visited her yesterday. Chief Inspector Anderson. Gentle, humorous, intelligent, even handsome, though in a quiet understated way, with none of James's florid dark beauty. It wasn't that she fancied him. He wasn't her type, and besides, he was a policeman, for God's sake. But he made her hope that her future might hold something different.

Plenty of other women would be foolish enough to take James off her hands. Someone probably already had. He was such a bloody dog in the manger he would hit her if she so much as looked at a man, but she'd suspected him of screwing around for years. As she got to the door of the studio and took a deep breath she told herself firmly that she didn't care.

Her fist hammered on the door. 'James!'

'Fuck off,' he replied. He sounded so angry that her courage faltered. He was always in a filthy temper after sleeping in the studio.

'James, let me in.' Her voice was getting shrill, but she couldn't help it. At least on a Sunday there would be nobody else in the building to hear. 'We've got to talk.'

The door flew open, making her jump. James scowled at her. 'Talk about what? Mealy-mouthed Chief Inspector Anderson?'

She clenched her hands at her sides. 'James, I've had enough. I want a divorce.'

'*What?*' He looked truly astonished. After a second he grabbed her shoulders and pulled her in to the studio, staring. 'You what?'

'I want a divorce,' she repeated. Her voice was trembling. Now he would hit her. She was ready for it. She could take it, if she could get free.

But he didn't. He lifted his leonine head and laughed. 'Don't be stupid, Andrea. You can't live without me.'

'I bloody can!' she retorted, stung.

'You can't.' He was grinning, so confident and arrogant that she wanted to kill him. 'You love me.'

'I don't love you,' she said, though as she spoke the words she knew she did. 'You're a bastard. You're selfish and vicious and –' He was still smiling. She wasn't hurting him. She hunted around for something more effective, and then inspiration struck. '– and you're a bloody awful painter!'

Suddenly he was very still. His dark eyes gleamed oddly as he stared at her. Well, that had worked! It was years since she'd succeeded in bating him. 'I can't sell your bloody paintings, can I?' she taunted him. 'Only the ones you do in other people's styles. And that's because you're technically competent but you're not an artist. You're just a bloody imitator!'

She expected him to lunge at her, but he didn't move. His lips were trembling. She felt a sudden surge of guilt. It wasn't true, any of it. She liked his art, she'd always believed in him. But it felt so good to get her own back for once that she didn't retract.

At last he said, 'Stephanie doesn't agree with you.'

Stephanie? What the hell did it have to do with her? 'She's a bloody researcher. What does she know?'

'She likes my art,' James said, slowly and clearly. 'Perhaps that's why I like her. Perhaps that's why I fucked her yesterday.'

Andrea's ears seemed to be ringing. She blinked hard, trying to decide if she was imagining things. Then she said, 'You did what?'

'I fucked her,' James said, smiling grimly. 'She was dying for it, she did a great job of seducing me. We didn't even get to bed, she was so desperate I screwed her on the sofa. She's got a nice body, good tits. But then she's younger than you, of course.'

She could see them together, Stephanie with her mane of hair tangled and glossy and her legs wide apart to let James plunge into her. It was unbearable, unbelievable. 'No,' she whispered. Her eyes were stinging with tears of rage. 'I don't believe it.'

'Oh yes,' James smiled. 'Go and ask her. Ask her to show you the picture I drew her afterwards.'

'You drew her a *picture*?' It was the ultimate betrayal. Andrea knotted her hands in the air, consumed by jealousy so violent that it was a physical pain. 'James, how could you? How could you do that for her?'

'You see?' James mocked her. 'You do love me. You can't live without me.'

'Bastard!' she screamed, and she ran at him and pounded him with her fists.

He pushed her away, holding her easily at arm's length as he laughed at her. When her frantic lunges turned to sobs he let her go, still chuckling. 'Told you so, Andrea, darling.' He gave her a little shove and she staggered back, weeping with fury, her head swimming with images of James doing it to Stephanie. It was no use trying to pretend that she didn't care. She did care, more than she could have believed.

'Well,' said James, at the door, 'I'm off home. Then I'm going to go to the pub for lunch. Don't follow me in there yelling like a fishwife, will you.'

'James!' she screamed, a wild helpless cry of anger and longing. But he didn't turn back. She stood for a moment, still sobbing, listening to his quick footsteps running down the stairs. Oh God, had he believed that stupid insult about his art? It was too late to take it back. If she had lost him, what would she do?

Then she remembered what he had said about Stephanie, that she had done a good job of seducing him. Her tears stopped and her hands tightened into white fists. Cunning, manipulative bitch! How long had she been planning this?

There was no way that she was going to let her get away with it.


Mud and gravel crunched beneath Anderson's feet. He was running much faster than usual and was already past the two-mile marker, but he didn't care. Exhaustion would help him to deal with his anger.

What in God's name was the matter with Catherine? It wasn't him she was afraid of, it was herself. Every time they slept together it was better, more intense, more exciting, and she just couldn't cope with it. In bed she trusted herself enough to submit to him, to charge him with her pleasure. In the morning that trust was gone.

Sweat ran down his throat and soaked his singlet. Damn her! What did she want from him? There wasn't anything more that he could do, and no point in wasting mental energy trying to sort out her problems. His mind turned without prompting to Andrea Maguire, and the ferocious speed of his running slackened slightly.

Poor woman, trapped by her savage husband in a marriage that must be torture to her. How could she bear to be shackled to a man who offered her violence? People who said that women liked to be treated roughly didn't understand the difference between games and reality. Catherine, for example –

Catherine! Unless he made it impossible to think he would be thinking of her. He gasped in a breath that chilled his lungs and increased his speed.

Stephanie clutched the phone with both hands. 'Hello? Mrs Pritchard? It's Stephanie here. Could I speak to Jane, please? Is she up?'

'Oh, hello, Stephanie, dear. How are you? Are you all right? You don't sound well.'

She thought she had kept her voice steady, and even her flatmate's mother could see through it! She swallowed hard and said with false cheerfulness, 'I'm fine, thanks so much, fine. But I really need to speak to Jane.'

'She's just having a coffee. I'll get her.'

In the moments of silence that followed Stephanie fought the tears. But when Jane's cheery voice said, 'Hi, Steph, what's up?' everything collapsed.

'Jane,' she wailed. 'Clive chucked me!'

'He what? You're kidding!'

'I've been awake all night, I couldn't sleep, I'm so wretched. Please come back, I've got to tell you about it, it's awful.'

'Can't you tell me about it now? Mummy's making a big lunch, I can't just leave.'

'Please, Jane, please. I can't talk about it over the phone.' She couldn't. If Jane was there it might be possible, but not electronically. How could she describe Clive kissing her belly, moving down between her legs, sweeping his tongue across her – and tasting James.

'Oh –' Jane sounded torn. 'Look, all right. I'll explain to Mummy and Daddy. I'll get out of it. They'll understand. But it'll take a while to drive back, Steph. What time is it now? Eleven? I won't be back for three hours.'

'Thank you,' she sobbed. 'Jane, thank you.'

She put the phone down and wiped her eyes, then went

to the bathroom and splashed her face with cold water. Thank God she had a flatmate. What did women do who lived alone?

The doorbell rang. Stephanie jumped, thought about ignoring it, then suddenly thought that it might be Clive, contrite, ready to apologise. She blotted her eyes again, shook back her hair and ran to the door.

She opened it and her jaw dropped. It wasn't Clive. It was Andrea.

'You bitch,' Andrea said, pushing past her into the living room. Stephanie turned to stare at her, so taken aback that she couldn't reply. Andrea stopped by the coffee table and looked at it. There was an empty bottle of champagne on it and two glasses. She spun back to face Stephanie and folded her arms. 'Did you have to get him pissed before he would fuck you?'

The champagne had been for Clive, not for James, but Andrea's words turned Stephanie's upset instantly to anger. 'None of your bloody business,' she said, slamming the door. 'What the hell are you doing here?'

'What the hell were you doing, seducing my husband?' Andrea demanded.

'Go away,' Stephanie said. Andrea's lips were white with rage and her eyes were wide. She actually looked threatening, although she was almost a head shorter than Stephanie. She looked dangerous, like a tiny ferocious carnivore.

'No chance,' snapped Andrea. 'Not until you promise never to touch James again.'

Anger made Stephanie's lips quiver. 'I don't have to promise you anything.'

'You ungrateful bitch!' Andrea hissed, clenching her fist. 'How much money have you made out of my ideas?'

'I do the work. Me and James do the work. You do fuck all. You don't appreciate him. I do.'

'Appreciate him?' Andrea laughed bitterly. 'Christ, do you know what he's like?' She unfolded her arms and pushed up her sleeve and showed Stephanie a ring of dark red bruises, livid as weals on her pale skin. 'He's a bloody good artist and a bloody brute. Are you stupid as well as greedy?'

There was no way that Stephanie was going to admit that

she had a bruise on her wrist, too, nor that she had already realised that James could be a violent bastard. How dare Andrea come here and curse her and call her names and patronise her? As if she'd never guessed, she said, 'You mean he hits you?'

'Yes,' Andrea whispered. She looked suddenly deflated, as if she was ashamed. After a second she asked hesitantly, 'Do you mean he – didn't, with you?'

Stephanie shook back her hair and smiled in the most superior way that she could manage. 'No,' she said. 'Obviously you don't do all the right things for him the way I do.'

For a moment Andrea didn't move. She stood staring, while a dark flush rose in her pale cheeks and then ebbed away. Stephanie was expecting abuse, and when suddenly Andrea reached out and grabbed the champagne bottle by the neck and lunged towards her she was so surprised that she didn't even think of resistance, just cowered away, turning her head and flinging up her hands to try to protect her face. Out of the corner of her eye she saw the bottle coming towards her, a green blur, and she whimpered and flinched and then pain burst in her head and everything went white, then red, then black.

Andrea stood over Stephanie's slumped body, gasping as the first violence of rage left her. She looked at the bottle in her hand, amazed that it hadn't broken. She had wanted it to break so that she could push it into Stephanie's face. That would have shown her.

But the bottle was in one piece. Champagne glass was tough. So now what would she do?

And as she looked down at the golden-brown tangle of Stephanie's hair she knew. It would be deliciously ironic, and it would be certain to terrify Stephanie so much that she'd steer clear of James in future. That's all she needed to do, just scare the snotty little bitch enough to keep her in her place.

The bag from the wine shop was underneath the coffee table. Andrea nodded, then looked around for something to tie Stephanie's hands with. She walked through to the bedroom and found a pair of dirty tights discarded on the floor. What a slut.

When she came back Stephanie was beginning to stir slightly. Andrea grabbed her shoulders and pulled her to a kneeling position. It was difficult. Stephanie was at least five feet eight and strongly built, What had James been thinking of, wanting to fuck this Amazon? He'd said often enough that he loved Andrea's tininess, her slender limbs, her little feet and hands.

Stephanie almost slumped to the floor again, but Andrea caught her and pushed her back until she was balanced securely on her knees. Then she tied her hands together, fingers laced, just as James had described it. Stephanie moaned and her eyes opened a little.

Snatching up the champagne bottle, Andrea said thinly, 'Wake up, bitch.'

Stephanie swayed and her eyelids fluttered. Then she opened her eyes and moved as if she would get up. 'Don't move,' Andrea snapped. 'Stay where you are, unless you want me to hit you again.'

'No,' Stephanie whispered, sinking back to her knees.

'Listen to me,' Andrea hissed, reaching down for the bag. 'I want you to keep your hands off James. Understand me? Don't go near him. He's mine.' She held the bag before Stephanie's face. 'See this? I mean it. Promise.'

'Don't,' Stephanie moaned, her eyes fixed on the bag.

'Promise, you bitch,' Andrea said, and with a convulsive, determined gesture she jerked the bag open and forced it down over Stephanie's head. Stephanie let out a sound like a sob and tried to get to her feet, but Andrea's hands were on her shoulders, holding her down, holding the bag down. The white plastic snapped inwards, outlining Stephanie's face as she tried to breathe. There was a concave O over her gaping mouth and tiny indentations where her nostrils sucked vainly for air. Andrea kept pressing the bag downwards, counting. How long to scare her? A minute? A minute should be enough.

The bag went slack. Andrea released it, but didn't take it off. Bitch, bitch, she deserved a good fright.

She counted a slow 60, then lifted off the bag. 'All right,' she said, 'I –'

Something was wrong. She expected that the moment the bag was off Stephanie would suck in a deep breath, choke, struggle, scream. But she didn't do anything. Her eyes were slightly open, but her eyelids weren't moving.

'Stephanie,' Andrea said hesitantly. She reached out to touch Stephanie's shoulder. 'Stephanie.'

Stephanie slumped slackly forward until her forehead touched the floor. She didn't move. Andrea's hands began to shake, and when she reached out to feel Stephanie's throat for a pulse she could hardly guide her fingers.

There was no pulse. She recoiled, panting. How could it have happened? A minute without breathing wasn't enough to kill anyone. For a moment she was struck with panic. She almost jumped up and grabbed the phone, ready to dial 999, ready to scream for help.

But then she stopped herself. It was too late. Ambulances took ages to come, they wouldn't be able to save Stephanie. And then they would know that Andrea had killed her. Too late, too late, too late, she had to save herself, get out, hide the evidence. Thank God Stephanie had been alone!

She swept up the bag and dumped the champagne bottle in it. Had she touched anything else? Only the tights that bound Stephanie's wrists. That must be OK. She couldn't bear to touch Stephanie again, anyway. She twisted the lock on the door with the plastic bag and let herself out.

To begin with she was shaking so that she could barely drive. She headed into the middle of the town and found a recycling bin, dumped the bottle in it and heard it shatter, pushed the plastic bag into the litter bin beside it, jumped back into the car.

Then she thought of someone finding Stephanie's body, left just as James had left Francesca. Everything just the same. If they tracked down James for the first murder, wouldn't they blame him for the second one, too?

It was funny, really. She began to giggle, then to laugh. Her laughter got louder and louder, and then the tears came, but she still didn't stop laughing.

# NINE
## Sunday 12.30 p.m.

Anderson let himself into the flat and headed straight for the shower. His legs were shaking. He had run so far that he could barely manage the stairs, but at least he seemed to have sweated out his anger.

The shower was bliss. When he emerged, rubbing his hair briskly dry with a clean towel, he felt almost human.

There was a message on his answering machine. He hesitated before he pressed the button, reckoning up the chance that it might be from Catherine. An apology, perhaps? He stabbed the button and waited tensely as the tape rewound.

A female voice, a voice that made him stiffen. It had changed. There was an American shading to it which set his teeth even more on edge. 'John, well, guess who, it's Sarah. No contact for a while, huh? Well, guess what, I'm back, my time in the States is up. I called you because I've lost Phil and Barbara's address and I thought you'd have it, you're always so efficient about that sort of thing. Maybe you're out running. I'll call again later, it would be good to find out how you are. And I guess I'll see you around, Guildford's a pretty small place, isn't it.'

The tape clicked off and ran back. He let it erase itself. Who was she trying to convince, with her 'it would be good to find out how you are'? If she wanted to talk to him it was because she thought it would be to her advantage. A lost address was just an excuse.

Since the divorce he had cut himself off from their circle of acquaintances, most of whom had been Sarah's anyway, since she hadn't liked to socialise with his colleagues from the police. It was therefore quite unlikely that he would 'see her around', and he had no intention of talking to her. He wasn't going to step back into that maze of manipulation and self-serving and deceit. He dressed quickly, found the address and wrote it on a plain piece of paper. He hesitated, then signed the paper with just his name and put it in an envelope. He'd send it care of her parents.

There was an easy way to ensure that she didn't catch him at home. He pulled on his jacket and left, and on the way down the stairs he let out a short, ironic laugh. When they had been married Sarah had often driven him to seek refuge in the office, and now, after nearly two years, with one phone call she had done it again.

Bill McKie was in charge of the weekend shift. When Anderson came in he was on the telephone, but his eyes widened. As soon as he put the phone down he said, 'Morning, sir. Didn't expect to see you today.'

Why not? The answer was obvious. Fielding had noticed his eagerness to be away last night and had put two and two together. He would have done as much himself, but still he was angry. If they knew about last night, they would know by his appearance this morning that he had failed, and that was unbearable.

McKie didn't seem to notice his discomfiture. 'I've just spoken to Pat, sir. She's picked up Allen no problem, he was at the fair. She's driving back with him now.'

Anderson nodded. That was gratifying, and promised a conclusion to the Lyons murder that was both tidy and swift. 'Good. Maybe I'll join her in the interview.'

At his desk he sat for a moment abstracted, his mind returning again to Catherine. It was true what he had told her, he had been sexually cautious. Perhaps he had been wrong to be. After all, he was free. Why shouldn't he take the

126

opportunity for sex when it presented itself, rather than waiting until he realised he didn't really like the woman anyway? He had slept with Catherine on their first date and it had been wonderful. And if he did happen to meet Sarah, he didn't want her to think that he was short of company.

Perhaps on Monday he would look up Kim Baines, the WPC who had made her interest so apparent not long ago. She was good-looking and bright and it was obvious that she wanted to get him into bed. Why not? Everyone else did it. The police were probably the most incestuous, voracious group of people in the country.

He hadn't convinced himself, and Catherine was still lurking in the back of his mind. To evict her he went and got himself a cup of disgusting station-issue coffee, then returned to his desk and reached for his in tray.

He was still struggling to immerse himself at 2.10, when suddenly his door flew open and McKie said, 'Sir.'

McKie's breathing was fast and his face revealed volumes. Anderson put down his pen and got up. 'What's happened?'

'Another murder, sir. Another woman. The emergency switchboard just called.'

'Where?'

'Guildford, sir. Eastern edge. Uniformed branch are already on their way. I've got the details.'

He glanced at his desk. There was nothing there that couldn't be left. 'All right. Let's go.'

McKie hesitated. 'Sir, shouldn't we call the Super?'

Anderson's head went back and McKie flinched. 'Why?'

'You know he likes to be rung if anything like this happens weekends, sir.'

Yes, he knew perfectly well, and he knew why. Senior officers didn't get overtime, but if they got calls at weekends they got extra pay. Parrish had all of CID well aware that anything significant on a weekend meant a call to him at once. He would listen, nod, call another officer to deal with it and pocket his call-out pay.

It was a disgrace: a waste of money and an abuse of privilege. And Parrish was by no means the only offender. Once, as a new DCI, Anderson had spoken to Parrish about it. Parrish had sneered and said that everyone did it. Everyone, that is, who was not as lucky as Anderson, whose wife was so rich he didn't even care whether he was paid or not. Anderson was sensitive about Sarah's money, and as Parrish had intended, this jibe had prevented him from ever raising the subject again, even after his divorce.

However, there was no need to let Parrish get away with it this time. 'You don't need to call him,' Anderson told McKie crisply. 'I'll take responsibility.'

McKie looked uncomfortable, but didn't argue. 'All right, sir.'

Anderson didn't like being driven, so they headed for the crime scene in his BMW with the headlights flashing and the siren wailing occasionally. Sunday traffic melted to the side of the road, astonished. As they cut across the road to run a red light Anderson said, 'Details, Bill.'

McKie shuffled further down in his seat. Anderson glanced at him. He looked as if he would have liked to close his eyes. Fielding had stronger nerves. 'Yes, sir. The dead woman's name is Stephanie Pinkney. A young woman called 999, Stephanie's flatmate. She'd just come home and found her. She was pretty incoherent, apparently, so we haven't got many more details.'

'So this might just be a sudden death?' His foot slackened on the throttle.

'She seemed very clear that it was murder, sir.'

'I hope they told her not to touch anything,' Anderson said, leaning slightly into the next bend.

They were at the address within ten minutes. Two police cars were parked outside and a knot of interested bystanders was gathering. Anderson and McKie got out of the car and looked at the house, a tall Victorian monstrosity subdivided into flats. Someone took good care of the front garden.

The uniformed PC at the door said, 'First floor, sir,' and waved them through. They stood at the bottom of the stairs for a moment, looking for anything unusual. There wasn't anything. 'Have to wait for Forensics,' Anderson said, and led the way up.

The door of the flat was open and someone was crying inside it. He went in and took in the scene. A big living room, typically Victorian with high windows and ceiling, bright classy posters decorating the walls, a three-piece suite and a coffee table. And a dead woman lying on the floor, face up, with a pale PC standing beside her. Anderson's eyes were drawn to the woman's hands. They were tied in front of her, the fingers laced as if in prayer. His stomach lurched.

'Jim,' said McKie, who seemed to know every PC in the nick. 'Is this how you found her?'

'No sir,' said the PC, looking hunted.

'You moved her?' Anderson snapped.

'She was warm, sir,' said the PC quickly. 'Warm, and she wasn't stiff. I had to try to revive her. But she was gone.'

'What position was she in when you found her?' Anderson asked, coming a little forward. He was afraid that he already knew.

'She was —' The PC hesitated. 'She was kneeling by the coffee table, sir. Kneeling down, with her head hanging forward.'

McKie drew in a sharp breath and Anderson knew what he was thinking. 'All right,' he said to the PC. 'Get a leaf of your notebook. I want you to draw on it a plan that shows exactly how you found her, where she was, and the position she was in. Draw stick figures if you have to,' he added, seeing confusion in the PC's face. 'Where's the woman who called the police?'

'Her flatmate? In the kitchen, sir. WPC Baines is with her.'

Anderson restrained a snort of surprise. Speak of the devil! To McKie he said, 'Bill, look around here. See if you can find a weapon, anything. Get Forensics set up when they arrive, and the surgeon. I'm going to talk to the flatmate.'

'Sir,' McKie said quickly. 'Sir, you know what this looks like, don't you.'

'Don't jump to conclusions,' Anderson said, turning away.

The kitchen was big and bright, with a bleached pine table and chairs for six. WPC Kim Baines was sitting at it next to a young woman whose head was buried in her hands as she sobbed. Kim looked up as Anderson came in. Her hat was off and her dark blonde hair was disarranged, and it suited her. When she saw him her face brightened and she looked as if she was about to make a cheeky remark, but then sober professionalism returned. 'Sir,' she said. 'This is Jane Pritchard. Jane.' She touched the young woman's arm. 'Jane, this is Detective Chief Inspector Anderson. He's here to find out what happened.' She looked again at Anderson. 'She's very upset, sir.' It was a coded request to him to be gentle. As if he'd be anything else with a young woman who'd just found a friend dead.

He sat down at the pine table opposite Jane Pritchard. She glanced up, revealing a plain, freckled, snub-nosed face smeared with snot and tears. Kim Baines got up and said, 'Sir, I'll make you some tea.'

'Thanks.' He kept his voice soft. 'Would you like some tea, Jane?'

Jane sat up and wiped her nose with a tissue, Kim's no doubt. In a choked voice she said, 'I'd rather have gin.'

'By all means,' he said. Jane looked a little startled. 'Where d'you keep it?'

'In the cupboard at the end,' she said. 'Can I really have some?'

'I'm sure WPC Baines can mix you something.' Kim smiled and nodded. In a few moments she had found the gin and some tonic and put a long glass in front of Jane. 'There,' Anderson said. 'Wrap yourself around that.'

Jane took a long swig of the drink, then put down the glass and closed her eyes. Tears leaked from beneath her eyelashes and trickled down her cheeks. 'I'm sorry,' she said.

'It's OK.' She sounded quite composed, despite the tears. 'Jane, tell me what happened today.'

She took a deep breath and let her eyes focus on the view out of the kitchen window. 'I was visiting my parents for the weekend. About eleven Stephanie called. She was terribly upset. She said she'd had a row with her boyfriend Clive and he'd chucked her. She asked me to come home. It wasn't easy, but she sounded so upset. So I said I would. I drove back straight away and I got home about two and – she was there, where she is now, kneeling on the carpet, and her eyes were open and I could see she was dead and I didn't know what to do –' She buried her head again in her hands, as if she couldn't bear the memory.

'You did the right thing,' he assured her. There was a movement in the doorway and he glanced up and saw McKie standing there, his eyes fixed on Jane. Anderson nodded and McKie came in and sat down beside him. 'Jane,' Anderson said, 'This is Detective Sergeant Bill McKie.' She nodded, not lifting her head.

'Sir,' McKie said, 'It looks as if –' He broke off, then said, 'Jane.'

She lifted her head. McKie asked, 'What did Stephanie do for a living, Jane?'

'She was an art researcher,' Jane said, and Anderson felt as if a cold trickle of water was running down his spine under his shirt. 'She worked at the Tate.'

'Look,' said McKie bluntly, 'was she into dirty paintings?'

Jane narrowed her eyes. 'She specialised in –' She hesitated, pressed her lips together and swallowed, then lifted her head and finished coolly, '– erotica.'

Beside Anderson McKie stiffened like a hound catching a scent. Damn it, was he infected with Fielding's psychopath theory, too? Before he could pursue it any further Anderson said, 'Do you know what Stephanie was doing while you were away this weekend, Jane?'

Jane shook her head and wiped her eyes. 'Not really. She was planning to see Clive last night. She said she might do some shopping. I –' She made a confused, rueful face. 'I don't understand about her and Clive. They'd been going out for ages. I can't think what can have happened. I mean, I know Stephanie wasn't Littie Miss Perfect, she was always telling me how she fancied other blokes, but it wasn't as if she ever actually did anything about it.'

'I think we ought to speak to Clive,' Anderson said, 'and find out from him what happened last night.'

Jane's head went up with a snap. 'Oh my God,' she said. 'You don't think Clive could have killed her, do you? He couldn't. He –'

'We just need to talk to him,' Anderson said gently, 'to make sure.'

'Tea, sir,' said Kim Baines, holding out a cup. 'Sarge?'

'Thanks, Kim, love,' said McKie. When he had his tea he said, 'Sir, can I have a word with you?'

Anderson nodded and got to his feet. 'Jane, excuse me. I'll be back with you soon. Kim, is everything OK?'

'Fine,' said Kim brightly, and she flickered her eyebrows at him and moved her lips in the faintest suggestion of a kiss. Obviously she hadn't given up.

'Sir,' said McKie when the door to the kitchen was closed, 'you heard what she said.'

Anderson looked again at the dead woman. She was young, in her late twenties perhaps, and very attractive. Her hair was beautiful, a long thick cascade of golden brown. There didn't seem to be a mark on her. 'Did you find any weapon?' he asked.

'No, sir. Sir, look at her hands. Look at how they're tied. It's the same killer.'

'It looks superficially the same.' He knelt down beside the dead woman, looking at her more closely. No wonder the PC had tried to revive her. Her parted lips and half-open eyes made her look as if at any moment she would get up and walk away. A waste, another bloody waste of a life.

McKie took a quick step towards him and dropped his voice. 'Christ, sir! The same position, kneeling, no visible cause of death, her hands tied like that when nobody knew how they were tied, and she's an art researcher working in the same bloody field! It's the same killer, sir. It must be.'

'And I suppose you think it's Pat's mission psychopath,' he retorted icily. 'For God's sake, Bill, you heard what our witness said. She rowed with her boyfriend last night. We have to rule out the obvious first. And Pat's just arrested Allen on suspicion of Francesca Lyons's murder. His fingerprints were found on her body, if you recall. Are you suggesting that he committed this murder as well?'

The withering sarcasm made McKie wince, but he didn't give up. 'Sir —'

'If that's not enough for you, Bill, look at her hands. Look at the knot.' McKie hesitated, then knelt reluctantly beside the corpse for a closer look. 'That's a reef knot. The other knot was tied in some sort of a hitch. Wouldn't you have thought that the same person would have been inclined to tie the same knot?'

McKie shook his head and got to his feet. He was about to say something else when the police surgeon arrived and shortly after him the Forensic specialists, ready to take the place to pieces. Anderson said, 'Bill, sort things out. I'm going to talk to Jane again.'

'If it's not the same killer, sir,' said McKie, 'how do you account for the similarities?'

'It could be coincidence. It could be that more than one person is involved. We don't know, and we shouldn't make assumptions. Sort things out here. Then get the address of the boyfriend and go and find him. We want to interview him as soon as possible.'

'Yes, sir.' McKie sounded sullen, but Anderson didn't care. If two women in the same field of art had died, it made more sense to believe that something was going on in that field that to invent a psychopath. And the knot was different, although that was by no means conclusive. Anyone could explain that difference away. Why did they all want a complex outcome rather than a simple one? Blinded by the glamour of the serial killer. As Dr Reid had said, they'd all been watching too much television.

In the kitchen Jane had finished her gin. She looked up as Anderson came in. Kim Baines said, 'Your tea will be cold, sir. D'you want me to freshen it up for you?'

She looked as if she'd like to freshen him up. At the sight of her obvious, eager interest his own merely theoretical interest in her waned. Where would be the fun in bedding a woman who had no need to be persuaded? 'No thanks, Kim. You can go and help Sergeant McKie, if Jane doesn't mind.' Jane shrugged, and Kim made a little face and went to the door.

Anderson sat down beside Jane. She asked wanly, 'What's going on?'

'The police surgeon's here,' he said, 'and the Forensics team. They'll be lifting fingerprints and looking for evidence. I'm afraid there'll be quite a mess.'

'Do you know how she was killed?' Jane's eyes were hazel, very quick and penetrating, and suddenly she was totally focused on him. 'Do you know what happened to her?'

'No,' he replied honestly. 'Did you find anything, did you see anything that might suggest how she died?'

Jane shook her head. 'No, nothing.' She regarded him again with those sharp eyes. 'Are you sure you don't know?'

He took a deep breath. 'I have a suspicion, Jane. But I don't know.'

'What do you suspect?'

If he told her she might give something away. It was risky. But she seemed intelligent and sensible. She could handle it. 'I suspect,' he said slowly, 'that she was stunned and then smothered with a plastic bag.'

The blood drained from Jane's face and she moistened her lips with her tongue. 'Oh,' she said softly. 'Oh, God, how –' Her voice faded out, then returned strongly. 'Why do you suspect that?'

'Because this killing looks like another murder I saw recently.'

Jane lifted her head and her nostrils flared as she took a deep breath. 'Do you think the same person might have done them both?'

'It's possible. Jane, tell me about Stephanie. Who might have done this?'

'I thought,' she said blankly, 'I thought you thought that Clive –'

'We need to talk to Clive, but I'm not assuming anything. Tell me about Stephanie.'

'She –' Jane shook her head. 'I don't know. I knew her from college, we'd been sharing this flat about a year, we got on fine, I liked her. She worked in town, at the Tate. She liked her job, she said she was lucky to get it. The pay was crap, but that's life in the art world, she used to say. She never told me she was in any sort of trouble. She and Clive seemed happy. They'd been going out for ages, years. She didn't have trouble with him or with men generally. I can't think —' She covered her face with her hands. 'I truly can't think of any reason why anyone would want to kill her.'

'You said she wasn't Miss Perfect. What did you mean?'

'Oh.' Jane leant her head back and looked at the ceiling as if by doing so she could stop the tears from running down her cheeks. 'She was a flirt. Nothing worse than that. She fancied men, she liked to look at them, she admired them. Clive was used to it. I never saw them row about it.'

He nodded slowly and asked after a moment, 'Can I see her room?'

The room was at the back of the house, overlooking the garden. It was a tip, strewn with clothes and cosmetics and correspondence. Jane looked at the mess, then sat down on the bed and began to cry again. Anderson gazed steadily around him. Too complicated for a quick search, too much that he might disturb. But —

A picture on the wall caught his eye. He stepped closer to look. It was a male nude, drawn in pen and ink in a harsh, striking style that he thought he recognised, though there was no signature. He said, 'Do you know where Stephanie got this?'

Jane looked up and wiped her eyes with the sheet, then shook her head. 'She used to pick them up all over the place.'

'Did she know a man called James Maguire?'

There was no reaction in Jane's face. 'I don't think I ever heard the name.'

Kim appeared at the door. 'Sir. Sir, the bloody Press are here already. There's a TV crew downstairs.'

Damn! No time to look more closely at anything. He touched Jane's shoulder. When she looked up he said, 'Jane, they'll all be after you. The TV, the papers, everyone. I would very much appreciate it if you said as little as possible about what you found when you came home.'

'Is it important?' she asked, eyes wide.

'Yes. It could be.'

'All right. I hate the way they do this, anyway. I won't say anything.'

'Thank you.' He turned away and went through the living room, full now of apparatus and the searing light of flashguns. 'Press alert, Bill. Keep low.'

'Yes, sir,' said McKie, but his face was shuttered. Who had leaked the details of the Lyons murder? Could it have been Bill, and if so, why?

The TV crew was standing at a respectful distance, all set up. They started filming as soon as he appeared. The reporter was a young man whose turned-up collar and dark glasses revealed his pretensions to higher things. He stuck out his microphone and said eagerly, 'Can we have an interview, Detective Chief Inspector? Is it true that this looks like another killing by the Gallery murderer?'

Christ, where did they find these things out? And why did they have to make everything so melodramatic? When the time was right he would use the media to ask the public for assistance, and until then he just wanted them to keep their noses out of the case. He put on his coldest, most official face and voice and said, 'We're treating this death as suspicious. Until relatives have been informed I have no further comment to make.'

Then he walked to his car. The reporter followed him like a dog yapping at his heels, throwing question after question, but Anderson ignored him and took a certain quiet pleasure in shutting the car door in his face. Then he lifted the radio. Fielding needed to know that there might be a problem with the collar she had given up her Sunday to make.

# TEN
## Sunday 2.30 p.m.

'I have nothing to add to my original statement,' Richard Allen said for the tenth time.

Pat pushed herself back from the table and glanced across the room at Gerry Hart, who was leaning against the wall as usual. They had been in the interview room for twenty minutes and so far Allen had maintained an impression of studied calm, unruffled by everything that she threw at him. He had brushed off the sighting of his car and what had quite possibly been him in Wressingham on Wednesday evening, and he was now exchanging looks of polite exasperation with his solicitor. His expression said, These police, honestly! So unreasonable. But what can you do?

She watched him now, sizing him up. A big man, fleshy, with heavy features and massive hands and feet. He was good-looking in a sort of Roman-Emperorish way, but in her view not a patch on Chris Lyons. What had Francesca seen in him? There was no accounting for love. Mind you, he had a big nose, and everyone knew what people said about men with big noses.

He didn't know that she had the last piece of evidence up her sleeve. It was time to reveal it and watch his reaction. 'Mr Allen,' she said. The formal mode of address was suitable for this interview. It gave her status and power, it made her as important as him. 'You're under arrest for the murder of

Francesca Lyons. I am quite confident that we have enough evidence to convict you. Aren't you even curious about what it is?'

'If it was something to do with all those samples that you so disgustingly took,' he said, 'I'm sure you would have said so. And as I'm innocent, I find it hard to be curious.'

'Not the samples,' Pat said, propping her elbows on the table and studying Allen's face. He did look remarkably calm, but his high forehead and eyelids were beginning to shine with sweat. Nerves, or was the interview room just hot? 'Not the samples, Mr Allen. Fingerprints.'

He laughed. 'Fingerprints! I told you, I visited Francesca's gallery about a week before she was killed. I told you all about it. I'm not remotely surprised that my fingerprints are there.'

'The prints weren't on the premises, Mr Allen,' Pat said softly. She heard Gerry behind her straighten up, watching with eager attention. 'They were on Mrs Lyons's body.'

There was a long silence. Allen's solicitor, who had been sitting in a corner in an attitude of unconcealed boredom, sat up and gaped at his client in apparent disbelief. Allen himself stared at Pat open-mouthed. He looked like a fish out of water, gasping for air. After a moment he said, 'What?'

'Fingerprints were found on the skin of Mrs Lyons's abdomen,' Pat said steadily. 'They match the fingerprints you gave on Friday exactly. Would you like to make any comment, Mr Allen?'

Allen's big body seemed to crumple in on itself. He turned to his solicitor, who said in a strangled voice, 'You don't have to reply, Mr Allen.'

Slowly Allen turned back to face Pat. She looked him in the eye, enjoying the little thrill of power that she always felt when a man who was bigger and older and better off than her was suddenly at her mercy. She said, 'Mr Allen.'

Allen made a choked sound and put his face in his hands. Pat said for the benefit of the tape recorder, 'Mr Allen has covered his face with his hands.'

As if her commentary was more than he could bear, Allen flung up his head. 'All right,' he said, 'all right.'

Was this going to be a confession? She held back the flicker of a smile. 'What do you mean?'

'I was with her that night,' Allen said. His voice sounded leaden. 'It's my voice on the answering machine. I called her because we had arranged to meet. I went there and we –' he swallowed hard '– we made love.'

'I'd like to confirm this, Mr Allen,' said Pat. 'In your previous statement you said that you had not been at the Lyons Gallery on Wednesday night. Are you now retracting that statement?'

'Yes.' He covered his face with his hand. So did the solicitor. 'My previous statement was – inaccurate.'

She took a deep breath of triumph. 'Well, then, I think you'd better make an accurate statement now. We'll talk about why you lied later on.'

'Made an inaccurate statement,' the solicitor corrected hopelessly.

'Lied,' she said, with satisfaction. 'Now then, Mr Allen.'

Allen supported his temples on his splayed fingers. 'I was her lover,' he said to the surface of the table. 'Since March. We were in love. But – her husband, my wife, the kids – we were going to keep it secret – until the children were older. I did see her that night. I got to the gallery about 8.30 and I left after about – I don't know – an hour.' His eyes lifted to Pat's. They were suddenly wide and dark. 'I didn't kill her,' he said. 'I loved her.'

'And you made love,' Pat said softly. He nodded. She said, 'Mr Allen nodded.' Then she went on, still softly, 'Did you use a condom?'

Again he nodded. Aloud he said, 'So I didn't mind giving you a semen sample.'

For a moment Pat wondered how she was going to ask the next question. At last she said, 'Did Francesca have any other lovers?'

His head jerked up and his mouth was tight with anger. 'What the hell are you getting at?'

She kept her voice very steady, but she was tense with eagerness. 'We found the spermicide from the condom. But there was also semen in Francesca's vagina. Did she have any other lovers?'

For a moment Allen stared at her as if she was crazy. Then, unexpectedly, he laughed. 'Not unless you count her husband.'

'What?'

'Her husband. Chris. When she came to the gallery that night he'd already made love to her. She said he was trying to keep her back.'

Pat couldn't prevent herself from glancing round at Gerry, but his face was blank. He hadn't realised the significance of this. There was no second man that Francesca loved and trusted. Either Richard Allen or Chris had killed her, or whoever had killed her had done it without making love to her. The mission killer was back in the frame.

Concealing her excitement, she turned back to Allen. 'You said you left after about an hour.'

'I suppose I left at about a quarter to ten.' His face was beginning to twitch with a tic that might be guilt or might be an attempt to prevent tears. 'I was home by 10.15. It's a good half hour drive.'

That was true. And if Francesca had made that phone call just before 10, then if Allen had really got home at 10.15 he was off the hook. Pat said, 'Can anyone vouch for the time you got home?'

He shook his head, more and more violently. 'Only my wife, and I won't ask her. She'd find out about Francesca. I've gone to all this trouble to avoid –'

'Good Christ,' Pat burst out, 'you're sitting in the nick under arrest and you're worried that your wife'll find out about a love affair? What were you going to tell her about today?'

'Nothing,' he said baldly. 'Just that I had a bad day at the fair.'

'One of us will be speaking to your wife.' That thin-faced, angry woman, who had already guessed about her husband's lover anyway.

'No!' Allen surged to his feet and Gerry took two quick steps forward, looming. For a moment the two big men stared at each other, then Allen sank back down to the chair and hid his face.

A knock sounded at the door. Pat jumped, then nodded

to Gerry to open it. The desk sergeant stuck his head around it and said, 'Pat, your governor's on the phone. Has to talk to you straight away, he says.'

Gerry raised his eyebrows. Pat tugged at her plait, then snapped, 'Interview terminated at –' she glanced at the clock '– 2.50 p.m. Gerry, take him back to the cells.'

She hurried to the desk and picked up the phone. 'Yes, sir, Fielding here.'

'Pat.' The crackly line revealed a radio connection. 'There's been a development. We've got another murder. It looks extremely similar to the Lyons killing.'

'Christ,' she said, hardly breathing.

'How are you getting on with Allen?' said Anderson's sharp voice.

She made herself concentrate. 'He was her lover, sir. He was there that night. The fingerprints on the body got that out of him. But he says he left her at about 9.45, and if anyone backs it up that means he couldn't have committed the murder. And sir,' she said, 'he's explained the semen and the spermicide. He used a condom, but when Francesca came to the gallery she already had semen in her body. Her husband had made love to her before she set out.'

There was a silence. Anderson was no doubt imagining, as she was, how Chris had hesitated and prevaricated and told them half truths. Eventually Anderson said, 'If he left before ten, the phone call gets him off the hook. Either Francesca made it, or Chris did.'

'Yes, sir.'

All right.' He sounded decisive and unfazed. How could he be so cool? Everything pointed towards a serial killer, a psychopath stalking their patch looking for women to smother. 'I'm coming back now. Bill's gone to pick up the new victim's boyfriend, we have to interview him. Can you get corroboration on that time of departure for Allen right away?'

Allen's wife. God, Gerry could do that job. 'Yes, sir. No problem.'

'Good. OK, Pat, when I come in we'll have a briefing. Hold on to Allen.'

'Yes, sir.' She heard him hang up and stood for a moment

staring into nothingness, the phone held limply in her hand.

Anderson didn't run from his car to his office. He was still thinking hard, trying to assimilate what Fielding had told him.

One thing was amply clear. There was no point in Allen lying about Chris having made love to Francesca earlier in the evening: the DNA samples would prove everything. So the two men were explained. And if Allen was off the hook, then either Chris was the killer or someone else was, someone they hadn't yet found, a stranger.

Fielding met him at the door, her face pale and tense. 'Sir, I think we ought to call Dr Carroll.'

'No,' he said, and his voice was so emphatic that Fielding actually took a step back. He made himself speak more softly. 'We have suspects, Pat. Eliminate them first. Then we'll think about other possibilities.'

She turned away, clearly angry. She was so wedded to her theory that she couldn't keep an open mind. Without looking at him she said, 'Bill called. He's got the boyfriend. He's bringing him in now.'

'Good.' She still wasn't looking at him. Had he spoken so roughly? For a moment he wanted to make a gesture, to restore relations. But it shouldn't be necessary. She was a professional, and he was her boss.

But there was something. 'Pat,' he said. 'I'd better brief you on this next killing. We're going to be very busy when Parrish hears about this.'

She turned around, her eyes wide. 'Didn't someone call him? He always wants us to call when –'

'Nobody called him. It's my responsibility.' He looked into her eyes, letting her see that he knew all about Parrish's little game, that he had done it on purpose.

After a moment her face relaxed, though she didn't smile. 'God,' she said, 'the lengths people go to once they stop getting overtime. Is the same thing going to happen to me when I make Inspector?'

'It never happened to me. Come in my office, Pat. I'll fill you in. It's your case, after all, and I thought you would want to interview the boyfriend with Bill.'

Now she smiled at him. 'Yes, sir,' she said. 'Thank you.'

He'd just about finished briefing Fielding and gathering all the information from her interview with Allen when McKie called to say he was ready to interview Stephanie's boyfriend, whose name was Clive Hardwick. Fielding got up at once to go, her face set and eager. At the door she turned and said, 'Are you going to come in, sir?'

'Maybe in a little while. There's some things I want to do.'

She nodded and turned away. He sat for a moment looking after her, then swivelled his chair to look out of the window at the Guildford townscape, grey with rain.

He was condemning Fielding and McKie for being so set on the mission killer theory. But wasn't he just as set against it? Oh, he could justify the way he felt about it. But justification wasn't good enough. If he forced himself to be honest, he had to admit that his resistance to the psychobabble explanation was unfounded in fact. If anybody else had felt that way, he would have called it a hunch.

Rapidly, he ran over all the possible factual explanations. Chris Lyons, Richard Allen, Paul Johnson; all the suspects for the first murder. Allen might be off the hook. And this second murder had flung everything into confusion. It was so similar, identical, in fact, except for that recalcitrant knot. And nobody outside the police had known about how Francesca's hands were tied.

He shook his head, angry with himself, and looked for something else to do. There on his desk was the tape recorder, with a copy of the tape from Francesca's answering machine in it. He rewound the tape and played it again.

'Fran,' said the voice which he now knew to be Richard Allen's. 'Pick up the phone, it's me. Fran –' And then another voice. 'I'm surprised you're not there. I'm coming anyway.'

He hesitated, rewound the tape and played the second message again. It was crackly, blurred, poor quality, the machine had been old. But –

'I'm surprised you're not there. I'm coming anyway.' A deep voice, with a harsh, abrasive edge. Or was that just the tape? He played it again, and again, and each time he was

143

more certain that he had heard that voice and that it belonged to James Maguire.

He buried his head between his hands and rewound the tape. Was he going mad? What possible connection could there be between Maguire and Francesca? Was his mind playing tricks on him because he had seen a picture on Stephanie's wall that had reminded him of the pictures he had seen in James's studio?

The tape was useless as evidence. Only a few words, and the quality was too poor to stand up in court. Voiceprints were pretty novel anyway, England lagging behind the States as usual, and a decent defence counsel would tear any voiceprint evidence from this tape to shreds without even trying.

It wasn't enough. It was too like a hunch. If he mentioned it and he was proved wrong, he'd be as bad as Fielding with her pet psychopath. He turned off the tape recorder and got to his feet. Muscling in on the interview with Hardwick would take his mind back to where it belonged, the facts of the case.

He opened the door to the interview room and walked in. Fielding's voice said, 'DCI Anderson has just entered the interview room.'

Fielding was sitting with McKie beside her opposite a young man of thirty or so, whose gangling limbs seemed to have given way so that he was sprawled in his chair, shivering. Beneath his shielding hands his face was streaked with tears. Anderson glanced at Fielding with a frown. He hadn't expected her to be so hard on Hardwick even before he was arrested.

She met his look with equanimity. 'Clive,' she said, and the young man flinched. 'Clive, tell DCI Anderson what you told me.'

Clive slowly lifted his head, revealing a pale, good-looking face with hollow cheekbones and very bright blue eyes. He would have to be handsome, to hang on to a girl as beautiful as Stephanie Pinkney had been. At present he looked absolutely terrified. 'Tell him what?'

'Tell him what happened last night.'

A scarlet flush crept up on Clive's high cheekbones. 'Again?'

'Again.' Fielding's voice was flat and unanswerable.

The blue eyes flashed up to Anderson's. 'Last night,' he said hesitantly. 'I went around to Stephanie's. I took a takeaway. We drank a bottle of champagne and then we went to bed.'

Anderson came a little closer. He'd seen the glasses on the table, but he hadn't noticed a bottle anywhere. 'What happened to the bottle?'

Clive hesitated. This clearly hadn't formed part of his earlier recital. 'We – I think we left it on the table, on the coffee table. Steph didn't – she wasn't –' He turned his head aside and whispered, 'She wasn't great at clearing stuff up.'

Anderson glanced at Fielding. She opened her mouth, closed it again, then said, 'Bill, make a note that we ought to look for that bottle.'

'I interrupted you,' Anderson said courteously to Clive. 'Go on.'

Clive swallowed hard. 'We went to bed and I –' The flush rose again, brighter this time, staining the whole of his face and throat.

'Just tell DCI Anderson what you told me, Clive,' Fielding said.

'I – I.' Clive shut his eyes and began to speak more quickly, as if he wanted to get it over with. 'We were going to make love. I, I went down on her.' He swallowed again. There was sweat on his brow under his soft brown hair. 'She was wet. It wasn't just her. She'd been with somebody else. I could tell. So we – argued about it.'

'What did she say?' Anderson asked softly.

'At first she denied it. Then she didn't. But she wouldn't tell me who. And I was so angry. I yelled at her and I wanted to – to hit her but I didn't. I got dressed and I left and I said I would never see her again.' Suddenly the tears were there, trickling from his blue eyes. 'And now I won't. I won't. Steph.'

Anderson looked at Fielding. She puckered her lips uncertainly and waggled her head. Clive didn't appear to have convinced her. 'Clive,' she said, and her voice was cold. 'Tell him about today.'

'There's nothing to tell,' Clive said anxiously, wiping his face. 'I told you. I slept late and I went to get a paper about 9.30 and then I sat in my flat and read it and I got to the pub about one.'

'By which time Stephanie had probably been dead for an hour at least,' McKie put in.

'Don't!' Clive wailed. 'I didn't kill her. I didn't go back there. I swear it!'

'Stephanie's neighbours say they heard someone going into the flat about 11 a.m.,' McKie said. 'Just after she called her flatmate. How do we know that wasn't you, Clive?'

'Because it wasn't,' said the young man, wringing his hands. 'I was at home. I was there all morning.'

'Who can corroborate that, Clive?' Fielding persisted.

'No one. No one. Oh God help me, I didn't kill her,' Clive said. He looked up into Anderson's face and held out his hands, palms up, the universal gesture of appeal. 'Please,' he said. 'These two don't believe me. Please believe me. I didn't kill her. I loved her.'

Anderson looked into the tear-stained, agonised face for a moment, then glanced at Fielding. 'Have you asked for intimate samples?'

She shook her head. 'Waiting for you, sir. Senior officer on duty, you know.'

He nodded. 'Clive, I'd like to ask you to help us by giving samples of your blood, semen and saliva.' Clive's story suggested that they would find semen in Stephanie's body, just as they had in Francesca's. And if Clive was lying, he would find this daunting.

Clive's long face lit up. 'Yes,' he said at once. 'Of course. I didn't make love to her. You'll be able to prove it. But my fingerprints will be everywhere: I was at her flat nearly every night.' Once again he seemed to be struck by terrible reality, and the brightness left his face. He whispered Stephanie's name again and began to sob.

'Who do you think killed her, Clive?' Fielding asked sharply. But Clive didn't respond, just covered his face with his hands.

Fielding looked up at Anderson and shook her head. 'Interview terminated at 3.40 p.m.,' she said. 'Clive.' Clive didn't open his eyes. 'Clive, I'm going to leave you here for the time being. I'll be back shortly.'

'Am I under arrest?' Clive asked faintly, still with his eyes shut. 'Can I go?'

Fielding hesitated, and Anderson got the feeling that if he hadn't been standing there she might have responded differently. But she said, 'You're not under arrest, and you're free to go whenever you want. I'm asking you to stay here to help us further.'

'Yes,' Clive said. He opened his eyes. Their blue was startling. 'I'll cooperate. Of course I will.'

Fielding slammed the door. 'No alibi,' she said as the three of them walked down the corridor. 'He caught her cheating on him and he's got no alibi.'

'But we've got no evidence,' said McKie. 'Not yet, anyway.'

They returned to CID offices. Gerry Hart was there, waiting for them. 'Sarge,' he said, as soon as Fielding appeared, 'I went to the Allens' house but his wife was out. The neighbours said she was gone shopping. I came back in case you wanted to go and talk to her yourself.'

Fielding glanced at McKie and Anderson. McKie said, 'You go, Pat. I'll handle the samples. We can leave Clive and Allen to stew for a while.'

She said, 'Sir?'

'All right,' Anderson said. 'Bill, when you've taken the samples, check out the whereabouts of Paul Johnson this morning. And bring in Chris Lyons. Pat, I want you to reinterview him. Gloves off this time.'

McKie's eyes flashed. 'You think it does look like the same killer, then, sir?'

'It's possible,' Anderson said evenly. 'It's worth checking, isn't it?'

'I'd say so, sir,' McKie said.

He walked away without a smile. Fielding watched him go and raised her eyebrows at Anderson. 'What's got into him?'

There wasn't any way to put this that would sound pleasant. 'I think Bill believes in your mission killer, Pat.'

Fielding gave a little, tight smile. 'I'm not surprised. After today, it looks pretty persuasive. Doesn't it, sir?'

The trouble was that she was right. Anderson went into his office and shut the door. What good were the suspects now in the station? Allen might well have a workable alibi and Clive looked as innocent as anyone Anderson had ever seen. The two crimes were so similar. And yet –

He tilted his head back and stared at the ceiling. Some similarities, hardly any differences. But the similarities in themselves might be misleading. Take the semen, for example. Anyone looking at the cases from outside would assume that the semen in both women came from the same source. But according to Allen Francesca had been with her husband, and it seemed exceptionally unlikely that Chris Lyons would have been with Stephanie Pinkney before her evening with Clive. So appearances were deceptive. The semen was probably from different men.

Did that mean that Dr Carroll and Fielding were right, and that the killer was the same person in both cases, and that in neither case had he, assuming it was a he, had sex with the woman he killed? Was it time to broaden his search, open a nationwide enquiry, call other forces to help?

It didn't feel right. Stephanie, especially, had done something unusual the day before she died. She had had sex with a man not her boyfriend, and she had refused to reveal who it was. And the next day someone had killed her. A jealous lover? A spurned lover? An impulse pick-up, proving just how dangerous random sex could be?

She'd had a picture on her wall that reminded him of the ones on the walls of James Maguire's studio. He opened his notebook and found the telephone number of Andrea Maguire's office. She wouldn't be there, but he could leave a message on the answering machine, make some excuse, get back to the gallery, look at the pictures again and check out his memory of them.

The phone rang. To his surprise, after three rings a female voice said, 'Andrea Maguire, good afternoon.'

'Mrs Maguire, hello. It's DCI Anderson here.' What would he say to her?

'Oh, Mr Anderson, hello!' She sounded actually pleased to hear from him. A warm glow began somewhere in his midriff. 'How are you? Is there something more I can do to help?'

His thoughts had smoothly run their course. 'Mrs Maguire –'

'Andrea, please.'

He hadn't expected that. 'Andrea. I was a little concerned that I had – ah – overstepped the bounds when I was speaking to you yesterday. I think I may have upset your husband.'

'Oh,' said her voice, light and dismissive, 'that's just James. Ignore him.'

She must be alone. She hadn't treated James so lightly when he was there, clutching her arm with his big hand. 'You're sure there's no problem?'

'None at all. But thank you for asking.'

Fair enough. He wasn't surprised. 'I'm very relieved to hear it. I was wondering, though, if I could come and talk to you again. There are a couple more points I just wanted to clear up.'

'Yes, of course.' Her voice was eager and expectant. 'Are you working now? I mean, if you are, I'm here in the gallery, I've got some things to do but we could talk if you'd like to.'

He made a quick calculation. He trusted Fielding to handle things at this end for a couple of hours. 'Thank you. That would be very helpful. I'll come straight over.'

'I'll be looking forward to it.'

He put down the phone and found he was smiling. It was a pleasure to talk to someone who seemed to be genuinely glad to hear from him.


Why did he want to come back again? Andrea paced up and down her office, twisting her wedding ring round and round. What did he want?

It wasn't possible that he should suspect her of having killed Stephanie. She hadn't left any clues, she was certain, and besides, he couldn't have sounded so open and relaxed with her if he thought she might be a –

Her mind refused to form the word 'murderess'. She wasn't a murderess. It had all been a mistake, an accident. Stephanie had asked for it, anyway.

But why was he coming? If it wasn't to do with her, it must be to do with James. Andrea stopped by the window and leant her hands on the windowsill, staring downwards at the quiet street below. Did she want to try to protect James, as well as herself?

As soon as she asked herself the question she knew the answer. James had betrayed her, and if it was a choice between her safety and his she knew what she would do. She wouldn't give him away outright, but she'd protect herself first. If that meant that Anderson pursued James for one or both of the killings, well, so be it.

On his first visit Anderson had touched her. He had been very gentle, and she had seen something in his face, a kindling in his eyes, which wasn't just pity. He thought her attractive, she was sure. And just now, on the phone, when she had told him to call her Andrea, his dark voice had spoken the name like a caress.

James had had Stephanie, and that was just the first one he had admitted to. He had probably screwed dozens of women over the years, models, sitters, anyone he could get. Why shouldn't she revenge herself in kind? Why not try to seduce Anderson? He was so totally different from James that he had an almost perverse appeal. What would he be like as a lover? Surely not fierce and brutal. Subtle, gentle, understanding. Everything that she hadn't experienced for years.

Why the hell not? If James didn't like it, she could say that she was just trying to keep the police off their tail.

Below her a big grey car drew up. Anderson got out of it and glanced upwards. She flinched back from the window, suddenly afraid of him. He was a policeman, for God's sake. What if he suspected her, and was cunning enough not to show it? She turned away, taking deep breaths in an attempt to slow her pumping heart.

The entryphone rang and she didn't bother to lift it, just pressed the button. Steps on the stairs, and then a knock on the door. She folded her hands together for a moment, then went to open it.

'Hello. How nice to see you.' Her voice didn't sound right

– strained, tense, unnatural. What would he think? He'd be bound to suspect. 'Do come in.'

He smiled at her. 'Thank you.' She closed the door behind him and he turned to watch her. 'Do you often work alone? There aren't many people around at weekends, and you've got valuable things in here.'

'There's the entryphone,' she said.

'But you just let me in. You didn't even ask who I was.'

It was rather sweet that he was concerned for her safety. She said, 'Honestly, it's very secure in here. There's a burglar alarm, and there's a panic button under my desk. I just have to press it and the security company ring up and if I don't give them a codeword they call the police. You don't have to worry.'

'You still ought to ask people ringing the entryphone who they are.'

With a little smile she confessed, 'I watched you arrive out of the window. So I knew it was you.'

His face softened. She wasn't wrong, he did like her. His expression showed it, and the warm sparkle of his dark blue eyes. After a moment he broke the eye contact and said, 'Andrea, I have to ask you again, did I cause trouble for you the last time I came? I thought your husband was angry. I didn't like leaving you with him.'

Honesty could only help. 'Well,' she said, avoiding his eyes, 'he was angry. You were – touching me.' She stroked her wrist, as if remembering how he had held it. 'We argued about it.'

'Did he hit you?' The voice was soft, but it expected an answer.

'No.' She could be honest there, too, for once. 'No, he didn't. He threw me out of the studio and I went home in the car, and he stayed here overnight. He often does when we've – argued.'

His brows were tilted slightly in concern. He was worried about her! Not suspicion, anxiety. 'I'm sorry to have been the cause of an argument,' he said.

She shrugged one shoulder. 'Don't worry. We would have been arguing soon anyway. He – he's been sleeping with someone else. Some other woman. I only just found out.'

His face was still and intent, focused. It was James he was suspicious of, for sure. 'Really?' he asked, in a carefully casual voice. 'How did you find out?'

'He told me. The swine. He really wanted to rub my face in it. Perhaps he wouldn't have come out with it, but seeing me with you —'

'Did he tell you who she is?'

Should she make it absolutely clear by mentioning Stephanie? No, better not. 'No. I get the idea it's someone else in the art world, but it would be, wouldn't it? That's who he meets.' Suddenly she began to enjoy herself. She was misleading Anderson and making herself attractive to him and getting James into trouble, all at the same time. Unable to resist, she added another lie. 'I get the feeling that he may have argued with her recently. Maybe that's why he told me about it.'

He nodded. Was that concealed excitement in his face? 'So,' he said, 'James spent the night here. But he's not here now, is he?'

Oh, he was subtle. He wanted to find out where James had been when Stephanie was killed without making it obvious that that was what he was asking. Casually she said, 'No, he's not here. I came back this morning about 10 a.m. to work, and he went home then.'

'He went home. On foot?'

'That's right. He walks everywhere. Because we've only got one car.' Anderson nodded, and she decided to volunteer some more information. 'He said he was going to go to the pub for lunch. But to be honest we were hardly on speaking terms, so God knows if that's what he really did.'

His face was smooth, not revealing what he was thinking, but she could guess. He was wondering whether James would have had time to walk to Stephanie's house and kill her. Well, as it happened, he would, just about.

Chew on that, James!

Anderson watched Andrea with a mixture of compassion and admiration. She was clearly very distressed. Her face was pale, there were streaks under her enormous green eyes, and her hands were trembling. But she was making a brave effort to conceal it, to try to appear calm and relaxed. It was kind of her to try to protect him from the consequences of his actions, but he still felt guilty. Because he had tried to find out about her, she had got into even more trouble with her brutish husband.

He didn't want to reveal to her that his primary interest was in James, but it was difficult not to. James could have walked to Stephanie's flat this morning in plenty of time to kill her. 'Where is James now?' he asked casually.

'God knows. Probably still in the pub.' She smoothed back her short, fine hair. Her ears were very small and neat and adorned with tiny, delicate filigree earrings. 'Well,' she said, 'this isn't getting us anywhere, is it? I'm sure you didn't come to talk about James. He's my problem, not yours. Would you like some tea?'

'That would be lovely,' he said.

'Kitchen's in the corridor. Come and talk while I make it.'

He followed her out of the office. Today she was wearing casual clothes, mocha brown leggings and a ribbed cream-coloured top which clung to her body. It had long sleeves and a high, close collar, hiding her wounds from the world. She was as slender and delicate as a fawn, so fragile that she looked as if she would break if she was handled roughly. How had she survived her husband?

'How is your investigation going?' she asked as she put on the kettle and rummaged for tea bags. Her movements were very deft.

'Things are becoming a bit complicated,' he said. 'Tell me, have you ever had any business dealings with a woman called Stephanie Pinkney?'

She emerged from the cupboard, shaking her head. 'I don't know the name. Who is she?'

'She's a researcher at the Tate Gallery. She works in the field of erotica and I'm trying to track her down in connection with the Francesca Lyons murder.' That was easier than explaining about another death, and less upsetting for Andrea, too. 'I wondered if you knew her.'

'I'm sorry, I can't help.' She poured the hot water into the teapot. 'I don't have much to do with researchers. I just buy and sell.'

'Might James know her? I mean, through his work?'

She shrugged. 'Possibly. I don't know.'

There was silence for a moment while she stirred and poured the tea. Then he said, 'Does James usually get to know your business contacts?'

That was rather a clumsy question, but she didn't seem to have noticed. She laughed. 'Not often. The gallery owners tend to avoid him, to be honest, because they think he's going to try to talk them into selling his pictures and they don't want to. More fools them. He is a good artist, you know.'

He wanted to ask her if James had ever tried to talk Francesca Lyons into selling his pictures, but that would have been just too obvious. 'I remember,' was all he said.

They walked back down the corridor to the office. He glanced at the wall, reminding himself of the style of James's pictures. He was sure that he wasn't mistaken. 'Your husband has a very recognisable style,' he commented.

'Yes, he does.' Andrea came and stood beside him, looking up at the portrait of her. She was very close, close enough for him to smell the faint, delicious fragrance of her skin.

'Would you be able to identify a picture of his?'

'Oh, yes.' She laughed again. 'He usually signs them, anyway, but I'd know his work anywhere.'

He had everything that he had come for. There was no reason to stay, other than the pleasure of drinking tea with Andrea Maguire. Reluctantly he said, 'I'm afraid I have to go. I'd like to find James and ask him about Stephanie Pinkney. You said he might be in the pub. Could you tell me which pub that is?'

'Of course,' said Andrea, with a wide-eyed glance. 'The Spotted Cow, in the valley. Do you know it?'

'Yes. Thank you.' He finished the tea and turned to the door.

'But —' Andrea said, and he turned back. 'If you're going to see James, he'll be angry with me again. Won't you protect me?'

A request for protection from a potential witness was a

serious matter. And besides, he would have liked to protect her personally. 'If you need protection from him,' he said seriously, 'of course I'll do everything I can.'

She stared, then laughed. 'Oh,' she said, 'I was joking!'

'Joking?'

Suddenly the laugh had gone. Her face was pale and still. 'What I was really asking,' she said in a very small voice, 'is whether you would come and see me again. Here, I mean.'

The thought rocked him. It was clear that their attraction was mutual, but to ask him to visit her – The prospect was entrancing, but he had to resist it. 'I'm sorry,' he said gently. 'I can't possibly.'

She made a rueful face and watched him as he went away. When he got into the car he glanced up at the high windows and saw her standing there, the palms of her hands pressed against the glass, looking down at him.

# ELEVEN
## Sunday 5.15 p.m.

The BMW wove along the narrow roads leading down to the valley and the Spotted Cow. Anderson drove mechanically, without his usual enjoyment. Did he have enough evidence to arrest James? Certainly not. Enough even to interview him formally, under caution, tape recorded, with all the trappings of police power to try to frighten him into a mistake? No. There was no overt link even between James and Francesca, and the only link he had found between James and Stephanie was that picture on the dead woman's bedroom wall. She might have bought it.

He didn't even have an inkling of a possible motive for the killings. Why had someone killed Francesca? Why had she been anxious and preoccupied in the weeks before her death? And what about Stephanie? Could there be a thread linking them, something to do with the world of art in which they had both worked?

More data, he had to have more data. Track down James, interview him informally, take it from there.

The Spotted Cow was only a couple of miles from the centre of Guildford, but it was half hidden in a delightfully rural spot. The food was famous, too, and Anderson would have frequented it himself except that it was on the wrong side of town and he wouldn't drink and drive. The car park contained several executive vehicles, their glossy sides freckled with mud from the approach road.

A thin persistent rain began as he got out of the car. He turned up the collar on his jacket and hurried over the car park, and once inside the protection of the pub he brushed the drops carefully from his sleeves. The jacket was only a few weeks old and he was afraid that it might watermark, but there didn't seem to be any damage done.

James was not in the pub. Anderson went over to the bar and caught the eye of the girl serving. She came over with a smile and he returned it, because she was very pretty, fresh and appealing, with freckled pale skin and red hair twisted up into a pre-Raphaelite mass on the top of her head. 'Hi,' she said. 'What can I get you?'

'Actually, I'm looking for someone. I think he was in earlier. I wonder if you know him: James Maguire?'

The girl's expression changed. Her face showed very clearly that she knew James well and found him attractive. She took a deep quick breath, making her breasts lift under her tight T-shirt. Was Andrea right in suspecting her husband of sleeping around? Looking at this girl, it was easy to believe. Anderson felt a gnawing of anger. He would have liked to protect Andrea.

'Yes,' the girl said, 'he was in. He went not long ago, actually. I think he's gone home. Do you know him?'

'Oh yes,' Anderson said easily. 'I'll track him down at home. Thanks.' He turned away, and then as if he had only just thought of it turned back and asked, 'When did he get in today, by the way?'

'Oh, first thing.' She picked up a glass, blew on it and began to polish it. Her hands moved sensually beneath the linen cloth. 'He's usually here for lunch Sundays. Sometimes with his wife, but not today. He must have arrived just after we opened.'

Anderson frowned. 'When's that? Twelve o'clock?'

'That's right.'

'Thanks.' He went to the door and ran across the car park in the strengthening rain, still frowning. The timing was tight. Stephanie Pinkney had been alive at 11 a.m., someone had visited her then and killed her, and her house was a couple of miles from the Spotted Cow. James would have had to have walked fast.

157

Tight, but not impossible. He checked the Maguires' home address and set off. It was no distance, less than half a mile. The house was detached, a small cottage standing some way from its nearest neighbour. The grey evening light showed it to be a little dilapidated in appearance, with peeling window-frames and spalling brickwork, as if nobody really cared about looking after it.

A light was on in the hall. Anderson pulled up on the drive and went to the door.

Nobody answered his first ring. The rain fell more heavily. He rang again and called out, 'Mr Maguire.'

A door slammed within the house and heavy footsteps stalked towards the door. It flew open with a jerk and he looked up into James Maguire's dark, handsome face. Maguire was scowling, and when he saw who it was his expression became even more aggressive. 'What the hell do you want?'

'As before, Mr Maguire. I'm investigating the death of Francesca Lyons. I'd like to talk to you about it.'

'I'm cooking myself dinner,' James said, not making any move to admit him.

'I'm sorry if it's inconvenient. But I'd like to speak to you.'

'Oh, for fuck's sake.' James turned away from the door. 'Come in. You'll have to stand and watch.'

Anderson entered the house and closed the door behind him. It was small inside, too, and although the hall was well decorated and quite tidy, he got the feeling that wherever James was, chaos was not far below the surface. Andrea's office, on the other hand, had been pristine. So she had to pick up after her violent slob of a husband, too. The tolerance of women never ceased to amaze him.

There were a lot of pictures on the walls, some by James, some not. He didn't have a chance to look at them, because James walked straight down the hall and pushed open the door to the kitchen.

A delicious smell emerged. Anderson's nose instantly identified beef and wild mushrooms. He realised that he hadn't eaten all day, and he was starving. Watching James cook was going to be purgatory.

The kitchen looked as if a bomb had hit it. James was

preparing *risotto ai funghi* and steak, and every implement, ingredient and piece of crockery that he had used was still where he had left it, abandoned among puddles of olive oil and stock and little piles of herbs. A glass of white wine and an open bottle stood beside the stove. James stirred the risotto, threw the wine into it and refilled the glass. 'So,' he said, ostentatiously taking a gulp of the wine as if he wanted to emphasise that he wasn't offering Anderson any. 'Get started.'

Anderson's mouth was watering. His dislike of James, already strong, became full-blown, icily controlled anger. 'I want you to confirm where you were last Wednesday evening.'

'Oh, for God's sake. I was at home with Andrea, sketching. She's already told you that.'

'Did you know Francesca Lyons?'

He shook his head. 'No. She was one of Andrea's clients, that's all I know about her.' The risotto had absorbed the wine, and now James added a large knob of butter and a ladleful of stock. The steam smelled fragrant and delicious. Anderson liked cooking, but his approach to it was completely different. He could hardly believe that a dirty kitchen and a cook as disorganised as James could produce a dish that looked so appetising.

Time for another tack. 'Mr Maguire, there's somebody I want to speak to in connection with the enquiry, a Tate Gallery researcher by the name of Stephanie Pinkney.' Was that a fractional hesitation in James's stirring of the risotto? If only they were face to face. 'Do you know her? She worked in fields like yours, and I wondered –'

'Never heard of her,' said James. 'Who is she? Why do you want to talk to her?'

'In connection with the enquiry,' Anderson said vaguely. 'I'm concerned for her safety.'

If James had killed Stephanie, wouldn't that ring alarm bells with him? But he gave the risotto another stir and then looked over his shoulder, apparently genuinely curious. 'Her safety? Why?'

Anderson shook his head. He was getting nowhere. 'Please tell me what your movements were this morning, Mr Maguire.'

James scowled. 'What the hell does that have to do with your enquiry?'

'It might be relevant.'

'Am I a suspect?'

'You sound as if you've got something to hide.'

James let out an angry snort of laughter. 'Bollocks! I just object to the police assuming that they have the right to barge into people's lives and demand information on things which have nothing whatever to do with them.'

'If you've got nothing to hide, you can tell me what you were doing this morning.'

A hiss from the saucepan announced that the risotto had caught. 'Fuck!' James exclaimed, stirring frantically and adding extra stock. 'Look,' he said, 'I slept overnight at my studio. This morning I came back here about, I don't know, eleven o'clock, I suppose, I didn't notice. Then I went to the pub. I got there just after opening time. All right? Dull enough for you?'

James certainly didn't look as if he was lying, but he was an intelligent man and quite possibly an excellent actor. However, there didn't seem to be anything more to gain from further questioning, and Anderson couldn't stand the smell of James's supper a moment longer. 'Thank you,' he said, carefully maintaining courtesy despite his intense and increasing dislike. 'There's nothing else for the moment.'

'Good,' said James, without looking round. 'Show yourself out. I'm busy.'

So where did that get him? Precisely nowhere, except to pique his appetite and reaffirm that he detested James Maguire. There was nothing to connect James to either murder, and he didn't seem to have any discernible motive, either.

The rain was bringing a premature twilight. Anderson slammed the door of the BMW and turned on the lights.

He still didn't believe in Fielding's mission killer, but he was increasingly convinced that there must be some common thread between the two murders. The similarities couldn't be just coincidental. Something to do with their work, something to do with erotic art, and probably something to do with one person, the killer.

If that was true, then the suspects he had to date looked very unlikely. There was no point in hanging on to Allen and Hardwick. Each of them was involved with one woman only. He and his team would have to do more work to uncover the missing link.

Pat leant back until her chair was in danger of tipping over and rubbed her face with both hands. She was tired and pissed off. All the way to Lyme Regis, setting off at six on a Sunday morning, and for what? To collar someone with a bloody alibi. So much for Sunday. She and Gerry had phoned for a takeaway pizza, and by the time they had got to eating it it was cold. What a bloody day.

'Cup of tea, Sarge?' Gerry asked.

She straightened. 'Thanks, Gerry. Yeah.'

He had already made it, the star. 'There you go, Sarge. Bit of a bugger about this, eh?'

It certainly was, and she was about to agree with Gerry when the phone on her desk rang. Could that be Anderson? She picked it up. 'Detective Sergeant Fielding.' She didn't usually bother to announce herself in full, but if Anderson was on the other end of the line she would take the care to be precise.

'Gosh,' said a slightly drawling voice, 'don't you sound formal.'

Daniel! She couldn't stop herself from glancing guiltily up at Gerry, as if it was wicked to have a man call her at the office. Gerry wasn't looking, and she turned away, trying to give herself some privacy. 'Hi,' she managed.

'Do you always work Sundays? How awful.'

'No, no, not at all, it's just this case, I —' She didn't even know why he was ringing. Perhaps it was about the case, perhaps he'd thought of something else that might be useful. 'What can I do for you?' she asked, trying to keep her voice businesslike.

'Come to dinner with me,' said Daniel's voice.

'Daniel, I —'

'I've got everything in,' he said. 'All sorts, and some lovely wine. I won't take no for an answer.' Pat glanced up and as she had feared Gerry had heard her say Daniel's name and was now looking at her with a curious, amused expression. 'You've got my address, haven't you?'

'Daniel –' What could she say? She couldn't speak with any conviction. She wanted to see him.

'Well, then, that's agreed.' He sounded as if he was grinning. 'Everything's quick and easy, it doesn't matter when you turn up, I'll just start as soon as you put in an appearance, OK?'

'Daniel, I can't,' she managed.

'Oh, rubbish,' he said. 'Live dangerously.' And the phone clicked and purred into her ear.

'Well, well, Sarge,' said Gerry, 'do I detect –' and no doubt more was to come, but suddenly Anderson appeared at the door and Gerry immediately became very interested in his paperwork.

'Sir,' Pat said with relief, jumping up, 'I'm glad you're back. I –' She swallowed. 'I'm afraid we're going to have to release Richard Allen. His wife confirmed that he was home a little before 10.15 on Wednesday evening, and that means he couldn't have been at the gallery after the time Francesca rang home.'

She expected him to look angry, but he seemed quite unperturbed. He was carrying a brown paper bag, and he put it down on her desk as he nodded. 'All right,' was all he said. 'What about Clive?'

What indeed? She shrugged. 'I can't see the point in holding him, sir. He's cooperated, he insists he's innocent, and I've got no reason to hold him. There's just insufficient evidence for any sort of a charge against either of them. I'm sorry, sir.'

'I agree. And did you get Chris Lyons?'

'Bill brought him in. I talked to him. He has an alibi for today, and for Wednesday he stuck to the same story. He –' How to describe it? 'He was very distressed, sir. Almost unbalanced, I'd say.'

'But you believed him.'

'Yes, sir, I suppose so.' He had been sobbing like a lost soul. She hadn't felt so awful for years. She'd had to believe him.

'All right,' Anderson said equably. Why didn't he look more concerned? His suspects were melting away around his ears and he didn't seem to care. Perhaps she had shown her puzzlement, because he added, 'Pat, there's more to this than meets the eye, one way or another. We've got more work to do. If the DNA results back up Allen's and Clive's stories, we'll have more certainty that they're innocent, and if they don't, well, we know where to find them.'

'You may not find Allen,' Pat said soberly. 'He's in big trouble. His wife says she's not going to let him back into the house.'

Anderson lifted an eyebrow. 'Well, make sure you have a contact address.'

'Yes, sir.'

'Pat, go home. There's no need to do anything else today.'

'Sir –' She got up and cast an anxious look at Gerry. 'Sir, could I have a word with you?'

He raised his eyebrows and picked up his paper bag. 'Of course. Come in.'

In his office she closed the door as he sat down at his desk and began to unpack the bag. He had been to a delicatessen, and he flattened the bag on the desk and arranged his food neatly on it. Everything he did was always so exact. There was a halt baguette filled with what looked like Parma ham, a small plastic tub of black olives and one of tomato salad, a packet of Italian breadsticks and a bottle of some expensive herbal drink. She watched for a moment, intrigued despite herself. Then Anderson looked up and said, 'Go ahead, Pat.'

She knew what she wanted to say, but somehow she couldn't think of the right words. Moving jerkily, she pulled up a chair on the other side of the desk and sat down. 'Sir, it's about, it's about Daniel Gough.'

He glanced up at her. 'He's asked you out.'

It shouldn't have surprised her that he should guess, but she closed her eyes all the same. Sometimes when working with Anderson she felt as if her head was made of glass and he could watch all her thoughts going round and round. All she said was, 'Yes, sir.'

'And you want to go.'

She opened her eyes and looked at him. He didn't look as if he was making fun of her. When she said, 'Yes,' she felt a tearing inside her and suddenly realised quite how much she wanted to go. She wanted Daniel as much as any man she had ever known. 'Yes, sir, I do. But he's a witness, potentially, anyway. I know it's risky. I wanted – I wanted to ask your permission.'

He looked at her steadily. She didn't say anything else, just sat there, her heart thumping. Put up, Pat, then shut up. Additional argument would be pointless. It was a simple enough situation, for God's sake.

Anderson steepled his fingers and frowned. He looked as if he was about to advise her against it, and for a moment she wondered what she would do if he did. But then he said, 'Well, Pat, I agree that he's a potential witness, but he's a pretty useless one, isn't he. His testimony may be necessary, but I doubt that it's crucial. And I trust you to know where to draw the line. I don't see why you shouldn't see him, if you want to.'

She took a deep breath. Her fingers were tingling. She was so relieved and excited that she didn't even react to his deprecating remarks about Daniel. She said, 'Thank you, sir. Thank you very much indeed,' and then she hurried to the door.

She parked her battered Ford Escort a little way down the road from Daniel's house and got out, and as she did so she realised that any normal woman in this situation would have gone home to change. She hadn't bothered. She had been so delighted, so excited, she just had to get there as soon as possible. She'd only stopped to buy a bottle of wine, and that had been hard enough. Daniel probably knew all about wine. She'd paid twice as much as she would usually have done, and now she was wondering whether the wine merchant had diddled her.

So should she go home and change now? She looked down at herself in the glow of the street lights. Well, she looked neat enough, but nothing special: closely fitting faded jeans, a smart long-sleeved T-shirt and her much-loved black jacket. She looked like a plain-clothes copper, not like a woman going to dinner with the man she fancied.

But she wanted to see Daniel, and quickly. Going home to

change would take an hour. Aloud she said, 'Oh, bugger it,' and locked the car, then walked with quick purposeful steps towards the house. There was one thing she could do, and she did it. She unfastened her plait and began to tease out her heavy hair with her fingers.

The street was all Victorian houses. Somehow she had expected that Daniel would own a whole house. Anyone with an accent that posh surely ought to be rich. But he didn't. He had the top-floor flat. The house was tatty, too. She rang the doorbell and after a moment the entryphone said, 'Hello!'

'Daniel,' was all she could say.

'Well hello!' said the voice, and the door clicked open.

She took a deep breath and pushed open the door. The light was on in the hall. The stairs went up in a dog leg, she couldn't see the top of them. She ran up the first flight and turned and Daniel was standing in front of her, backlit by the doorway, blond hair glowing, smiling at her.

'There you are,' he said. 'You came.'

'Yes.' God, he was gorgeous. That voice! She wanted to go to bed with him, now. But he was wearing an apron, he must have gone to some trouble. She walked up three more steps and said, 'Hello.'

He was looking at her in silence, as if he was amazed. At last he said, 'Well, I know this is a cliché, but you look smashing with your hair down.'

'Thanks,' she said. She was on the step below him. She looked up into his face and for a moment she thought that he would kiss her, but he didn't. He smiled and said, 'Let me get you a glass of champagne.'

Now that was more what she had expected. She followed him into the flat. It wasn't particularly big, and it wasn't in very good repair, but it was full of beautiful things. The hall table had slender legs and little claw feet, and there was an oil painting on the wall that looked really old and valuable, and in the dining kitchen the table was a round wooden job whose soft gleaming patina spoke of great age and ancestry. There were candles everywhere, on the mantelpiece, on the sideboard, and on the table, too, a huge candelabra that looked as if it was made of solid silver.

'Daniel, what a beautiful place,' she said.

He grinned at her. 'Actually, it's a horrid flat, isn't it? But at least it's old. I don't have two beans, you know, just all this stuff. It was my grandmother's mostly. We had to sell the house to pay the tax, so me and my brothers and sisters have got little tiny flats all crammed full of gorgeous furniture. It's most peculiar, really.' He turned into the kitchen, which was small and cramped and full of odds and ends hung from the ceiling. 'Champagne!' he announced, as he opened the fridge.

'Wonderful,' she said weakly.

'Well, I have to celebrate you coming to your senses at last.' He opened the bottle deftly, without the slightest pop, and filled two glasses. 'Here you are.' He handed her one. 'Well, here's to us. To our first evening.'

She took a sip of the champagne. It was delicious. His eyes met hers over the rim of his glass. He was smiling, that mischievous, boyish smile. How old was he? Not as old as her, that was for sure. Cradle-snatching, Pat! She glanced down at the bottle of wine in her hand and offered it to him, rather shamefaced. 'Sorry it's not champagne.'

'Oh, for goodness' sake.' He picked up the bottle and read the label. 'I say, very nice. Nice and cold, too. I'll stick it in the fridge, it'll go with the salmon.'

'Salmon!' She was impressed. She had expected spaghetti.

'Oh, I'm no great cook. Melon for a starter and salmon roasted in the oven. I was going to make a hollandaise sauce, but it all went to pot.' He nodded at a forlorn china basin, languishing in the sink. 'Look, it's late, I'm starving. Shall we start? The salmon will be ready by the time we've finished the melon.'

'Suits me. I had a gruesome pizza for lunch and I've been up since half five.'

'Half five on a Sunday morning? God, is there such a time?' He toasted her again in his glass of champagne. 'Sorry there's only one bottle. Do you know what the collective noun for champagne is?'

'The collective noun? No, I don't.'

'An insufficiency,' he said with a grin. 'An insufficiency of champagne.'

She laughed and took another sip. The bubbles began to whirl around in her head. What about drinking and driving? What about it? She didn't intend to be driving back to her house that night.

'Here,' he said, 'sit down.' He held her chair for her. 'Let's get started.' He brought out a couple of plates with half a small melon on each and a little dish. 'Ginger,' he said, 'if you like it.'

She hadn't previously considered putting ginger on melon. She watched what Daniel did and imitated him. It was surprisingly good, and she was really hungry. She finished the melon in no time, then rested her head on her hand and watched Daniel eating.

He was very neat and tidy in the way he ate. Good manners, of course. His heavy blond hair fell over his forehead and she wanted to sweep it back and push it out of his eyes. Beneath the apron he was wearing another collarless shirt, this time plain pale blue, and it set off the sturdy column of his neck beautifully. She wanted to touch him. She was sure that she could smell his skin from where she sat.

He looked up and for a moment their eyes met. He looked almost anxious. Was he shy? Was he not used to women who were as predatory and determined as she was feeling? He said, 'Gosh, you must have been hungry.'

'Starving. Bring on the main course.'

'I like a girl with a healthy appetite,' he said. He finished his own melon and then got up and came over to collect her plate. As he did so he hesitated, then said, 'Pat, I'm really glad you could come here tonight.'

'So am I,' she said honestly.

Would he make a move now? She was ready for it. But he didn't, he took the dishes away into the kitchen and began to bustle about, organising things. Everything seemed to take him twice as long and twice as many actions as it needed, it was quite funny to watch. As he sorted things out he asked her questions. How long had she been in the police? Why had she joined? Had she been to university? He seemed a little surprised that she had, and then not so surprised when she said, 'Well, it was a poly, actually, Daniel. My A Levels were crap.'

'Join the club, so were mine. What was your excuse?'

'I discovered boys,' Pat said truthfully. 'What about you?'

'Sheer bloody laziness,' Daniel said. 'Good school and all that, frightfully disappointed in me. My old man pulled a few strings to get me to Exeter. Didn't do any work there, either.'

Pat had worked like a dog at college, but working like a dog didn't seem to be Daniel's style. He was refreshingly laid-back. He brought through the main course, plain roasted salmon with jacket potatoes and salad and sour cream. It was very good, simple and tasty. As they ate he asked her more and more questions about the police. What was it like? Did she like it? Was it horrible?

'Horrible?'

'I mean –' His eyes were pale, pale grey, with a dark ring around the iris that made them look incredibly bright. 'I mean, you have to do things like – like deal with murder victims and things. Horrible things.'

'It's not really a dinner conversation,' Pat said. She wasn't squeamish, but she thought he might be.

'But I'm curious.' That was obvious! 'I mean it,' he said. 'It's just so hard to believe, someone like you, small and – and really attractive, dealing with all these awful things. What's the worst thing you've ever seen?'

She put down her knife and fork. 'Daniel, do you really want to know about this?'

'Yes.' He nodded earnestly. 'Yes, I do. I want to understand.'

'Look, most of the time it's routine. When I was in uniform I used to hate going to car accidents. But if you really want to know, the worst thing I've ever seen –' She closed her eyes briefly, dealing with the memory. When she spoke again it was in her courtroom voice, cool and detached. 'A teenage mother delivered her baby sitting on the loo, and she left the baby there, in the bowl of the WC. We never knew whether it was stillborn or not.' She took a deep breath and returned to her salmon. She was proud of herself. She'd told him the truth, but she didn't think that he could possibly conceive the horror of it, the blood, the squalor, the dead baby.

'Jesus,' Daniel said. He looked vaguely disappointed, as if he'd expected a gangland disembowelling.

'Look,' she said, 'your turn. Tell me about art. How do you get a job being a – a person who knows about art?'

He grinned and refilled her glass. 'Start off with a History of Art degree. Then pull every string you can, fail to get meaningful work in any gallery or research institute, and settle for working in a shop.'

That lazy smile made her want to eat him. He was beautiful, and she began to believe that he wasn't intending to make a move at all. Was she being stupid? Was he just – careful?

Well, she didn't want to wait. When he put down his knife and fork for the last time she got to her feet. He said, 'Are you all right?'

'Yes,' she said. 'I'm fine.' She walked around the table, watching his face in the light of the candles. He looked up at her with the bright eyes of excitement. Slowly she lifted her hand to his face and stroked his cheek, then ran her fingers through his hair. It was as soft, as heavy, as silky as she had dreamed it would be. He didn't say anything, but his lips were parted. She leant slowly forward, reaching for his mouth, anticipating, longing for that first touch of her lips on his.

And there it was, his mouth, soft and warm, tasting of the food and the champagne. For a moment he sat quite still. Then he put his hands over hers and ran them down her arms and pressed his lips on hers and his tongue slid into her mouth and she almost fell with the rush of desire that flooded through her. She couldn't stay standing, and she let herself sink down in front of him and he opened his legs and pulled her close and they kissed each other in silence, enfolded in each other, rapt with delicious novelty.

Her body was pressed against his, her face turned up to his. He was wearing jeans and beneath them she could feel his cock stirring, coming to life. She wanted it. When at last he lifted his mouth from hers she said, 'Daniel, let's go to bed.'

'You haven't eaten your pudding,' he whispered, smiling. 'It's chocolate mousse. I made it.'

'Let's eat it later,' she suggested. 'First things first.' She put her hand on his crotch, gently massaging the bulge of his swelling penis. He closed his eyes, his breath hissing. Then he pulled her hand away and got to his feet, lifting her up with him.

He picked up the candelabra from the table, casting guttering shadows. 'My lady,' he said in the voice of Franken-stein's assistant, 'allow me to light your way.' He stooped and halted ahead of her, dragging one leg like the Hunchback of Notre Dame. She laughed, unable to help herself, and followed him to the bedroom.

It wasn't a big room and it was full of furniture, a huge mahogany wardrobe, a tall chest of drawers, an old Empire bed like a sleigh. The bed was made up with dark blue sheets. Daniel put down the candelabra on the bedside table and turned to face her, his fingers working at the buttons on his shirt.

This was always the moment where her courage nearly deserted her. What if he didn't like her body? She was small, muscular. Her breasts didn't even merit a B cup. What if he liked women with big tits and soft haunches? She gritted her teeth and pulled her T-shirt over her head and dropped it on the ground.

Daniel finished unfastening his shirt. He pushed it off, never taking his eyes from her. He didn't look as if he found her unattractive. She was watching him, too, his eyes, his lips. His shoulders were broad and he was more heavily built than he had looked with his shirt on. His torso was hairless, smooth and glistening in the candlelight, and his flat belly was lifting and falling quickly with his breathing.

She unbuckled her belt and unfastened her jeans. At least she was wearing decent underwear, black stretch lace from M&S, about as pretty as made sense for everyday. And it matched! That was a lucky chance. She pushed the jeans down and stepped out of them and her socks at the same time.

After a moment Daniel came towards her. 'Pat,' he said very softly, 'you're lovely. God, you're beautiful.' He stretched out his hand and cupped the shallow curve of one breast. Her nipple tautened beneath his palm and she took a quick deep breath and reached out for him, deftly unfastening the buttons on his fly. They clung together, mouths reaching. His body was warm and hard. He smelt wonderful, of cooking and man. She pulled her lips free of his and reached up to bite his neck. She wanted to eat him, to consume him, she wanted to envelop him in herself.

His fly was open. She pushed her hand inside, found the waistband of his boxers, slid her fingers underneath it. His cock was hot and rigid with excitement. She gently pulled it free of his clothes and took a long breath of delight, then dropped to her knees to take it in her mouth.

'Christ,' he whispered as she licked him, wrapping her tongue around the smooth silky head. 'Christ, Christ.' His hands fumbled with the fastening on her bra and at last unhooked it. She shivered as the bra came loose and hung on her arms. Then she let the head of his cock enter her mouth and moaned with delight. She'd wanted him for what seemed like forever, and now at last she had him, one hand cradling his soft hairy balls, the other wrapped around the shaft of his cock, and her mouth working on him, sucking, licking, delivering pleasure.

His trousers fell around his ankles. He moaned and pushed his hips towards her, then just as suddenly pulled away. 'Don't,' he said. 'God, I'm so excited, I'll –'

She got to her feet, pulling off her bra. Daniel caught her in his arms and bent his head to kiss her breasts. She let her head fall back and whimpered with pleasure as he swirled his tongue around her long nipples, cooling them with his saliva, tormenting them with his lips and teeth. His hand slid into her panties, his fingers parted the dark curls of her pubic hair, he touched her clitoris.

'Oh,' she cried, her whole body jerking helplessly. 'Oh God, Daniel.'

He released her breast and knelt down to tug her panties down her thighs, down to her ankles. She stepped out of them and pushed his boxer shorts off and they were both naked, panting. His erect cock gleamed in the candlelight and the air was cold on her wet nipples. For a moment they looked at each other. He was as gorgeous naked as he had been clothed, and from the look in his eyes he felt the same about her. She reached out for him and together they swayed across the room and fell onto the bed.

Then things were frantic, out of control. He kissed her mouth and her neck and her breasts and her belly and she clutched whatever part of him she could reach and kissed him too and then they were head to tail, her knees on either side of his face, her face pressed to his groin, kissing and licking his throbbing penis. He wrapped his arms around her hips and pulled her downwards and his mouth was between her legs, sucking, exploring. It felt so good. She stiffened all over, tensing as she pushed herself against him, and then gradually she relaxed, yielding to the pleasure. She took his cock into her mouth and he moaned, his voice stirring against her body. She let her lips rise and fall on his slippery shaft and he thrust his tongue into her and sucked at her clitoris. Their bodies began to heave, lifting and falling with the rhythm of their caresses. Her nipples rubbed against his lean belly and his fingers clutched her buttocks, gripping the little tight orbs until she whimpered.

Bliss, it was bliss. She sucked him harder, feeling orgasm beginning in her breasts and her sex. But she didn't want to come this way, she wanted to feel him inside her. She lifted her mouth from his cock and pulled a little away from him.

He lifted his head. 'What's the matter?'

'Nothing.' She swivelled round and kissed him on the mouth. He tasted of her. 'Nothing's wrong. Everything's wonderful.'

'Don't stop, then,' he whispered, grinning.

'No. I want you.' She ran her hand down his belly and took hold of his cock, caressing it, then leant forward to whisper into his wide eyes, 'I want to feel your cock in my cunt.'

His pupils were dark with desire. 'Christ. Yes.'

'I've got a condom in my pocket,' she suggested.

'No need.' He indicated with his head. 'Bedside drawer.'

She leant across and pulled the drawer open and found the little packet and opened it with her teeth. 'Bloody hell,' he said. 'That always takes me five minutes.'

'Practice makes perfect.' She kissed the tip of his cock then rolled the condom onto it. He lay still, his breath coming quickly. She swung over him, straddling him, rubbing herself against his shaft. 'Daniel,' she said softly. Her flat belly jerked and contracted with pleasure as she moved. 'Daniel, I wanted you the moment I saw you.'

'Me too,' he said, gasping. 'I couldn't believe in you. I still can't.'

His hands grasped her breasts, trapping her nipples between his fingers. She bared her teeth, shivering. 'Oh God,' she said, 'I want your cock in me.' She reached down and took hold of him, lifting the head of his cock so that she could fit it between her legs, there where she was hollow for him. She arched her hips and slid downwards, impaling herself, swallowing him up .

Slowly, agonisingly, she lifted and lowered herself. Daniel gazed up at her, clutching her breasts. There was sweat on his forehead beneath the shock of his blond hair. She rubbed herself against him, forcing herself down, reaching behind her to cup and caress his balls as she ground herself down on his muscular body. His fingers tightened on her nipples and she groaned and her breath shuddered with urgency. The sensation of his cock sliding in and out of her was so wonderful that it was almost unbearable, and her breasts were swollen and aching with pleasure. She was coming, and when he put his hand between her legs and found her clitoris with his fingers and rubbed at it she gave a great cry and flung her head back, jerking as her orgasm flooded into her and filled her and left her shaking.

She fell forward and Daniel wrapped his arms around her and rolled her over so that he was on top of her, his heavy body pressing her panting to the sheets. 'Pat,' he said, kissing her neck. 'Pat, God, you're gorgeous.'

His cock was still inside her, moving, an aching ecstasy. She arched upwards towards him, her fingers clutching at his taut buttocks. 'Fuck me,' she hissed, pulling him towards her.

'Oh, God,' he said, as if her directness was more than he could bear. He began to thrust, first steadily, then with increasing vigour and desperation, slamming his body against hers with delicious ferocity.

'Fuck me,' she said, over and over again, every time he lunged into her. He was nearly there, she could feel it. 'Yes,' she said. 'Yes, yes.' And he roared and twisted above her and thrust himself into her as deep as he could, so deep that it hurt, a sweet, sharp pain. She pulled him down on top of her. His body was slippery with sweat and his hair was damp. After a moment he groaned, then lifted his head and kissed her mouth.

She clung to him, wrapping her legs around his to keep him there. He buried his head in her shoulder. At last he said, 'Oops, I'd better move. Bloody condoms.'

Reluctantly she untwined herself and let him go. He withdrew gently, making them both whimper with disappointment.

For a moment they lay side by side, still breathing fast. Then Daniel rolled over onto his belly and propped his chin on his hands, grinning at her. 'Well, gosh,' he said.

'Gosh yourself,' was all she could manage.

'I tell you what,' he said, reaching out to stroke down her body with one hand. He rested his fingers on her breast, teasing her nipple. 'There's some champagne left in the bottle. And would you like some chocolate mousse?'

'You'd like some,' she observed.

'Mm, I would.' He reached forward and drew her nipple into his mouth, sucking gently. When he lifted his head he was still smiling. 'I'll go and get it. I'm sure we can think of some way of eating it.'

Anderson had long since finished his meal and tidied the remnants of it into his waste bin. His desk was clear. Outside it was dark, and the office was nearly empty. How was Fielding getting on with Daniel Gough?

He didn't want to think about it. He rested his head between his hands and pressed the button on the tape recorder.

'I'm surprised you're not there. I'm coming anyway.'

Was it really James Maguire? The more he listened, the more he was convinced that it was. Normally he would have trusted himself, trusted his own senses. But now he wasn't so sure. His dislike for James and everything he stood for was so profound that it might be affecting his judgement.

And not just his dislike for James. He desired Andrea, there was no point in trying to ignore it. When she had asked him today for his protection he had felt an urge to help her, to defend her, so strong that it was almost physical.

It was hardly surprising under the circumstances that he felt an eager ambition to catch James Maguire doing something wrong. But he shouldn't let it affect him professionally.

He looked up at the clock. It was nearly 10 p.m. Time to go home. He had to sleep.

Too late for the gym, too late for squash. Perhaps before he went to bed he should try another run.

# TWELVE
## Monday 7.45 a.m.

All the way to the office Anderson couldn't shake off his dreams. Andrea naked, her hands wrapped around her slight body as if to shield her modesty, her green eyes lascivious. Catherine fully dressed, her eyes closed, tears trickling from beneath her lashes as his hands unfastened her crisp white blouse to bare her quivering breasts.

The dreams disturbed him. He didn't want them, and there wasn't anything he could do to prevent them. He hated to be reminded that there were parts of him which were not under his conscious control.

The sun was bright and it was already warm. He glanced at the blue sky as he walked across the car park, then ran up the stairs to the office.

McKie was already there, but there was no sign of Fielding. Anderson acknowledged a few 'Morning, sirs' with a nod, then said, 'Bill, we need to talk about the Lyons and Pinkney cases. Where's Pat?'

'Haven't seen her this morning, sir.' McKie shook out a few papers. 'I've got what you asked for on Johnson.'

He didn't want to start without Fielding. It wasn't like her to be late. 'Coffee first,' he said.

'In that case, sir, I'll nip along to the canteen. I fancy a bacon sandwich. Can I bring you anything?'

The canteen's idea of a bacon sandwich was the

176

opposite of Anderson's. 'No thanks.'

McKie lounged off, yawning. Anderson went to the coffee point and found that nobody had made any coffee yet. He assembled the machine. Most of it could do with a thorough wash. No wonder the coffee tasted revolting.

While the coffee was brewing he carefully washed a cup and saucer and dried it. The tea towel was dirty, too. Just as the coffee was ready, Fielding appeared at his elbow, breathing quickly. 'Morning, sir.'

'Coffee?' She wasn't exactly late. No need to mention anything.

'Mm. Please.' Her face was slightly flushed and her eyes were bright. Several strands of glossy dark hair had worked loose from her plait, something which didn't usually happen until much later in the day. And she was wearing yesterday's jeans and a blue and white wide striped collarless shirt which, if he was not much mistaken, belonged to Daniel Gough. Obviously she'd had a successful evening.

He poured two cups of coffee and went with Fielding back to his office. She looked uncomfortable, and he could understand why. Because she'd felt it necessary to ask his permission, he now had some sort of declared interest in her relationship with Daniel. An unfortunate bringing together of work and personal life. He would find it uncomfortable, too.

McKie appeared, munching. 'All right, Pat?'

'Morning, Bill.' Fielding's voice was scrupulously normal.

'Could have brought you a bacon sarnie.'

'No thanks.' She looked as if she shared Anderson's opinion of the canteen.

It was time to get down to business. 'Right, Bill. Let's hear what you've got on Johnson and Lyons.'

McKie hastily swallowed a mouthful of bacon sandwich. 'Yes, sir,' he said through the crumbs. 'Rock solid alibis for yesterday, both of them. Johnson was helping a friend to move house, he's got half a dozen people can vouch for what he was doing. When I picked Lyons up he told me he'd been at his parents-in-law's house with his kids.' McKie wiped his mouth with the back of his hand. 'He's in a bad way, sir. There was a bottle of Prozac on his kitchen table.'

'Shit,' said Fielding, 'Bill, you handed him over to me for interview and you didn't tell me that!'

'Didn't I?' asked McKie, unperturbed. 'Sorry.'

'Did he tell you why it was prescribed?' Anderson asked.

'Didn't ask, sir. Just depression, I reckon. He started crying as soon as I asked him a question.'

Fielding shook her head in stony disapproval. Anderson regretted having sent McKie, one of the less sympathetic and subtle of CID's sergeants. But there was nothing he could do about it now. 'All right. What about Stephanie's friends, family, connections? Any leads there, any thoughts?'

'No, sir.' McKie shook his head. 'We got through a good number of friends yesterday. We'll call her workplace today. No leads at all, no ideas. Sounds like she was popular. Bit of a goer, if you know what I mean, but no more than that.'

Fielding shuffled in her chair. It could be that she objected to McKie's phraseology, but she should be used to it by now. 'Pat?'

'Sir.' Fielding took a long breath. 'Sir, I think we're wasting our time looking for a connection between our suspects for the two killings. There isn't one, is there? What possible motive could someone have to kill Francesca and then to kill Stephanie? Nothing in their backgrounds seems to connect them. So what if Francesca had a lover? That doesn't relate to Stephanie. And Stephanie rowed with her boyfriend, and that doesn't relate to Francesca. There's no connection.'

It was obvious where this was leading. 'You want to call in Dr Carroll.'

'Yes, sir, I do. I want to suggest it in the strongest possible terms.' Fielding leant forward slightly and put her clenched fist on his desk. 'Sir, think about it. You know how closely the murders fit the type. We know now that the killer didn't have sex with Francesca, so that objection's out of the window. And for God's sake, sir, look at the period of these killings! One on Wednesday, one on Sunday. If the pattern stays, we have to expect another murder by the end of the week.' She opened her fist, her fingers tense, and met his eyes. 'Are you going to wait until another woman dies before you take any notice of this?'

That was pretty clumsy emotional blackmail, and it wouldn't work on him. 'Did you run the computer, Pat? Looking for other unsolved murders of this type?'

She checked slightly, as if she hadn't expected him to guess that she would do it anyway. 'Yes, sir.'

'To no result.'

'No.' For a moment she hesitated, then she came back even more strongly. 'But sir, that's not relevant. This could be a new killer, just finding out what turns him on. We've got the chance to stop him now. We have to call Dr Carroll.'

'And you know what he'll say? He'll say that our killer is a white male, because the majority of serial killers are, and that he's a well educated professional person, because the majority of organised serial killers are. How many men answering that description are there in Surrey, Pat? What do you suggest we do to make the net a bit finer?'

'If you don't bloody ask him, sir, you'll never know. Christ, I'm not asking for much, am I? Just call the psychologist. Call the expert.'

This had gone far enough. 'Sergeant, every piece of evidence you adduce in support of a serial killer theory could also relate to something linking these two dead women which we don't yet know. We haven't even finished investigating Stephanie Pinkney's work. There is no need to contact Dr Carroll at this point.'

She hadn't missed his pointed use of her rank, rather than her name. She sat back on her chair, breathing hard, folded her arms and stared at the desk.

McKie brushed crumbs onto the carpet. In a diffident voice he said, 'Ah, sir, I was wondering, do you need two sergeants on this one? Because there's lots else to do. That arson at the factory, they could do with another man on that case.'

Fielding gave McKie a poisonous look. 'Thanks for your confidence and support, Bill.'

'I don't have a problem with that,' said Anderson evenly. He despised McKie for trying to wangle his way out of a case that was becoming uncomfortable. He was the wrong man, anyway. He and Fielding would do better working together without him. 'Make sure Pat's got all your reports and anything else she needs.'

'Of course, sir.' McKie looked pleased. He got up to go. The wrapper of his sandwich fell from his lap.

'Bill,' Anderson said icily, as McKie ignored it, 'don't mess up my office.' McKie looked startled, then stooped to pick up the wrapper and slithered out of the room. When he shut the door Anderson said, 'Pat, as soon as we're on top of the paperwork this morning I want to go to Stephanie Pinkney's flat and look through it again. Forensics have finished there, and maybe there'll be something else for us to find.'

Fielding lifted her head and glared at him. 'Maybe, sir.'

'Make sure we can get in.'

'Yes, sir.' She tightened her folded arms. Anger radiated from her.

Should he try to smooth this one over? No. It was her problem, not his. 'Right,' he said. 'That's all for now.'

She got up without a word, gave him a blistering look and slammed the door.


What was that God-awful light shining in his eyes? James groaned and turned away, but the sunlight was inexorable. At last he sat up, scrubbing his hand over his face. His mouth tasted like the scrapings of his palette.

The bedside clock said ten to ten. Where was Andrea? Gone already? By the time she got home last night he'd had too much to drink, a whole bottle of white on top of what he'd drunk at the Spotted Cow, and he hardly remembered anything. She had been very quiet, or was he just imagining things? He did remember that he had ignored her. He wasn't going to forgive what she had said about his art. It didn't matter whether or not she had meant it. She had said it, and that was bad enough.

He staggered to the bathroom and splashed his face with cold water, then went down to the kitchen to make a cup of coffee. No sign of Andrea, and her breakfast coffee cup was already washed up on the draining board. He switched on the kettle and then flicked the radio on.

It was the news. He listened with half an ear as he made

the coffee. He was pouring water from the kettle into the cafetière when the announcer said, 'Police are still refusing to comment on the suspicious death yesterday of a Guildford woman. The detective in charge of the investigation, Detective Chief Inspector John Anderson, has now named the dead woman as Stephanie Pinkney –'

The water slopped over James's fingers, scalding him. 'Fuck!' he exclaimed, and turned on the cold tap. He ran his fingers under the cold water, listening to the rest of the report. There were no details. But he knew what had happened.

His hands were shaking. Christ, wasn't one killing enough? And on top of everything, Stephanie was part of their meal ticket!

After a few minutes the scald was bearable. He ran upstairs and threw on clothes, jeans, a sweatshirt, battered shoes, then grabbed his keys and hurried out of the house. His head throbbed as he ran along the road towards the centre of town. He ran with his thumb stuck out, just in case, but he knew he wouldn't get a lift. Nobody in Guildford ever gave lifts, they were all too bloody respectable.

What had got into Andrea? If she'd been that angry, why hadn't she taken it out on him? Why go to such lengths? He was so deep in thought that he almost crossed a road without looking, and an angry woman in a Saab sounded her horn at him and shook her head. He gave her the finger and ran on.

Shit, Andrea was tougher than he had thought. But killing Stephanie was doubly stupid. They needed her, and the police were already interested in them. And besides, he was the tough one. Who did she think she was?

He was there at last. He ran up the stairs two steps at a time, panting. The office door was open and he lunged through it and kicked it shut behind him. Andrea was on the phone. She glanced up at him and her eyes widened. He grabbed the receiver from her hand and slammed it down.

'What's wrong?' she asked in a trembling voice. So she was scared of him now! Bloody right, too.

'You are so fucking stupid,' he told her.

The phone rang. Andrea put out her hand to pick it up and he grabbed her wrist and twisted until she cried out and got up, bending half over to try to take the pressure from her arm. 'Don't!' she wailed. 'James –'

'Who's going to fix our provenances now?' he demanded, jerking her wrist so that she whimpered. 'Who else do you know at the Tate? Christ!'

She stopped struggling and swallowed hard. 'How did you find out?'

'It was on the bloody radio. The same bloody policeman is investigating!' A sudden thought struck him. DCI Anderson asking him about Stephanie, pretending that his questions related to the earlier investigation, saying that he was concerned for her safety. What had the manipulative bastard been getting at? 'Jesus Christ,' he said with dawning panic. 'The police'll probably think that I killed Stephanie! Andrea, what the hell got into you?'

The phone stopped ringing at last. 'Let go,' Andrea said, tugging at her wrist.

'No. What did you do? Jesus, what happened?'

'I killed her.' Her wrist was trembling. He gripped it more tightly. 'She deserved it. She slept with you.'

He felt a surge of fierce possessive joy. She loved him so much she would actually kill for him! But it didn't change the situation. 'What the hell do we do now?' he said, tightening his grip. 'We're in deep shit, Andrea. Never mind the bloody police, where's the next crust going to come from? Who'll buy my stuff without Tate-certified provenances?'

She tensed against his hand and glared at him. 'Why don't you start painting pictures I can sell?'

His fist came up automatically and she flinched. But he didn't strike. Why was she saying something that she knew would infuriate him? Was she trying to manipulate him, too?

Her green eyes flashed. 'Don't worry about Chief Inspector Anderson, either, darling. He was here yesterday. I can handle him.'

'What?' He flung her away from him, so hard that she almost fell. He couldn't believe it. 'You saw him here?'

She straightened, breathing hard. 'We have to cooperate with the police, don't you think?'

'Cooperate?' He could hardly see through a red haze of

mingled jealousy and fear. 'With that devious bastard? I saw the way he looked at you, Andrea! I saw the way he touched you!'

He swung at her but she ducked out of the way and dodged behind the sofa. 'Nothing happened,' she said. 'He asked questions, that's all. I can handle him.'

'Handle him –' He was almost bursting with anger. 'Shit! Don't you touch him.' He lunged towards her, but she kept dodging. She was quick, he'd never catch her. 'If you so much as look at him, I'll kill you,' he promised her, and he meant it.

'See?' she mocked him. 'You do love me. You can't live without me.'

The phone began to ring again. The sound burned in his aching head. Bitch! How dare she use his own words against him? He made another frantic grab for her, but she darted away from him. In a moment she would be laughing at him, and he couldn't bear it. He shook his fist at her. 'Remember,' he threatened. 'If you go near him, I'll kill you.'

She was shaking and her eyes were vivid. He thought his anger would split him in two. He wanted to hit her, to strangle her, to throw her down and force his cock into her and show her who was boss. But it would be too bloody ignominious to try to catch her and fail. Instead he turned to her desk and with one violent movement swept everything off it, papers, coffee cup, ringing phone, the works, all tumbled into chaos onto the floor.

He stared at her over the mess, panting. 'Remember,' he said, and stalked to the door.

Andrea raked her fingers through her hair, gasping for breath. James's footsteps retreated down the corridor, then faded as he ran down the stairs.

This time, this time she had beaten him. Normally she was so paralysed by her fear of him that she couldn't even run, she just sat there like a rabbit in front of a weasel waiting for him to hit her. But this time she'd kept her head, and it had worked. Her wrist hurt, but he hadn't landed a single blow. And he had wanted to, that had been clear.

For the first time it occurred to her that in some ways

James was pathetic. The thought that Chief Inspector Anderson was after him had really seemed to shake him.

She stretched, then went and looked down at the pile of papers and coffee. After a few minutes she knelt down and began to see what could be salvaged. It was still possible to get out of this in one piece. Priority one was to make sure that nobody connected her with Stephanie's murder. That should be OK, as long as Stephanie had kept to her side of the bargain. They had agreed from the beginning that it was safest not to keep anything which might link them: nothing in writing, nothing permanent.

What then? Make sure that the police didn't find out about the fraud. That shouldn't be too difficult, they were pig ignorant about art. Chief Inspector Anderson believed everything she told him.

And then, if she could, she would protect James too. It might be feasible. But if it looked as if one of them was going to face murder charges, she was bloody determined that it would be him and not her.

She put the receiver back on the phone. It rang almost immediately. She watched it for a moment, then picked it up. Her voice was absolutely calm. 'Andrea Maguire. Oh hello, goodness, what do you think happened there? Honestly, you can't trust British Telecom these days –'

Pat drew in a long angry breath and pulled another book towards her. There had been a surprising number of reference works in Stephanie's bedroom, and she and Anderson had split them into two piles for examination. Forensics had finished in here yesterday, and none of the books had carried any fingerprints other than Stephanie's. They were all about twentieth-century art and artists. Some of them were on erotic subjects, and Anderson seemed to have a disproportionate number of those in his pile, so she wasn't even getting the opportunity for a bit of a turn-on while she slogged through. She didn't like the pictures and she didn't understand them and in her current angry and resentful state of mind she thought that Stephanie's job was a complete and total waste of time.

She held up the last book and flicked through it. No pages were turned down, no papers fell out. What was she supposed to do? She put down the book.

Underneath it was a spiral-bound notebook, dog-eared and battered. She picked it up and as she did so a couple of pieces of paper fell from it. Frowning, she stooped to collect them. Her plastic-gloved fingers made them hard to manage. They were old and creased, round-edged papers about two inches square. She turned them over and saw that they were gallery labels. She was going to put them back in the notebook and forget about them when something caught her eye.

This first one had three lines of handwriting on it underneath the printed gallery name. She looked more closely. Superficially it looked as if the whole label was written in the same hand, but she knew enough about graphology to do a simple comparison of handwritten documents. The risers and descenders were the same, the slant was the same, but the final line of writing was different from the previous two. The tops of the o's and a's were open on the first two lines, closed on the last line.

She looked at the other label. This one was almost entirely printed, only the date was handwritten. She thought for a moment, then held the label up to the light.

Against the light it was possible to see that the numerals had been changed; a 3 to an 8, so that what looked like 1988 was originally 1983.

Why? She looked at the labels again, her head on one side, puzzled.

'What's up?' Anderson asked.

She really didn't like him today, and she almost said, 'Nothing.' But that wasn't a professional way to be. For a moment she didn't reply. Then she said, 'Look at these, sir.'

Without a word he put down the book he'd been examining and came over to her. He held out his hand and she gave him the labels. 'I don't know what these are, sir, but it looks as if they've been altered.'

He examined them as she had done. His face was intent. Under normal circumstances she would be congratulating herself for having found something, for having the chance to impress him. Now she half hoped that she hadn't found anything at all.

'They're exhibition labels,' he said. 'Pictures carry them around, like a history.' He squinted at the second label. 'This one, the alteration's been done so that if it was stuck to a picture, without the light coming through it, you wouldn't notice that anything had been changed.'

'Why would someone want to alter exhibition labels?' Pat asked, intrigued despite herself.

He met her eyes. The stillness of his face showed that he was excited. He always kept himself under tight control. 'To make it look as if a picture has been somewhere it hasn't been.'

'Fraud,' she said.

He nodded. 'Good work, Pat. Let's keep going. Perhaps there's something else here.'

They ploughed on through book after book, turning each page. Many of the books were battered and worn, with underlinings and sidelines in the margins. If they were going to go into this in depth somebody really ought to make a note of all the things that had been emphasised and consider them for similarities. That would be a pretty awful job. Pat determined that it wouldn't come her way.

'Sir,' she said after another half hour of silent labour, 'what exactly are we looking for?'

He didn't answer her at once and she looked at him curiously. After a silence he said, 'I'm not entirely sure, Pat. Anything that looks out of the ordinary. Like those labels.'

She lifted her eyebrows and said with a good deal of ironic satisfaction, 'Well, sir, since neither of us are experts in this sort of field, perhaps on this occasion you might consider calling in the specialists from Scotland Yard?'

His face showed that the irony was not lost on him, but he didn't rise to the bait. She expected him to resist, but he said mildly, 'Good idea, Pat. Let's see what else we can find, then we'll be able to give them a decent briefing. No use wasting their time.'

He was so bloody reasonable sometimes! Why couldn't he argue with her, so that she had a chance to beat him? She shut the book she was looking through with a snap and picked up another one.

At last she had finished her heap. There was nothing else in it that looked odd. She linked her hands and stretched. Oh, for a bit of exercise!

Anderson was still deeply engrossed in a reference book called *Erotic Art: A Revised Survey*. He seemed to her to be spending much too much time on each page. He was going to be a bloody expert by the time they had finished. She yawned and said, 'Sir, I –'

He looked up, and something about his face made her stop speaking. 'Pat,' he said, 'do you remember which paintings were missing from Francesca Lyons's gallery?'

She thought for a moment. '*Venus* by Eric Gill. *Making Love* by Mario someone, Mario Tauzin. And –'

'Look,' he said. He didn't move, and after a moment she got up and went to look over his shoulder.

The book seemed to be describing exhibitions at various galleries around the world, but she didn't give it a great deal of attention, because there was a note trapped between the pages. She recognised the writing as Stephanie's. It said, *Tauzin, man and woman coupling, unrecorded since 1939. Making Love?*

She met his eyes. He didn't need to tell her that this might be the link they had been looking for. Oh, shit, was he going to rub her nose in it?

'Interesting?' he said, lifting one eyebrow.

'Yes, sir,' she said through her teeth.

'Why should Stephanie have been undertaking research on a painting stolen from Francesca Lyons's gallery?'

'Don't know, sir.' God, now she sounded like a cross child. This wasn't correct behaviour from a would-be Inspector. 'Perhaps she was stealing paintings to order. Or she'd discovered a fraud, and she was killed because she found out.'

'Interesting thought. But equally she could have been involved in fraud.'

She wasn't going to argue about this. She straightened her shoulders and said crisply, 'Let me take all the details, sir. I'll get back to the office straight away and call the Art and Antiques Fraud unit. Maybe they'll be able to cast some light on it.'

He nodded. 'Good.' His eyes were quite opaque, as if he was thinking about something he wasn't going to tell her. 'I'll get back to the dealer who sold Francesca this picture. Perhaps she'll be able to add something.' He closed the book with the note still inside it. 'Got an evidence bag?'

She rummaged in her pocket and held the bag out, open. He dropped the book into it and met her eyes. He wasn't saying anything, but he was gloating. Damn him!

They continued through the remaining books and papers. There didn't appear to be anything left to find, and just before noon Anderson was satisfied for the time being. 'All right,' he said. 'Let's get back to the office.'

Fielding sat in the BMW with her arms folded, her body tilted away from him as if she was trying to pretend that he wasn't there. She didn't say a word all the way back to the office. She must have been so attached to her theory about the psychopath that she was finding it difficult to accept that there might be another explanation.

Well, it looked as if he was about to be proved right, so he could afford to be charitable. Otherwise he would have told her to pull herself together. As it was he'd let her sort herself out.

It was irritating that they still needed to call in outside help, but if he had to get advice from anyone he'd rather get it from a specialist police unit than from a psychologist. And he didn't have any objection at all to making contact again with Andrea Maguire.

Carrie Vickers met them in the doorway. 'Sir, Sarge. I'm just off to M&S, doing the sandwich run. Want anything?'

Fielding shook her head. She still looked sullen. Anderson saw Carrie give Fielding an anxious glance and he prompted gently, 'Not hungry, Pat?'

For a moment he thought she was going to go on sulking. She gave him a fierce look, then suddenly seemed to decide that it wasn't worth it. 'Oh, shit, yes. Carrie, get me one of those bacon and egg farmhouse rolls, will you? And a chocolate mousse.' There was something in her expression that betrayed restrained amusement. What was funny about chocolate mousse?

'Sure, Sarge. Sir, what about you?'

He was pleased that Fielding seemed to be coming round, and more excited about their discoveries in Stephanie's flat than he cared to show. 'Yes. Thanks, Carrie. Avocado and bacon, if they've got it, BLT if not, and a Greek yogurt with honey.' He found his wallet and took out a £20 note. 'Here, use this.'

'Bloody hell,' Carrie said in obvious astonishment. 'Have you won the lottery, sir?'

Every now and again he was reminded that he didn't often make this sort of gesture. 'You could say that,' he said.

As they walked in Nick Parker looked up and said, 'Sir, Sarge, the lab called about that DNA testing. They said they hoped to have a result by Thursday.'

Fielding harrumphed. 'We already know whose semen it is, don't we?'

Nick looked as though she was accusing him personally, not the lab. 'And Dr Reid's secretary called,' he said. 'Dr Reid's on a long weekend, back tomorrow evening. Do you want to leave the post mortem on Stephanie Pinkney till Wednesday, or get someone else to do it?'

Anderson glanced at Fielding. She shrugged. 'Are you expecting anything to show up at PM, sir?'

'No. But I'd still rather Reid did it.' He addressed Nick. 'Call his secretary back and say we'll wait.'

'You've spoken to Stephanie Pinkney's work, Nick, haven't you,' said Fielding. 'How's it going?'

'I spoke to a couple of her colleagues,' Nick said. 'Carrie spoke to her boss. Just what you would expect, really, you know, surprise, shock, all that stuff. Nobody had any ideas.'

Phone calls weren't good enough. 'We ought to speak to them in person,' Anderson said. 'You can't see how someone feels over the phone.'

'It would take ages to get up there, sir,' said Fielding. 'Let me call the Yard. If they're going to go there to look through her work, maybe they could interview her colleagues at the same time.'

That was a very reasonable suggestion from the manpower viewpoint, though it went against the grain. 'All right,' he said. 'See what they say.'

He closed the door of his office and sat down, thinking. Andrea Maguire had sold the missing picture. Should he be suspicious of her, rather than her husband?

It could be coincidence. He picked up the phone and dialled her number.

'Andrea Maguire,' said her voice, cool and delicate.

'It's DCI Anderson,' he said. He wanted to call her Andrea, but if she might be a suspect he shouldn't get any closer to her than he already had.

'Hello!' The tone of her voice changed, becoming warm, welcoming. She was pleased to hear from him. 'You seem to be on the phone practically every day. People will talk.'

That wasn't funny, under the circumstances. 'I'm sorry if I'm intruding,' he said stiffly.

'You're not, oh no,' she assured him. 'What can I do for you?'

'I just wanted to ask you something more about that picture,' he said, 'the Tauzin.'

'But you took the papers,' she said, sounding puzzled. 'You took photocopies, didn't you? So you've got all the details. What more can I tell you?'

That was true, of course. He must sound like a complete idiot. 'It wasn't about the provenance,' he said, quickly covering up. 'It was about the artist generally. I'd like some sort of background on him.'

She took a long breath. 'Really? Well, I'll help if I can, but I don't really know that much about Tauzin apart from the stuff that appears on provenances –' She broke off, and he heard noises in the background. 'Look,' said her voice again after a moment, 'I can't really talk now, I've got a client here. Could I get back to you?'

'Yes, of course. When would be convenient?'

'Well –' She sounded uncertain, then she dropped her voice. 'Look, don't you think it would be easier to do this face to face, rather than over the phone? I can show you reference works, you know, it'll all be much clearer. Sort of hold your hand through it, if you know what I mean. And I would really like –'

She stopped speaking, but her breathing echoed. The silence

drew out, ringing like a note of music. He had to say something. 'That would be very helpful,' he managed at last. 'When would be convenient?'

'Tomorrow,' she said, her voice so soft it hardly carried. 'Tomorrow evening. I've got a client coming at 4.45. Any time after that, I'd love to see you.'

'Thank you,' he said, carefully keeping his voice neutral. 'Five o'clock or thereabouts. I'll see you then.'

'I'm looking forward to it,' she said.

He put the phone down and left his hand for a moment on the receiver, staring into nothingness. She could hardly have made it clearer that she also felt the attraction between them. Perhaps he shouldn't go to talk to her himself. Perhaps he should send Fielding instead.

But no, that would be ridiculous. Didn't he trust himself to control his baser instincts? He was suspicious about a picture she had sold, and he wanted to watch her while she talked about it to determine whether she was sensitive on the subject. That was all. He had the best observation skills in CID. It wouldn't be professional to send anyone in his stead.

He got up from his desk and turned to the window. The sunlight was still bright. It was a beautiful day. When Carrie got back with the sandwiches he would go for a walk along to the river to try to clear his head.

Pat failed twice to get through to the Yard Art and Antiques unit, which was bloody irritating. She ate her roll in about four bites and then turned to the chocolate mousse. It wasn't a patch on Daniel's. Or was that just the orthodox way in which she was eating it?

As she finished the mousse she knew that she was about to succumb to temptation. It was a good feeling. She tucked the phone between her ear and her shoulder, found the number of the Lyons gallery and dialled.

After about eight rings she began to wonder if it was closed, or if Daniel was busy. Then his wonderful voice said, 'Good afternoon, Lyons Fine Art.'

'Hello,' she said. 'I wonder if you can help me. I'm a talent scout looking for nude chefs to take part in a new West End revue. Someone suggested that you might be interested.'

For a moment he was silent, then he laughed. 'That has to be you, Pat.'

'Pat?' she said. 'Who's Pat? This is the Cook Book Talent Scout Company.'

'I hope you're calling me to say that you can come round tonight.'

'Well,' she said, dropping the joke and speaking rather more quietly, 'actually, since I had to borrow clothes from you this morning, I thought that maybe you ought to come to my place instead, if you'd like to.'

'I'd love to,' he said simply. 'What time?'

'I don't know. Can I call you? I'm not sure when I'll finish tonight. It could be late, things seem to be hotting up here a bit.'

'Well, I hope that's good for you. But any time is fine, I can always open late tomorrow morning.' God, what a wonderful life he must have. 'If you're busy, though, won't it be a bit of a royal pain having to cook? Are you sure you don't want to come round to my place again?'

'Who said anything about cooking? I'm an appalling cook. Beans on toast is my limit. But there's a wonderful tandoori just around the corner from me, and they deliver.'

'Good lord, the cookery of the Empire! Wonderful. I'll bring a six pack, then, shall I? What do you favour?'

'Anything. Stella Artois.'

'It shall be even as you command, my mistress,' he said in his Frankenstein's assistant voice.

Her phone bleeped at her. Someone was waiting on the other line. 'Daniel,' she said, 'I'm really sorry, I'm going to have to go. I think this might be Scotland Yard trying to get through.'

'Scotland Yard? Good heavens, Holmes!' He was laughing. 'I still don't believe in you. Tell me all about it tonight. Goodbye.'

He broke the connection. She smiled and moved her lips in the shape of a kiss, then depressed the button.

The phone rang again at once. 'Fielding here.'

'Can I speak to DS Fielding, please?' said a middle-aged voice with a strong East End accent.

'You're speaking to her.'

'Bloody hell! Right, OK, hello, love. This is DS Hughes, Art and Antiques Fraud unit.'

She had expected a detective in such an abstruse field to have a small amount of class, but obviously not. 'Thanks for calling, DS Hughes.'

'Derek, love,' he said.

'Derek, OK. I'm Pat.'

'Hello, Pat, darlin'. How are you today?'

'I'm fine. And I'll be even better if you don't call me "love". Or "darling".'

There was a short silence. Bugger, had she misjudged it? She might need Hughes's cooperation, and not everyone took kindly to being corrected. But after a moment Hughes said, 'Right, well, that put me in my place, didn't it?' and he sounded really good-humoured.

She warmed to him. 'Look, Derek, we've got a case here which I think could be right up your street. We're wondering if you could help.'

'Tell Uncle Derek all about it,' he said.

'Let me find my notes.' She had organised everything very carefully. She didn't want to waste the Met's time, and she wanted to look bloody good, too, knowledgeable, efficient, cool. She described the case to date in as few words as possible, making sure that she included everything she thought might be relevant.

Hughes listened carefully. He didn't ask her to repeat herself, and he fired a few quick, pointed questions which revealed that he had been listening hard and that he wasn't as much of a plonker as he sounded. After about fifteen minutes he said, 'Yeah, all right then, Pat. It sounds as if you might have something going on. It's a bit small beer, though, isn't it? These little dirty jobs don't flog for more than eight to ten grand. Small-time stuff. I've got paintings worth more than a million to chase up here.'

She let her voice go cold. 'And are those paintings potentially connected to two murders?'

'All right, love, don't lose your rag, I'll look into it for you. Stuff it all on the fax or the scanner, will you? I'll go up to the Tate when I've got a minute, and I'll call you or your governor, what's his name, DCI Anderson, if anything comes up.'

'Thanks very much, Derek. When will you be able to go?'

'Dunno. Not today, probably not tomorrow. Day after tomorrow, I should think.'

'Can't you make it any sooner? We –'

'Look, love, your governor doesn't authorise my overtime, does he? I'll go as soon as I can.'

'But –'

'If you want it to get higher priority, you get your governor to call my governor. And he'll tell your governor just what I told you. You get that stuff on the fax, OK?'

'OK,' she said wearily. 'Thanks, Derek.'

'All part of the service,' he said, and cut the connection. Pat sighed, then got up and went over to the door of Anderson's office.

He was sitting looking out of the window. 'What is it, Pat?' he asked without looking around.

'I've been in touch with the Yard, sir. DS Derek Hughes. He said he would go to the Tate and look into it for us some time in the next couple of days.'

'Some time in the next couple of days?' He swung round to face her, frowning. 'Wasn't he more specific than that?'

She said reluctantly, 'The day after tomorrow, sir.' He looked angry, as if it was her fault. She couldn't resist the chance to get her own back slightly. 'Sir, with respect, I did suggest that we call the Yard three days ago. If we'd done it then, we'd already have this information.'

He stared at her, and for a moment she was afraid that she'd overstepped the mark. But all he said in the end was, 'We wouldn't have known to look at Stephanie Pinkney's research at that stage, Pat.'

'If you don't like it, sir, DS Hughes suggested you should speak to his boss at the Yard. But he didn't hold out much hope of increasing the priority.'

'No.' He turned again to the window. 'Is that all?'

'Yes, sir.' What had got into him today? God, he could be bloody difficult sometimes. She wanted to shake him. Instead she turned away and shut the door behind her with unnecessary force.

# THIRTEEN
## Monday 4.30 p.m.

Anderson rubbed his hand over the back of his neck and arched backwards. Why did he feel so stiff? He linked his hands behind his head and pressed his elbows back and his hands forward, trying to stretch his spine.

The walk by the river hadn't worked. He couldn't get Andrea out of his mind. Whenever he stopped consciously thinking about something else the images of his sleep reappeared, Andrea and Catherine, separately and together, beautiful as sirens.

Of course, there was a very straightforward way to stop himself from thinking about Andrea, and that was to call Catherine. If he could arrange to see her in the near future, his interest in Andrea would be purely theoretical.

He looked at the telephone on his desk. His fingers itched to lift it. He knew Catherine's number off by heart, her direct line at the firm of accountants where she was a partner. She would answer the phone in her business voice, cool and professional, and he would say it was him, and then what?

She would put the phone down, he was sure of it. She was afraid of him, and if he pursued her he would make it worse. He would have to wait, engineer another meeting by chance like the meeting outside the Fairfax Gallery.

God, why was there no work on his desk which could engage his mind? He didn't want to think about Catherine and he knew that he shouldn't think about Andrea. He was in a cleft stick.

He got up, raking his hands through his hair. A cup of tea, even station tea, might help. He pulled open the door and headed for the coffee point.

Fielding was there before him, filling the kettle. She glanced at him and then away, saying nothing. Why was she still angry? He could have been a lot harder on her than he had been. It was absurd, this sulking. He felt like leaving her to stew, but it was unnecessary and unpleasant not to be on speaking terms, and it was a challenge to try to bring her round. 'Pat,' he said, 'how's it going?'

She gave him a suspicious look. 'No further leads from any of Stephanie's friends, sir.' He nodded, and she hesitated, then said, 'Are you after a cup of tea?'

'Exactly that.'

'Right, well, I'm just making one.' She switched on the kettle and stood for a moment gnawing at her thumbnail. 'Oh yes, sir, Chris Lyons's GP called. He, well, he asked us to lay off. Apparently he's afraid that Chris might be becoming suicidal.'

'Definitely a mistake to send Bill round,' Anderson commented.

That got a reluctant smile from her. 'Yes, sir. He's not exactly Mr Charm and Tact, is he?' She covered her mouth with her hand, as if she hadn't meant to smile and was trying to conceal it.

She clearly wasn't ready yet to acknowledge that her theory had been wrong, and it wouldn't be tactful to mention it. Another subject, perhaps. 'How did things go last night?' he asked casually.

Her dark eyes flashed up to his and then away. She made a business of putting tea bags into the pot. 'Fine, thanks, sir.'

Was that the beginnings of a blush? 'Where did you go, anywhere special?'

'Round to his place.' She poured boiling water into the pot and put on the lid, then looked up at him with a small smile. 'He cooked us dinner.'

'Very nice. What's his place like, is it artistic?'

'You could say that. It's full of antiques, he inherited them.'

'And how was the cooking?'

'Great,' she said, with a little half grin.

Where had he seen that expression before? That's right, when she was ordering her lunch. The connection was obvious. 'Good chocolate mousse?' he enquired delicately.

She stared at him. This time there was no mistaking it, her pale cheeks were flaring scarlet. Well, well. What had young Daniel done with his mousse?

'Tea's up, sir,' she muttered, pouring it out. He accepted the cup she offered him and hid his expression in the steam.

It sounded as though Fielding had enjoyed herself with Daniel. Lucky her. But he couldn't feel pleased for her. He covertly watched her face and saw it change as she thought that she was unobserved. The embarrassment disappeared, to be replaced by a look of reflection. Her dark eyes became very bright and she licked her lips and took a deep, luxurious breath. The memories must be arousing.

Damn it, he had given her permission to see this witness. He had condoned her sleeping with him. And it looked as if she'd had a bloody good time. Why was there one law for her and another for him? Why was she allowed to go to bed with Daniel, while Andrea was out of bounds?

As they walked back through the office Carrie called out, 'Sir. Sir, I've got the Met on the phone.' Into the receiver she said, 'He's just coming.'

He raised his eyebrows at Fielding and went over to Carrie's desk. She pressed the Silence button and held the phone out to him. 'Detective Sergeant Hughes, sir. Sounds like a right barrow boy.'

He took the phone. 'DCI Anderson.'

'Evening, sir,' said a voice whose chirpy cockney sparrow tones would have raised his hackles even on a good day. 'DS Hughes here. Art and Antiques unit.'

'Yes,' Anderson said. 'DS Fielding briefed me.'

'Oh, yeah, Pat. Sounds like a nice bit of fluff, governor, is she?'

That didn't even merit a response. 'Is there a problem, Hughes?' Anderson asked in his most glacial tones.

'Yeah, well, there is, actually,' said Hughes's voice. He didn't sound remotely concerned about Anderson's obvious disapproval. 'We've just had something come up, something big. It's got to be dealt with straight off. I'll be off this evening to look into it. To Barbados, as it happens.'

'Then give our enquiry to someone else.'

'Can't be done, governor,' said Hughes with unremitting cheerfulness. 'There's not many of us in the unit and we're at full stretch at the moment. It'll just have to wait till me or one of the boys gets back. Could be next week. Sorry if it mucks you about, nothing I can do and all that.'

Anderson's knuckles whitened on the receiver. 'I want to talk to your superior officer.'

'Sorry, guv, no can do. He's cut off early tonight, gone to the opera, all right for some, eh?'

'Tell him to call me first thing in the morning.'

'Sure, guv, no problem. I'll be in touch, yeah?'

The line went dead. Anderson stood for a moment getting himself back under control, then set down the receiver with exaggerated gentleness.

'Problem, sir?' Fielding's voice was tentative.

'Yes.' He trusted himself to turn around now. 'Detective Sergeant Hughes has other calls on his time. He finds himself constrained to fly to Barbados in the course of an investigation.'

'Barbados?' exclaimed Carrie, her mouth hanging open. 'Bloody hell, when can I have a transfer to the Met?'

Anderson picked up his tea and stalked towards his office. He didn't like to criticise other forces in front of his staff, and if he wasn't careful he was going to forget himself in a minute.

Fielding followed him, cradling her mug, and shut the door. 'What did he say, sir?'

'That nobody will be looking at our case for at least a week.'

'Shit,' she said.

'Exactly.'

'Well,' Fielding said, looking uncertain, 'I don't suppose there's an awful lot we can do about it, sir.'

'No.' He took a sip of tea and realised that what he really wanted was something stronger. A lot stronger. He was in luck. Fielding was one of the very few of his colleagues that he could easily ask. He lifted his head quickly and said, 'Look, Pat, do you fancy a drink?'

Her eyes opened very wide. 'A drink, sir?'

'Yes, a drink.' Why did she sound so bloody amazed? He couldn't keep the irritation from his voice. 'Remember drink? An alcoholic beverage, yes? I had whisky in mind.'

She looked away as if she was embarrassed. 'Sir, I can't. I'm – busy.'

'Seeing Daniel again,' he said, unsurprised, but disappointed all the same.

'Yes, sir.'

He didn't have to make her feel bad about it. He forced a smile. 'Your turn to cook?'

'My turn to feed him. I don't like cooking.'

She was twisting her toe on the carpet, clearly eager to get away. There wasn't much point in trying to keep her. 'Well, see you tomorrow.'

'Bright and early, sir.' She hesitated, then said, 'Look, sir, I've been meaning to say, on balance, I mean, I'm glad we found what we found today. I mean, that there's something odd going on, something that could link Francesca and Stephanie. I hope that is the explanation. I really mean it. I'll get really stuck in tomorrow, as much as I can without the input from Scotland Yard. We'll crack it, sir.'

He was glad she had said it. He returned her smile without too much effort. It wasn't her fault that she had a new man and he was stuck between Scylla and Charibdis. 'Thanks, Pat. Have a good evening.'

'Thanks, sir.' She gave him a shy smile and slid out.

Now what? His desk was almost clear, and he knew that beneath his calm surface he was ready to shout for frustration. What should he do?

'Something odd going on, something that could link Francesca and Stephanie.' Yes, Pat was right. That's what they had found. The key lay with the altered labels that Pat had found among Stephanie's possessions, and with that picture, the picture by Mario Tauzin, *Making Love*.

Stephanie hadn't kept that many working papers at home, just reference books. So it wasn't clear why she had been interested in that particular painting. Maybe her desk at work would reveal more. Why wait for Scotland Yard to get there in their own good time? What was so different and difficult about art fraud as opposed to any other sort of fraud? He would go to the Tate and do some detecting himself. Parrish wouldn't like it. Parrish could go to Hell.

He picked up the phone on his desk. 'Carrie, you made the call to Stephanie Pinkney's boss, didn't you?'

'Yes, sir.' Carrie sounded apprehensive, as if he was about to check up on her.

'Who is he? What's his phone number?'

'Just a second, sir.' The sound of frantic rummaging through piles of paper. 'Yes, sir. The number's 0171 887 8126. It's Dr Vaughan, Hillary Vaughan.'

'That's a male Hillary, is it?'

'Yes, sir.' She sounded startled, as if she'd expected him to get it wrong even though she hadn't corrected him when he had referred to Stephanie's boss as 'he'.

'Thanks, Carrie.' He broke the connection, then dialled again.

After two rings a languid voice answered. 'Hillary Vaughan.'

'Dr Vaughan, good evening. This is Detective Chief Inspector John Anderson from Surrey Police.'

'Anderson?' said the voice. 'Detective Chief Inspector Anderson?' It sounded wary. Everybody sounded wary when a policeman called unexpectedly, whether or not they had anything to hide. 'Is this about Stephanie Pinkney?'

'That's right, Dr Vaughan. I'm in charge of the murder investigation. I understand that you spoke to one of my team earlier today.'

'Yes. Is there a problem?'

'Not at all. I called because I had asked Scotland Yard to help us with this investigation, but they have a resourcing problem and can't give it the priority I'd like. So I would like to visit you tomorrow, if that's possible, and ask you a little more about Miss Pinkney.'

'Well, yes.' Dr Vaughan sounded hesitant. 'Do you believe this is necessary?'

If Stephanie was involved in something she shouldn't have

been, then her boss might be involved as well. 'It's more or less routine, Dr Vaughan,' he said reassuringly, and added in a confiding undertone, 'I would send a junior member of the team, but it seems like a good opportunity to get up to town and catch your latest exhibition. I've read a lot about it. I've got a great interest in English portraiture, and I don't often get the chance to visit the Tate.'

'Ah.' That even got a slight laugh. 'Well, of course. I'm free first thing, as it happens. If you come to the staff entrance and ask for me, I'll take you around to the exhibition afterwards. What time will you be here, Chief Inspector?'

'When would suit you?'

'Nine o'clock would be ideal.'

'Then I'll be there at nine. Thank you very much. I look forward to meeting you.'

He put the phone down and took a deep breath. Had he been disingenuous enough? Probably not. If Vaughan was involved, there would be nothing left among Stephanie's papers to find. But it was still worth a look.

His desk was clear, tomorrow was arranged. What now? A fast, aggressive squash match would fit the bill perfectly. He opened his address book, found the page for the squash ladder and picked up the phone.

Andrea pulled into the drive, switched off the lights and sat for a moment in the dark, thinking. What would it be like this evening? What would he do?

Everything felt quite different now. She had power over him. It was a novel sensation, and she relished it. She didn't have to sit here trembling, afraid in case he might be in a bad mood. She knew he would be in a bad mood, and she didn't care. He could hit her, but she could retaliate.

She opened the door and called out cheerfully, 'Here I am!'

Silence. No sound from the kitchen, but dinner smelt good. Was he out at the pub? Why had he left all the lights on? 'James. Are you there?'

No response. She went through to the kitchen and found that he had cooked dinner and eaten it, too. There were three dirty saucepans on the stove, two dirty plates on the table and a few more in the sink. She opened the oven hopefully, but there was nothing inside it.

The bastard! If he hadn't felt like cooking at all, fair enough, but to have cooked just for himself and left nothing at all was really below the belt. The detritus suggested that he had made salmon fishcakes, too. Bastard. He knew it was her favourite.

'James!' She banged out of the kitchen, into the living room. He wasn't there. She jerked open the door of the study, half expecting it to be locked, but he wasn't there either. Again she shouted his name, though now she hardly expected an answer.

'Where the hell are you?' she demanded, running up the stairs. The light was on in their bedroom. She stamped in and there he was, lying in bed, his big shoulders naked above the duvet, reading a novel. A half-drunk glass of wine was on the bedside table. As she came in he slowly, ostentatiously lifted his head to stare at her, as if he'd only just noticed that she was there.

'Didn't you think of leaving me anything to eat?' she snapped, trying to conceal a frisson of fear. It was all very well not being afraid of him when he wasn't there. His presence in the flesh was something else again.

'Cook it yourself,' he said, returning his gaze to his book.

She wasn't going to let him get to her. 'James,' she said after a few deep breaths, 'look, we need to talk. We need to make sure that we've got everything straight. Otherwise we could get each other into trouble.'

He lifted his brown eyes and gave her a cold stare. 'I'm amazed that you should worry about that. I thought you wanted a divorce. I assumed you were going to drop me into the shit,' his voice hissed venomously, 'just as soon as you could.' Before she could reply he leant forward, dropping the book to the floor. 'Well, just take care, my darling. If you try screwing with me, you'll regret it.'

How dare he threaten her? For a moment she could hardly get words together. Then she said, 'Christ, James, you amaze me. There's no question about who the brains is round here, is there? I'm bloody well thinking for both of us again.'

'Don't patronise me,' he said.

His voice was very cold, with a harsh edge to it that she recognised. It scared her, and her fear made her angry. What was the point of making any effort to try to protect him? His stupid male ego would wreck anything she did. Better just to look after herself. Well, she could manage that, too. She knew how to manipulate James.

'You may be interested to know,' she said coolly, 'that Chief Inspector Anderson is coming around to the office tomorrow evening.'

James's eyes narrowed. He flung back the duvet and got out of bed. He was naked, and his penis hung long and thick between his legs. As always, the sight of his body shocked her with the power of her own lust for him. He came towards her slowly, his head a little on one side. 'I told you,' he said softly, 'not to see him. I warned you.'

God, oh God, he was getting a hard-on. That meant trouble. She tore her eyes away from his crotch, shuddering, and said defensively, 'What am I supposed to do? He called me. He wants to talk. I can't say no, can I? That would look pretty bloody suspicious!'

James stood glaring at her, head down, like a bull getting ready to charge. 'Andrea,' he said thinly, 'I'm warning you.'

She hated him for threatening her. Suddenly she was ready to do just what he suspected her of. She was ready to betray him to the police, put the blame onto him, hand him over to Chief Inspector Anderson and laugh at him. But that was for tomorrow. For now, she couldn't detach herself from wanting him. His cock was almost fully erect, hard and dark and glistening, and she craved it. It was always the same. He was aroused by his own anger, and she was aroused by his arousal.

'Look,' she said, thinking fast, 'I tell you what. Why don't you come around to the studio while he's with me? You don't have to talk to him, you can just be there and make sure that everything's above board.'

He scowled at her and she gazed innocently back at him. 'Well,' he said after a second. 'When is he coming?'

'About six,' she lied easily. An hour should be time enough for her to engage Anderson in something more than conversation. Then James would come and find them together and he'd be so furious that he would be bound to do something violent. He'd probably beat Anderson up. And then he would be in deep shit, on an assault charge and maybe worse, and if ever it came to her word against his about the murders there was no question who the police would believe.

'All right,' James said, still watching her as if he thought she was trying to trick him. 'I'll be there some time after six. So you'd better make sure he doesn't come within spitting distance of you.'

'I promise,' she said. She took a cautious step towards him, saw his eyes blaze and took another step. 'James,' she said softly, and she reached out and touched his erect cock. It was hot and dry and so hard that it quivered against her hand. He glowered down at her, eyes and lips sullen and sensual. 'Does it turn you on,' she whispered, stroking her fingers very gently down his length, 'to think about me with Anderson?'

His reaction was explosive. 'No!' he shouted. He caught her by the shoulders and flung her onto the bed. She landed heavily, gasping, and before she could catch her breath he was on top of her, smothering her with the weight of his body. He flung up her skirt and dragged her sweater up above her breasts. The air was cold on her nipples and she cried out and twisted, knowing that if she seemed to resist it just aroused him more. She loved it when he was like this, like a wild animal, uncontrolled, savage, overcome with desire for her.

He caught her wrists and jerked her hands apart, pinning her down. His breath was hot in her face. 'Say you don't want him,' he snarled. The length of his hard cock throbbed against her thigh. She smiled and said nothing. 'Tell me!' he demanded, shuddering with rage.

Well, did she want him? She thought that she probably did. As a contrast to James. She couldn't see Anderson losing control like this, shaking and yelling and practically foaming at the mouth. Yes, she would enjoy working him into some sort of compromising position. But there was no need to tell James that, he was already angry enough to perform well. 'I don't want him,' she whispered, arching her back to offer James her breasts.

'If you let him touch you, I'll kill you,' James hissed. 'I swear it, Andrea, I swear it, I'll kill you.'

'Kill me now,' she breathed, pressing her body against his.

For a moment he was still. Then he let go of her wrists and caught her beneath her thighs and dragged her legs apart, hooking her knees over his arms so that she was held open to him, trapped and helpless under his heavy body. She drew in breath after gasping breath, waiting to feel him. He lifted himself over her, the muscles of his shoulders flexing as he took the weight, and then the head of his cock was at her entrance. She was slippery with longing and he penetrated her easily, sliding the whole length of his cock deeply into her. She cried out and closed her eyes.

He took her then, thrusting into her wildly, like a beast. She lay beneath him listening to his pants and curses and considering her own power. She was using him, using him for her sexual pleasure and to protect her from the police, and it was thrilling. She cried out in rhythm with his thrusts and let herself go, and her orgasm was so powerful that she almost blacked out.

'So how's work?' Daniel asked. He scooped up a mouthful of balti on a piece of naan bread and held it out for her to eat. 'I haven't heard anything about Francesca recently. What's going on?'

Pat accepted the mouthful. 'Phwaa, that's hot. Good, isn't it?'

'Yes, it's delicious.' They had decided against eating the balti in bed on the grounds of mess, so they were sitting on the bedroom floor, Pat in her dressing gown, Daniel in his shirt. The order of play had been obvious from the start; bed first, balti second. Daniel took a swig from the can of Stella at his elbow and said, 'What about your case?'

She gave him a rueful smile. 'I can't really talk about it, Daniel. We're not supposed to, you know.'

'What, in case I'm some sort of a spy?' He sounded flattered.

'If you like.' She scooped up a mouthful of her curry and ate it, then said reflectively, 'I tell you what, though, Daniel. I'm having trouble with my boss on this one.'

'Your boss.' Daniel frowned, trying to remember. 'Is he the overdressed chap, greying hair, looks as if his arse is, as they say, tighter than a gnat's chuff?'

She stared, then laughed. 'Christ, Daniel! But yes, that's him.'

'What's the matter with him?' Daniel sounded angry and protective. 'Is he giving you a hard time?'

'No, no, not exactly.' How could she describe what was happening and still be objective? 'We had different theories about the crime, and that was difficult for a while. And now that's sort of out of the way, but things still aren't back to normal. I don't seem to be able to get through to him.' She had been looking into the middle distance, and now she lifted her eyes to Daniel's. 'If I didn't know better I'd say he was having trouble with his love life.'

'Is he gay?' asked Daniel bluntly.

'What, my governor?' Not that unreasonable a question, really. 'No, he's not, Daniel. He was married for ages. And he likes women.'

'Could apply to lots of gay chaps,' commented Daniel, dipping another naan.

'He's not gay. And I think he's got woman trouble. And I –' She hesitated again, trying to uncover the truth of what she felt. 'Do you know, I feel sorry for him, but I'm really pissed off with him, too.' Yes, that was it! 'You know, he always likes to be in charge, he's a real control freak, and I think he's got a problem at the moment which he can't solve. But he won't talk about it. He got me talking about you today, and I don't know anything at all about what's happening to him, and I probably know him as well as anyone at the office.'

Daniel didn't look amused. 'I don't like the sound of him. Shall I challenge him to a duel for you? Pistols at dawn?'

'No, don't do that.' She laughed, dipped a naan and held it out to him. 'Our Superintendent – that's the big boss – retires next year. If DCI Anderson gets his job, then there'll be all sorts of empty spaces up the ladder and that'll be good for me. If you blow his brains out with a rusty pistol I'm done for, professionally speaking.'

'Why are you so ambitious?' he asked her.

She'd said enough about her work. 'Why aren't you?'

'My only ambition,' he said, 'is to be the best paid nude chef on the West End stage.' He dipped his finger in the raita, reached across the array of silver-foil dishes and drew a line of yogurt and mint across her collarbone and down between her breasts. 'Famous for my artistry.'

'Michaelangelo,' she said, pushing her dressing gown from her shoulders.

Anderson pushed open the plate glass door to the balcony which ran along one complete side of his apartment. Outside it was warm and slightly damp. He went out into the dark and leant on the balustrade. Beneath him something splashed into the river, startled by his unexpected appearance.

Winning three straight games of squash had tired him, but not enough. He stared downwards into the shifting reflections of the water. A slight breeze made the bulrushes rustle.

Normally he liked being on his own. He liked his flat, he took quiet pleasure in each one of his carefully chosen possessions, and he enjoyed surrounding himself with whatever stimuli exactly suited his current state of mind. Now even a glass of Beaumes de Venise and the brilliant joyfulness of Handel's *Dettingen Te Deum* couldn't lift him from his bleak mood. What the hell was wrong with him?

Nothing that a visit to Andrea tomorrow afternoon wouldn't cure.

But she might be involved. A witness, a suspect, anything was possible. He had to keep his distance.

'Damn,' he said. He turned with sudden decision and walked quickly back into the brightness of the flat. He sat down on the big sofa, drained his glass of wine, then picked up the phone and dialled. His heart beat strongly and fast.

After about five rings Catherine's voice said, 'Hello?'

'Catherine, I'm sorry to call you so late. Did I wake you?'

There was a silence. Then Catherine said very softly, 'John.'

Was she prepared to be reasonable? 'Catherine, I really want to see you again.'

Another silence, so long that he didn't know whether she was still there. 'Catherine?'

She said in a smothered voice, 'I'm sorry –' And then she put the phone down. The dialling tone buzzed in his ear, angry and reproachful.

Knowing that it was useless, he dialled her number again. It rang ten times before he slowly replaced the receiver on the hook. He shut his eyes so tightly that sparks flared behind his eyelids. What was the matter with her? Why was she being so irrational? It was obvious that she wanted him, but she wouldn't even speak to him. Anger brimmed up in him, fighting to break his composure.

'Shit,' he said, pressing the heels of his hands hard against his temples. 'Shit, shit, shit.'

# FOURTEEN
## Tuesday 9.45 a.m.

'Well, Chief Inspector,' said Dr Vaughan, draining the last of his coffee, 'I really don't think there's very much more I can tell you. I hope I've been helpful, but I have another meeting to attend at ten. Would you like me to escort you to the exhibition?'

'That's very kind of you,' Anderson said easily, 'but it occurs to me that while I'm here it would be sensible if I made some checks in your research department.' He watched Vaughan carefully for signs of surprise or unwillingness, but there were none, only polite confusion. 'I'd like to examine Stephanie's papers,' he explained, 'and also, if it's possible, try to trace an enquiry made by another woman, Francesca Lyons, several weeks ago.'

Dr Vaughan frowned. 'Do you believe that this might be related to Stephanie's murder?' he asked in tones of deep distaste. 'I hardly like to think of anyone at the Tate being involved in improper activities.'

'Dr Vaughan.' Anderson sat a little forward and opened his hands. 'At the moment I'm still looking for a motive for Stephanie's murder. And the nearest I've got is that it may relate to her work, to her research. I don't know why at this point, but who knows if her papers might reveal something.'

'Yes.' Vaughan nodded slowly. 'Yes, of course. Well, look, let me take you along to the archives. I'll introduce you to Geraldine, she manages the whole of Archive and Research.

She'll be able to show you where Stephanie worked, and she might be able to help on your other query as well.' He got to his feet. 'And then I must leave you, I'm afraid, Chief Inspector.' He opened his desk drawer and flicked through a number of white cards, then held one out. 'I'm sorry I won't be able to take you into the exhibition, it is rather special. Allow me to give you this instead. Perhaps you'll be able to come back another time.'

The card was an entrance pass for the exhibition, admitting two and allowing them to stay after the normal closing time of the gallery. Anderson looked at it, for a moment able to think of nothing but Catherine. If he had waited till today to call her, he'd have been able to use this pass as an excuse to see her. She wouldn't have been able to resist.

For a moment he could hardly bear it. Then he remembered himself and said, 'Thank you very much indeed, Dr Vaughan. That's very kind of you.'

It didn't seem as if anybody had touched Stephanie's desk. Like her bedroom, it was a tip, piled high with papers and books. Anderson sat down in front of it. He didn't know anything about art records and he didn't know what he was looking for. Well, never mind. He was confident in his ability to absorb and retain detail.

He read quickly and made notes of any underlinings or annotations in Stephanie's hand. Nothing emerged, no pattern, no unexpected comments. Time passed. It was hot in the office, and he stood up, carefully hung his jacket over the back of the chair, removed his lapis cufflinks and put them on a corner of the desk where they wouldn't be knocked, and rolled up his sleeves, three precise folds for each sleeve.

Towards the bottom of one of the heaps he found an old, battered catalogue. It was in German, and he knew only a few words of German, mostly music-related. He held it by the spine and riffled the pages, just to see if anything jumped out at him.

Yes, there was an underlining. He stopped and opened the page and his heart gave a skip as he read 'Mario Tauzin, *Das Liebe*'.

*Das Liebe*: love. Could it be the same picture? This was an old catalogue. He checked the date. 1933. And the note in Stephanie's book on her desk had suggested that this picture vanished from the record at the time of the Second World War.

A little way down the same page another picture was underlined: 'Rojanowski, *Erotische Idyll.*' He wrote it down, just in case.

He went on through the remainder of the books, but there was nothing else. What now?

Someone was behind him. He turned round to see Geraldine Wallace, the stony-faced guardian of the archive. 'I think I've found that enquiry you asked about,' she said, with quiet pride. 'Our tracing system is quite sophisticated, you know.'

'What have you found?' He got up to join her.

'Here.' She showed him the entry. 'Mrs F. Lyons. That's the right name, isn't it? She was interested in tracing the provenance records for a painting called *Making Love* by Mario Tauzin. I asked Stephanie to help, as that's her field.'

That was the connection! He concealed his excitement. 'That's very interesting, Miss Wallace. What was the date of that enquiry?'

'Fifteenth of September,' said Miss Wallace crisply.

That fitted with what Chris had told them about Francesca's anxiety and her trip to London. So there had been a link between the two murdered women. But what could it have been? 'Miss Wallace, if I wanted to look at the provenance records for that picture, what should I do?'

'Well,'said Miss Wallace, 'this lady wanted to look at the original documents; actually inspect them, you understand. But normally we wouldn't recommend that. Some of the documents are very fragile, and people can disarrange them and damage them and sometimes even lose them.'

'Tsk, tsk,' he said, since some deprecating comment seemed called for.

'So if you just want to read the records I'd suggest you use the microfiche. They've been promising us an on-line virtual-reality provenance database for years, but until we can come up with the funding I'm afraid we're still back in the Dark Ages.'

'Microfiche it is, then,' he said pleasantly.

'I suppose you want me to show you how it works,' grumbled Miss Wallace.

'If it wouldn't be too much trouble,' he said, in his most complaisant tones.

The microfiche was simple, but it was guaranteed to give the user a headache. The fiches were kept alphabetically, but there didn't seem to be any discernible pattern to the arrangement of records within a particular artist. It took him half an hour to find the painting by Tauzin which he wanted.

Here were microfiche copies of several of the documents which Andrea had showed him, together with others, extracts from exhibition catalogues, reviews, sale documentation. It all looked very convincing. There was a reproduction of the picture, and he stared at it for some time. It was a beautiful drawing, with a simplicity and purity of line that made him think of Japanese art, and a frankness in its depiction of penetration that was utterly untouched by modesty. It was so guileless that it was almost unerotic.

Almost, but not quite. In fact it was profoundly erotic. He moved the fiche, making himself blink, and zipped up to the beginning of the section.

One of the first entries was dated 1958 and was an extract from a newspaper article relating to art treasures thought lost to the Germans and retrieved several years after the war. Apparently the collection had included a large quantity of erotica by French artists including Tauzin, Rojan and Ballivet.

It looked as sound as a bell. But Francesca Lyons had wanted to check it up, and she had been murdered. How could he tell whether it was authentic or not?

One way, since he wasn't an expert, might be to compare this set of records to those relating to another picture. Why not use the other picture from that pre-war German catalogue, the one by Rojanowski?

He put aside the Tauzin fiche and hunted for the next one. It took time to find it. At last he had it, and he inserted it into the machine and switched it on.

He glanced through the provenance quickly, then went back to the beginning and started again. It began with the same 1958 newspaper article as the Tauzin entry. Well, perhaps that wasn't surprising, though it was coincidental that both pictures should have appeared in the same catalogue before the war and they were both found in the same cache after the war. Or was it? Perhaps it wasn't coincidental at all.

Frowning, he went on through the fiche, then hesitated and stopped. Was he going mad? He leaned across and turned on the microfiche reader at the next desk, picked up the Tauzin fiche and illuminated it. Now he could compare the two directly.

No, he wasn't going mad. The provenances of the two pictures were identical. It was as if they had passed through their entire lives together, from their first exhibition to their last recorded sale to one Esther Mansfield, a private collector. It was from Esther Mansfield that Andrea had purchased the Tauzin which she had then sold on to Francesca Lyons.

Now that was very, very coincidental. He remembered what Philip Fairfax had told him about invented provenances. It suddenly seemed possible that Stephanie was in the business of researching not twentieth-century art, but twentieth-century fraud.

But he didn't have a lot to go on. If she was a fraudster, where did she keep her records? Not on her desk at home, either.

Mind you, he and Fielding had not subjected Stephanie's bedroom to a proper search. They'd been looking for something obvious, not something hidden. If he took more care, who knows what he might find.

He returned to Stephanie's desk and picked up the phone to call Jane Pritchard.

The trip back to Guildford was purgatory, crowded tubes and delayed trains. How did commuters manage, dragging their way to London and back every day? It was after 2 p.m. by the time he got to Stephanie's flat, and Jane met him at the door. She didn't look well. 'This is very kind of you,' he said.

'By rights I ought to have a search warrant, you know.'

'As long as you're just looking through Stephanie's things,' she said, 'I can't see why I should mind. Anyway, you'll have to excuse me, I've got to get back to work.'

He stood at the door of Stephanie's bedroom, thinking. Should he call Fielding and get her to come and help?

No. He was on to something, and he might as well follow it himself. It might evaporate, prove to be a wild goose chase. That would be embarrassing. If he found anything in Stephanie's room, it would be different. He pulled out a pair of disposable gloves and tugged them on.

First the desk. Again he opened every book, shook them, checked for concealed papers. Nothing. He checked the drawers, the back of the desk, the blotter, the bookshelf above it. Nothing.

Time ticked on. He was conscious of it passing, bringing five o'clock closer and closer. Andrea would be waiting for him in her office.

The desk was clean. The wardrobe was next. It was crowded with clothes and lingerie and the washing basket, concealed at the bottom, was noxious. He took off his jacket and rolled up his sleeves again, wary of inadvertent contamination. The last time he had personally carried out a search in this much detail he had been with the Drugs Squad, looking for cocaine, not papers. At least this time he didn't have to stick his hand down the u-bend.

There wasn't anything in the wardrobe either, apart from a few silverfish and a rich seam of dirty tights. Stephanie reminded him of a lady of the eighteenth century, powdered and scented on the surface, grimy beneath it.

3.30 already. He knelt on the floor and lifted the covers to look under the bed. Several dusty suitcases met his eye. He sighed and pulled the first one out.

The suitcases held only mementos of holidays and old bikinis. He got up, brushed angrily at his dusty trousers, and looked at his watch. Christ, four o'clock! He had forgotten quite how long a thorough search could take. He couldn't be late for Andrea. Perhaps he'd have to come back tomorrow, and then he would have to bring Fielding. He could manage one day away from the office on his own without arousing too much comment, but two would be pushing it.

Time for the chest of drawers. It was a rather handsome piece of furniture, made out of knotty pine. He pulled it a little away from the wall to check that there was nothing taped behind it, then tilted it backwards. Nothing underneath it, either. One by one he pulled out the drawers and rifled through the contents. They contained nothing but clothes.

The last drawer stuck as he tried to pull it out. He gave it a strong jerk and at last it emerged. It was full of sweaters and nothing else.

He was about to put it back when he wondered why it had stuck, when the rest of the drawers had pulled out smoothly. He reached into the chest and tapped the bottom. It moved slightly.

He gave a little snort of satisfaction and felt around the inside of the chest until his fingers encountered a slightly protruding edge. He glanced around and his eye fell on a nail file, abandoned on the floor nearby. He used it as a lever. After only a few seconds what had looked like the bottom of the chest of drawers lifted out, revealing itself to be a false panel of hardboard, laminated in pine.

Not rushing now, he set the panel aside and put his hand back in the chest of drawers. There were papers in there. He smiled and brought the first one out. It was a handwritten list headed 'Prices fetched at auction 1995'. Beneath it was a notebook with 'Possibles' written on the front. In one corner of the secret compartment was a bank passbook, still in its plastic envelope. He pulled it out. It was from the Manx Bank. It would be, wouldn't it? If you were going to secrete ill-gotten gains, why worry about paying tax on the interest?

He opened the book and looked at the entries. A few thousand pounds at a time, two thousand here, three thousand there, building up to a pleasant little balance in excess of £25,000.

Now that he was almost there, he felt inclined to move slowly, to savour and enjoy each new discovery. He considered the bank book in a leisurely way, then put it back in its envelope and turned to the notebook.

The last entry in the book read, 'Tauzin, good for at least another 2'. Beside it, in the margin, there was a scribbled doodle of a pudgy cupid holding up a bleeding heart. The heart was inscribed with a single name: 'James'.

James! It hadn't been a hunch, he had been right. Was it James Maguire? It had to be. He flicked back through the notebook. There were occasional doodles on earlier pages, hearts and flowers, again mentioning James, sometimes linking the name to Stephanie. One page carried a long note about an artist called Gerda Wergener with a comment, 'Very marketable. But can James handle her style?'

So Stephanie researched the possibilities and James drew the pictures. That made sense. He flicked through two more pages and stopped.

There was a picture, a drawing, in a style he recognised. It was no more than a sketch, doodled in pencil on lined paper, but brilliant all the same: a woman lying on a sofa in a state of complete dishevelment, breasts peeping from her rucked bra, skirt around her waist, eyes and lips heavy with the aftermath of orgasm. The artist had even managed to suggest the glint of juice in the darkness between her open legs.

He knew the subject. It was Stephanie Pinkney. And he knew the artist. And in case there had been any doubt, the picture was signed, a long, racy scrawl.

*James Maguire.*

He put down the notebook and for a moment covered his eyes with his hands. He had the link between Stephanie and Francesca, between Stephanie and James. But what about Andrea? She had sold the pictures which James had painted to Stephanie's orders. Had she known what she was doing?

Slowly, painstakingly, he went through the notebook, page by page, looking for any reference to Andrea, any reference to the sale of the pictures. There was nothing. He picked up the list of auction prices and read through that as well, then knelt down and felt in every corner of the hidden compartment, looking for anything he might have missed.

There was nothing. He knew that there had been no reference to Andrea in any of Stephanie's other papers, it would have been picked up. So what was the conclusion he had to draw?

The obvious one was that Stephanie and James were a team of forgers, linked by their crimes and by the mutual passion which glowed from James's sketch of Stephanie. James despised and battered his wife. Perhaps she knew that the paintings she sold were forged, perhaps not. In any case, there could be little doubt that she had sold them under duress. She was terrified of her husband, as well she might be.

And the killings? Francesca's was easy enough to explain. Stephanie placed false provenances in the Tate's archives. When Francesca had come, asking awkward questions, Stephanie had mentioned it to James, and he had taken deadly action. And as for Stephanie, who could say? A lovers' quarrel, perhaps? James was mercurial and violent, capable of anything. Perhaps it would come out after the arrest. He looked forward to the opportunity to interrogate James.

Now it was time for him to go. Andrea was expecting him. She had asked for his protection as a joke, but James was a killer, and Andrea would be the key prosecution witness. She would need protection more than she had dreamed.

# FIFTEEN
## Tuesday 4.45 p.m.

Pat was thinking about calling Daniel and making a move for home when the phone rang and the voice at the other end said, 'Pat, it's Anderson.'

'Sir!' She couldn't keep her amazement from her voice. 'Sir, where have you been? The Super's been asking questions.'

'I'll speak to him tomorrow. Pat, there've been some developments.'

'At the Tate?'

'At the Tate, and at Stephanie's flat. We missed some things. They're with me now, but I've got to go over to Andrea Maguire's office. I'll come in afterwards.'

'Sir, what's going on?' Jesus, was he determined to try to crack this whole case all alone? Hadn't he heard her yesterday, climbing down, offering her help?

'Haven't you got it yet?' He sounded almost as if he were teasing her. 'You were spot on. It's nothing to do with jealousy, it's all about money. Stephanie Pinkney and James Maguire were in it together. She did the planning and created false records. She told him what to draw, he drew it, and they sold the pictures through Andrea Maguire's usual distribution channels. Obviously they chose erotica because it was what she was particularly equipped to sell. Between £5,000 and £10,000 for an afternoon's work. Not bad, eh?'

That made sense, and he must have found the evidence in

his searches at the Tate. But – 'What was Andrea's involvement?'

'James beat her. He probably forced her. Or maybe not. I'll check it out. Speak to you later, Pat.'

'And Francesca discovered one of the fakes?'

'That's the hypothesis. She visited the Tate to check it out and spoke to Stephanie. All Stephanie had to do was tell James.'

'But why did James kill Stephanie?'

'Look, Pat, I can't tell you everything now. I'll brief you when I get in.'

'Sir, the evidence –'

'Tell the Super he'll have a result by tomorrow. See you later.'

He cut the connection. Pat stared at the phone, then said, 'Shit,' and put it down.

'What's up, Sarge?' asked Gerry.

She shook her head. 'That was the governor. He's broken out. If he's not back within a couple of hours we'll have to send out a search party and get his mug shot on the 9 o'clock news.'

'Saving the world again?' asked Carrie.

Pat shook her head. 'God knows what he's doing. But if he –' She broke off and turned away. It wasn't right to criticise Anderson to Gerry and Carrie.

But her mind finished for her. If he wanted to help me get my promotion, he'd involve me. What does he think he's doing, bollocking off on his own, not even stopping to drop in the evidence? If he had half a brain, he'd involve me. If he –

She shut her eyes and pinched the bridge of her nose between her fingers.

– If he trusted me, he'd involve me.

Anderson pressed the entryphone button and stood looking up, waiting. The door buzzed open and he shook his head. Didn't she care who walked in? She ought to.

He ran up the stairs. As he got to the top floor he heard voices in the office and realised that a client must be there. Perhaps that's why she hadn't bothered with the entryphone.

Andrea's kittenish face appeared at the doorway of the office. She smiled at him, a smile so disarming that he couldn't help returning it. 'Hi,' she said. 'It's nice to see you.'

There wasn't any acceptable response to that, so he just nodded.

'Look,' she said, with a quick glance behind her and a rueful expression that made him want to smile again, 'I'm so sorry, I've just got someone here. Would you mind waiting in the studio? I won't be a few minutes.'

'Of course,' he said. As she closed the door he heard her talking to the client, her voice calm and self-assured.

If he was the sort of detective who went with his gut, he would take her innocence for granted. She couldn't welcome him so cheerfully if she thought he might be about to discover her involvement in a murderous fraud. But he wasn't that sort. He liked to have proof to back up whatever he suspected. He couldn't relax yet.

James glanced at the clock. Just after 5 p.m. He held up the sketchbook and looked critically at his latest composition for the next Tauzin. It was a beauty: two young women side by side, their slender bodies displayed in all their lovely nudity. Their long elegant necks turned to allow their parted lips to touch, and you could just see that one girl was putting her soft tongue into the other girl's mouth as she slipped her hand between her lover's legs, prising open the delicate lips of her sex, just beginning to penetrate her vagina.

'Very nice,' he said, 'very nice indeed.' It was just right, the perfect combination of restraint and graphic realism. All he needed to do now was prepare the paper, though that took long enough, God knows.

He put the sketchbook in a drawer and locked it. When the final drawing was finished he would destroy the preparatory sketches. That always hurt, watching a piece of himself crumple into smoke and ash. But the original was there, and delightfully valuable, after all.

And now it was time to wander along to the studio and make sure that Andrea didn't get up to anything with that foppish copper Anderson. Not that she would dare, if she valued her skin. He hadn't been joking when he promised to kill her if she let the bastard touch her. He'd killed before, after all. It had been shamefully easy, almost enjoyable, in fact, and he hadn't found that it troubled his conscience.

The studio walls glowed with artificial life. Anderson walked slowly around the room, looking at the pictures, trying to ignore the effect that they were having on him. He could have wished that Andrea hadn't asked him to wait in here. How was he supposed to look at this panoply of sexual activity and maintain his composure?

It wouldn't be so bad, except that so many of the women had Andrea's face. He hardly knew her, and yet it was as if he had seen her naked, as if he had made love to her, as if he knew how she would react when he touched her.

This was not the right way to keep a clear head. He tore his eyes from the pictures on the walls and made himself look around the studio without registering the details of any individual picture, as if he was searching for evidence, not passing the time before Andrea could see him.

Gradually he brought himself back under control and focused on details. What a mess the room was, pictures everywhere, piled on every flat surface, stacked against the wall. He'd probably have to arrange a search in here. He didn't envy whoever it was got the job.

One stack of pictures drew his eye. Why was that? He put his head slightly on one side and narrowed his eyes. In a moment he would have it.

Yes, that was it. There were at least ten pictures in the stack, all framed, pushed up one against the other. The pictures at the front were thick with dust, as if they hadn't been touched for years, though God knows it wouldn't take long for dust to accumulate in this smoke-thick, filthy atmosphere. But at the back the dust was disturbed on the penultimate picture, and the picture closest to the wall had no dust on it at all.

Why put a picture right at the back of the stack? He glanced over his shoulder. Was Andrea coming? No, he could still hear her voice in the office, behind the closed door. He didn't want to put his gloves on in case she came and found him there, hunting for evidence. Well, Forensics would have to cope with his prints as well as anyone else's. He reached down and drew the picture out of the stack.

It was an ordinary work, the sort of thing he had come to expect from James, about 60 centimetres by 45, a painful, ugly portrait painted in pastel on dark grey paper. He didn't recognise the subject. There was nothing special about it, and for a moment he felt a stab of disappointment. Perhaps the chain of connection that had led him so far was broken.

But perhaps there was something strange about the picture, after all. The frame felt odd, uneven. He turned the frame round to look at the back, and saw that the mount had been disturbed and replaced with transparent Scotch tape.

Slowly, not even trying to imagine what might result, he peeled back the tape from three sides of the mount and lifted it.

Behind the mount, laid against the dark grey paper of the portrait beneath the glass, was another piece of paper, white this time, hiding. On its back were a number of gallery labels. He knew before he turned the picture over what he was going to find.

There it was, the picture he had last seen on the microfiche in the Tate Gallery, the picture that had been in Francesca Lyons's gallery before she was killed. It was signed *Mario Tauzin*, but he knew who had drawn it. This picture, hidden as carefully as a messy, careless man like James could manage, was the evidence he needed to convict James of murder.

And perhaps that wasn't all. Perhaps it could help to establish Andrea's innocence, too. Why had James taken the picture? Waste not want not, perhaps, to sell it again once the furore had died down? If Andrea knew what had happened, she would know that this picture was hidden in her husband's studio.

Sounds from the office suggested that Andrea's client was about to leave. Moving quickly and being careful not to touch the hidden picture, he reassembled the mount to conceal the fake Tauzin.

The door of the office opened and Andrea and her client emerged, chatting amicably. Anderson went over to the window and stood holding the picture, apparently contemplating the portrait.

God, it was ugly. He couldn't imagine any sitter ever actually paying to be portrayed by James Maguire.

'That's it,' Andrea said, coming in with a sigh. She was wearing a long fluid wrap skirt and a jersey blouse fastened with tiny pearl buttons. The blouse skimmed her slight body elegantly, but the points of her small breasts showed through it. She met his eyes and said with a slight smile, 'I'm all yours.'

As casually as he could, he held out the picture. Would she react, would she recognise it? 'Who's this?'

Her face became a blank for a moment. 'Goodness,' she said, 'I haven't seen that one for a while. It's an old friend of mine who dared to sit for James. Do you like it?'

He hesitated, and she looked up and met his eyes. That was what he had been waiting for, that eye contact, so that he could see exactly what happened when he turned the picture around. Slowly, he reversed it and showed her the botched mount. 'It's a bit of a mess at the back,' he said evenly.

There was no reaction, none. She looked at the mount, then met his eyes with a smile. 'God,' she said, 'James will insist on doing his own framing. He's no good at it, is he? Look at that!' She ran one slender finger along the Scotch tape, then looked up into his face. 'Mind you, until I can make some money selling them perhaps he'd better frame them himself, eh?'

She couldn't be so good an actress. At that moment he would have testified in court that she had no idea at all that the fake Tauzin was hidden behind the portrait. It must be as he had imagined. Stephanie and James were the forgers, James was the murderer. Andrea was innocent, her husband's dupe. He still wasn't sure why James had killed Stephanie, but he would find out.

He slowly set the picture down, leaning it against the front of the stack. Andrea looked up at him, fragile, wide-eyed, lovely. For a moment he examined her high cheekbones, her soft lips. She returned his gaze, and as he met her eyes her pupils dilated, darkening with longing.

She was a witness, an important witness. But it didn't matter any more. She was innocent, and her green eyes revealed that she desired him. He lifted his hands very slowly to cradle her delicate face, and she didn't move, didn't pull away, just smiled very slightly. His fingers gently, gently lifted her fine-boned chin, turning up her mouth to his. He glanced once around the room, at the images of Andrea moaning in her husband's embrace, and then he stroked her baby-fine hair and lowered his lips onto hers and kissed her.

Guildford was full of people leaving their offices and making their way towards their homes. James watched the faces as he walked through them, looking for inspiration. He was walking past one of the little trendy shopping galleries carved out of the old buildings in the middle of the town when he saw a face he knew.

'Hi!' he said, stretching out a hand to stop her. 'How are you?'

'Oh,' said the pretty girl, rather flustered, 'James, hello.'

It was Rachel, the barmaid from the Spotted Cow. She was dressed very smartly, in a long skirt, tight jacket and high heeled shoes. 'You look rather different,' he said with a smile. 'Is this the day job?'

'Yes.' She looked up at him with bright, eager eyes.

'What do you do, then?'

'I'm a receptionist,' she said, and added hastily, 'and I do some PA work, for the directors, you know.'

'Of course,' he said smoothly. He glanced up at the clock on the shopping arcade. 'Look,' he said, 'I'm a bit at a loose end at the moment. Do you fancy a quick drink?'

'Oh –' She hesitated. 'I've got to be at the Spotted Cow by 6.30, James, or Bob'll kill me.'

'Plenty of time,' he said with a smile. The girl was obviously keen on him, and asking if she would sit as a model had always worked in the past. 'Look, do say yes. I want to ask you a favour.'

She was so slight that he was almost afraid of hurting her, even with the gentlest of kisses, and she quivered between his hands. Her fragrance was sweet and faint and when his fingers brushed against the front of her blouse he felt her nipples, hard tight peaks to the slight swells of her little breasts.

Every time he lifted his lips from hers she whimpered and clung to him more tightly. Her helplessness, her need for him were irresistible. He concentrated entirely on the sensations of kissing her, her taste, her smell, the touch of her skin and hair, the beauty of her fluttering eyelids, the sweetness of her soft moans. A part of his mind was trying to get his attention, trying to make him stop, and he didn't want to.

Her eyes opened. She glanced at the walls, a hunted look. Of course, she wouldn't want to be in here, in the studio, surrounded by her husband's pictures, her husband's representations of her sexuality. He slid his hand down to the small of her back and smiled at her as he guided her gently towards the door of the studio and across the corridor to the office. She didn't resist.

The door of the office closed behind them. He took off his jacket and hung it carefully over the back of a chair, brushing his fingers against the smooth harshness of the wool as if it were some sort of talisman. He could leave now, if he wanted to. He could just walk away.

But her eyes were on his. She took a faltering step towards him and whispered, 'Please. Please, don't stop.'

And he couldn't stop. He took hold of her shoulders and very slowly pulled her towards him. She closed her eyes and let him guide her, and this time when he put his mouth on hers he let his hand rest on her breast, cupping her nipple in his palm.

She lifted her hands and laid them around his neck, moaning softly. Her tongue touched his as his fingers began to unfasten the tiny buttons of her blouse. She whimpered as she felt his hands exploring the naked skin of her breasts, and her body moved against his, a faint shudder of desire and acceptance.

The blouse was open. Her breasts were so shallow that his hand could cover them completely, and her nipples were the palest pink. He moved his lips to kiss her throat. Her head fell back and he stooped over her and his mouth moved down. She cried out as he flickered his tongue against her nipple and then took the nipple into his mouth, sucking gently.

'Oh God,' she gasped. He continued to caress her breasts

with his mouth and as he did so he slid his hand under the wrap of her skirt, onto her slender thigh and then upwards.

His fingers touched the soft swell of her pubic mound. He ran his fingernail over her cotton panties and her whole body stiffened. The plump cushion of flesh between her legs was warm and yielding. For some time he stroked her through the fabric of her panties, watching her eyelids flutter and her lips tense and move as if she was trying to speak. Then he gently eased his hand into the enclosing fabric and down through the crisp curls of her pubic hair.

He kissed her again as he explored the silky folds of her sex, already moist with need. His fingers traced the edges of her labia and then probed between, seeking her heart. She moaned into his open mouth and swayed as if she would fall. Quickly he withdrew his hand and caught her up into his arms. She seemed almost weightless. Her head hung back, exposing her pale throat. He carried her to the sofa and set her on it in a sitting position, then pushed off her blouse and unfastened her skirt. She opened her eyes and watched him as he eased her panties down her thighs and off.

Now she was naked, looking up at him with her great eyes. It was profoundly erotic to be standing over her, fully clothed, while she slumped beneath him, at his mercy. His cock was hot, engorged, chafing inside his trousers. He leant down, bringing his mouth to hers, and she lifted her lips to meet him.

As he kissed her he slipped slowly to his knees and cupped her breasts in his hands, then began to kiss his way down her body. He wanted to give her the purest pleasure, pleasure untainted by fear or violence, pleasure with no strings attached.

His lips brushed against her silky fur and she moaned again and lifted her loins towards his mouth, parting her thighs instinctively, offering him herself. He took a deep breath, drawing in her sweet scent. Then with his hands he very gently parted the lips of her sex to expose the hidden pearl of her clitoris, and he kissed it.

He caressed her with infinite gentleness, and she responded with little trembling cries of bliss. As her excitement increased he slowed the tempo of his kisses, drawing out the ecstasy, until as she approached her climax he was hardly touching her, only the slightest tremors of his tongue and lips lifting her over the edge of orgasm. She gave a high, gasping cry and her body arched up from the sofa as the spasms ran through her. Then she fell back, panting and shivering.

Now she would be ready for him. He kissed her quivering belly and got slowly to his feet. There was a condom in his wallet. When he walked back towards her, tearing the packet open, she gazed at him with an expression that combined fulfilment and longing.

Her body was beautiful, as fine-boned as a dancer's, almost boyish in its slenderness. He stood over her for a few moments, admiring her. Then he knelt again between her open legs and leant forward to kiss her as he rolled the condom onto his erection.

She caught at his shoulders and pulled herself upright, clinging to him. 'Yes,' she whispered, pressing her breasts against him. Her hard nipples scratched against his shirt. 'Please.'

He guided the head of his cock, finding the spot, then thrusting very gently. Her body opened for him, her warmth surrounded him. He closed his eyes, momentarily over-whelmed by the sensation of penetrating her. He was in her, buried up to the hilt, enfolded. Slowly he began to move, withdrawing to the very tip, easing himself back into her, opening his eyes to watch her face as he took her. For a little while she held up her head and kissed him, and then, as his movements grew stronger, deeper, she began to cry out, urging him on. She clutched at him and lifted her hips to meet his thrusts, gleefully accepting his body within hers.

Gasping, he held her tightly and lunged into her. It was good, so good that he closed his eyes and breathed through his clenched teeth. The pace of his movements increased and she responded, flinging her head from side to side, panting and moaning.

But something wasn't right. Her movements and her cries said that she was coming, but he had felt her orgasm and he could tell that it wasn't happening again. The moist clutch of her body around his plunging cock didn't change, and when he bent his head to kiss her breast he felt that her nipple was softening.

She was faking it. But he couldn't stop now, there was nothing he could do but surge onwards, driving himself to a lonely climax. He snarled as the sensations claimed him, spreading from his throbbing buried cock through his entire body.

Then he bowed his head, hiding his face from her. His breathing slowed, and gradually the pleasure ebbed away, leaving him drained and empty.

Andrea stroked her fingers tentatively through Anderson's strong silver-streaked hair. Had he noticed that she hadn't come, that second time? She hoped he hadn't. He was a real expert with his mouth, her first orgasm had been incredible. But somehow when he entered her his restraint, his gentleness, hadn't turned her on as much as she had expected. Perhaps she'd got more fond of James's animal fervour than she had realised.

And where the hell was James? She looked over Anderson's bowed head at the clock on the far wall. It was already five past six. Of all the bloody times to choose to be late!

Anderson seemed to be coming to life again. She wriggled a little away from him to allow him to withdraw from her. Fancy him having a condom! She hadn't even considered little necessities like that. He was certainly very organised.

He tidied himself up, then looked up at her. Something shadowed in his face made her think that her acting efforts hadn't been appreciated. What would he rather she had done? At least she'd tried to salve his ego. She concealed her twinge of irritation and smiled at him. 'That was wonderful,' she said softly.

He stroked his hand down her body. His eyes followed its path, down her throat, around the curve of one breast, across her belly. She shivered. There was something almost unnatural about his calmness, his steady deliberate inspection. What was he looking for? What was he seeing?

At last he looked up at her and said, 'You're very beautiful.'

'Thank you,' she said uncertainly.

'Now,' he said, handing her her panties, 'I think you'd better get yourself dressed.'

But if she was dressed, how would James know what they had done? She tried to think of a reason to stay as she was, but he didn't look as if he would buy an eager request for more sex. So slowly, reluctantly, she took the panties from his hand and pulled them on.

He watched her for a moment, then got to his feet and turned away, raking his hand through his hair. He went over to her desk, straightening his tie and tweaking at his sleeves. Then he took his jacket from the chair, put it on, and brushed at the lapels as if his exertions on the sofa could have mussed it.

As she fastened the buttons on her blouse she realised with an odd sinking of her heart that she didn't even like him. She had been curious about him because he was so different from James, and that was all. She didn't particularly want to repeat the experiment, either. Would she have to, just to make sure that James got the message?

Suddenly she heard the faintest of sounds from downstairs. The door opening. James! Christ, if Anderson heard him coming – She thought frantically, then said, 'Do you know, I – I don't even know your name. You must have told me, but I –'

He turned and looked at her, his expression unreadable. 'It's John.'

'John.' She walked towards him, moving with a seductive sway. 'John it is, then.' James's footsteps were drawing closer. He was walking softly, she could hardly hear him. She had to do something to compromise Anderson, right now. 'John,' she breathed, 'kiss me.' She reached up and buried her hands in his hair and dragged his mouth down to hers.

It was hard to walk quietly up Georgian stairs, but James did his best. He kept his feet towards the edges of each step and they hardly creaked. If Andrea was up to something, he wanted to be able to surprise her.

The office door was closed and he couldn't hear anything. But the door of the studio was ajar. He frowned. Had she taken Anderson into the studio? Why? He had no business going in there.

Still moving softly, he opened the studio door and went in. For several minutes he didn't notice anything out of place. Then he saw the portrait that had been at the back of the stack of pictures, leaning on its side. He went close to the picture and stood looking down at it, breathing shallowly through open lips. Then he picked it up and turned it around. The Scotch tape holding the mount in place was furred and sticking badly, as if it had been lifted and replaced.

He put the picture back on the floor, then went over to his desk and looked at the clutter covering its surface. After a moment he moved aside a few sketches to reveal a heavy glass ashtray. He picked it up, dumped its contents in the direction of the waste bin and hefted the ashtray experimentally.

He wasn't sure who had betrayed him to whom. But one thing was clear, and that was that he had been betrayed.

Anderson jerked his head up, then caught hold of Andrea's hands and pulled them away, more roughly than he needed to. She gave a little shocked cry. He held her wrists and stared down at her, his breath coming fast.

She hadn't wanted to kiss him. She had wanted to distract him. He had heard the footsteps too, he wasn't a fool. Had this whole thing, this entire encounter been some sort of conspiracy? Christ, had she been using him?

For a moment he couldn't think of what to say to her. A wave of anger swept over him. His hands tightened on her wrists and she said sharply, 'Don't!'

'Andrea –' he said.

And then the door burst open. James stalked in, his face distorted with rage. Andrea whimpered with fear and Anderson let her go and turned to face James, his neck prickling with reaction to the fury in the other man's eyes. He said, 'James Maguire, I'm arresting you –'

James roared, a furious animal sound, and lunged at him. Anderson ducked and slammed his fist into James's stomach. James staggered and grunted and folded over and Anderson set his teeth and reached out to grab James's arm and twist it up behind his back to bring him to his feet. James began to stand up, then writhed and brought his left hand round, fast and hard, straight at Anderson's face. Anderson cursed and swung aside, but he wasn't quick enough. The blow caught him along the side of his head and the world roared and faded.

He felt pain first, a throbbing in his brain, like sickness. Then, slowly, the pain became more localised. An intense, pounding ache by his right eye, as if –

Something hit him in the face, not hard, but sharp enough to jolt him. His head swam, and then gradually things made sense. The pain by his right eye was where James had hit him with something heavy. He was sitting on a hard chair. He tried to move and realised that he couldn't, his hands were tied behind him. He couldn't move his feet either. He wasn't surprised when the burning in his lips told him that there was parcel tape over his mouth.

'Wake up,' said James's voice. It was quiet, but with a tinge of glee. 'You don't want to miss this.'

He forced his eyes open. James was leaning over him, grinning. 'Look,' he said, gesturing. 'Pretty as a picture, hmm?'

Anderson's vision swam. He shook his head, trying to clear it, and then tensed hopelessly as he saw what James was showing him. Andrea, stark naked, sitting in the armchair, her hands bound in front of her, her feet bound too.

'Imagine what a field day the Press will have with this,' James crowed. ' "Today a senior police officer and a naked woman were found dead in a Guildford office building. The woman appears to have died in some bizarre sexual experiment, after which the officer, whose name has not been released, killed himself in remorse." Brilliant, eh? Worth televising?'

'James.' It was Andrea's voice. She didn't sound particularly afraid. 'James, that's not brilliant, it's absurd. Nobody would ever believe that.'

She was certainly right there. But it didn't look as if her calmness was justified. James snarled at her furiously, 'I've told you before, Andrea, don't fucking patronise me.'

'But James,' she whispered, undulating as if her naked body could distract him, 'honestly, darling, truly, nobody would believe you. You'd be in even bigger trouble.'

James smiled over his shoulder at her. 'Maybe. But you'll never know, will you, Andrea my darling? You'll be dead.'

'James.' Now she sounded really frightened. 'James, let me go.'

James turned away from Anderson and walked over to stand in front of his wife. At once Anderson began to twist his wrists, trying to determine what his hands were tied with. It was both rough and slippery and after a moment he realised that it was his own silk tie. Damn it, it would be wrecked! But it was tied tightly, in knots that would become more recalcitrant the more he tugged at them.

'Let you go?' James said to Andrea. 'No way, darling. What were you talking to this bloody detective about before I arrived? Don't think I don't know. I just happened to stroll into the studio before I came in here.'

My God. He had found the picture. He knew!

Panic surged up in Anderson, threatening to overwhelm him. If only he could speak, there'd be a chance that he could talk James out of this, make him realise how hopeless it was. After all, Fielding knew where he was. If anything happened to him she would fit things together. But he was silenced, bound and impotent, helpless. The parcel tape burned against his lips, smothering him. He closed his eyes tightly and took quick, deep breaths, fighting the urge to struggle.

After a moment he was calmer, though the panic was still there, not far beneath the surface, beating at him. Andrea said, 'I don't know what you're talking about.' Didn't she? He wasn't sure now. With infinitesimal movements he swivelled the tie binding his wrists until two fingers could reach the knot, and began delicately to worry at it. It was fastened very tightly. Unknotting it would take some time. He might not have enough time.

'Don't play the innocent, Andrea,' James said. 'What sort of a yarn have you been spinning your pet policeman here? Have you got him eating out of your hand? I suppose the poor sod doesn't know that you're a killer.'

*What?*

Anderson opened his eyes, staring. Andrea glanced at him, one quick bright glance, then writhed and snapped angrily, 'James, don't be stupid.'

'Still trying it?' James laughed. 'How long will you keep it up? Until I've put this on you?' He picked something up from the floor and held it out for Andrea and Anderson to see. It was a large plastic bag, quite plain, transparent.

Anderson swallowed hard and fought the shaking in his hands as he picked at the knot. He closed his eyes, trying to concentrate. Andrea's voice said, 'James, don't. Don't joke.'

'I'm not joking, darling,' James said softly. 'A little bit of Be Done By As You Did. How do you think Stephanie felt when you put a bag over her head?'

'I didn't,' Andrea whimpered, but there was no conviction in her voice.

'Why did you do it?' James persisted.

'Don't,' Andrea wailed, desperate now. 'James, don't, don't. I only meant to scare her. I didn't mean to hurt her. I didn't know she would die so quickly! James, please!'

She was a killer. He had just – fucked a murderess. Oh, Christ.

He felt sick and faint. His hands wanted to stop their pointless, hopeless working at the knot, but he made himself go on. Was he deceiving himself, or was it beginning, imperceptibly, to loosen? He had to try. Otherwise he might as well just sit there and wait for James to kill him. Or would that be a better option, under the circumstances?

'James,' Andrea said again, 'please, please, don't hurt me, James, don't –' And then her voice cut off.

'You,' snarled James. 'You bastard, look here!'

Anderson opened his eyes. James flung out one hand, showing off the ghastly sight of Andrea writhing, struggling, her lovely face hideously distorted by the transparent plastic that clung to her mouth and her nose and plastered itself against her pale cheeks. 'Watch this,' James hissed. 'You're next.'

He kept his eyes open, but let them go out of focus so that he wouldn't have to watch. There was nothing he could do, nothing until his hands were free. Then he stood a chance. The panic button was under Andrea's desk, no more than six feet away. He could summon help before James knew what was happening.

His half-focused eyes registered Andrea's weakening struggles. Her heart would stop in between thirty seconds and two minutes. From that time he had five minutes to help her. After that she wouldn't be worth reviving, because her brain would be dead.

And wouldn't that be more convenient? Only she knew what had happened between them. If she was dead, she couldn't ever tell anyone.

He fought down the thought and worked feverishly at the knot. It was loosening now, definitely loosening. Don't rush it, take your time, if you rush it you'll make a mistake –

Andrea wasn't moving any more. The bag was limp over her face. James looked at her with his head on one side, then stepped forward and delicately removed the bag.

He turned to Anderson, the bag held open, smiling.

And then the last knot came undone. No time to free his feet. Anderson's heart was pounding. He waited until James came close, then reached out and grabbed him and levered himself up. James rocked back, open-mouthed, and Anderson pushed himself sideways and fell headlong towards the desk, his feet still tied to the chair.

'Bastard!' James roared. Anderson dragged himself forward on his elbows and lunged towards the panic button, concealed beneath the apron of the desk. He couldn't reach it. James was coming for him, and he lifted his feet and kicked out with all his strength, using the chair as a weapon. James grunted and staggered and with one last desperate lunge Anderson reached the button and pressed it as hard as he could.

With an incoherent shout of rage James grabbed the chair and dragged him out from under the desk. He kicked out again and James wrenched at the chair and it broke, showering them with fragments of wood. James lashed out with his foot, aiming at Anderson's head, but Anderson twisted out of the way. James's foot landed in his ribs and he curled up in agony as the breath whistled out of him. He knew that the next kick was coming and he couldn't do anything to stop it, he just wrapped his arms around his face, trying to protect himself, and then he felt the blow and his eyes darkened again.

He wanted to give up, to sink into unconsciousness, but he knew that he couldn't, that there was some reason he had to stay awake. He lay very still and struggled with the swimming in his head. The parcel tape was stopping him from breathing, choking him, but he felt too weak to pull it off.

Then the phone rang and he knew why he had to stay awake. It was the security company, making their checkup call. If James gave the codeword, they would think it was a false alarm and stand down.

He braced himself for a final effort and lifted his head. Waves of pain swept over him, he had to struggle to keep his eyes open. There was the telephone socket, there in the wall, not ten feet away. He had to get to it.

'Hello,' said James's voice, cool and drawling. 'James Maguire speaking. Oh goodness, has the alarm gone off?'

Anderson staggered to his feet and half fell across the room and pulled the cord from the socket. Then he propped himself against the wall, tore off the gag and hissed, 'Shit.' James stared at the useless telephone, dropped it, then turned and looked at him with murder in his eyes.

'Not sensible, James.' His lips were stiff and bleeding, he could hardly make the words. He made a weak gesture, taking in the carnage of the room. 'Name one person who would be convinced by this as some sort of bizarre sex tryst.'

James snarled and came a step closer. His brown eyes were glittering, hard as stone. There wasn't anything more Anderson could do. James was going to kill him, despite everything. At least there was no chance he would get away with it. That was some comfort.

But then James stopped. Anderson saw him hesitate and tried to pull himself up straighter. 'If you kill a police officer on top of everything else,' he husked, 'they'll make sure you never get out of prison.'

'Fuck you,' James whispered. Then he turned and ran. The door of the office slammed behind him and his footsteps rattled on the stairs.

It would be good, now, to slump back into senselessness. But there was something else he had to do.

He dragged himself over to Andrea. It was hard to move, and a stabbing pain caught his lungs with each breath. Her eyes were open, her face still contorted with terror. She didn't look beautiful now.

The police wouldn't arrive for ten minutes. He had to revive her, now. She could be brain dead in the time it would take him to plug the phone in again and dial 999.

If she was dead, nobody would know what he had done. But he would know. And he would know that he had let her die, rather than admit his error. He would be a murderer then, just as much as James. Just as much as Andrea.

He pulled her down from the chair onto the ground and dragged her head back, opening the airway. Then he leant over her and drew in a deep breath. The pain made him moan. He pressed his lips to hers and forced air into her lungs. Her chest lifted, stirring her bare breasts.

Again and again he breathed for her, his shoulders shaking, fighting the pain and the terrible, gnawing knowledge of his own incompetence. She was a killer, and she had manipulated him and James to try to protect herself. Sweat fell from his face onto hers as he held her in an embrace more intimate than sex.

Her heart wasn't beating. He put his hand flat on her chest and struck it with his fist, hard, three or four times. Was he hitting her to save her life, or because he hated her?

She shuddered and he felt her heart start again, fluttering at first, then steady. He put his mouth over hers and breathed and now her lungs responded, filling for themselves, sucking the air from him. He pulled away from her and watched as she began to cough and choke and struggle.

It was a relief to let himself collapse.

# SIXTEEN
## Wednesday 3 p.m.

Detective Superintendent Parrish was a bulky man, and his broad shoulders and big belly entirely blocked the miserable view out of the window of the little room. He leant against the windowsill and folded his arms, tapping his fingertips impatiently against his elbows. 'John.' His voice was soothing, but he always tried to present a politician's unruffled face. Anyone who knew him could detect the anger and disapproval beneath the surface. 'Relax. I've got everything under control. You needn't worry. The CPS are quite happy.'

Anderson lifted his hand to rub his fingers against his temples, felt the bandage and lowered his hand again. It was humiliating to be lying in bed in vile hospital-issue pyjamas with his boss physically looking down on him. Why hadn't anybody warned him that Parrish was going to visit, so that he could have got up and at least made himself look halfway decent in a dressing gown?

Oh, God, if only his head didn't ache so abominably. Hadn't he been speaking English? Why wouldn't Parrish understand him? He said painfully, 'Sir, you don't understand. Andrea Maguire confessed to the murder of Stephanie Pinkney. I heard her.'

'I understood you perfectly.' Parrish's voice was sharper now. 'You're the one who doesn't understand. You're concussed, for God's sake. I'll repeat this another time.'

He walked past the bed, apparently intending to leave. Anderson pushed back the sheets and swung his legs to the floor. 'Sir –'

'Stay in your bloody bed,' snapped Parrish. 'Two broken ribs and a fractured wrist –' The Superintendent seemed suddenly furious. He stalked back towards Anderson, stabbing his finger at him. 'Who do you think you are, John? The fucking Sweeney? What's a DCI in his forties doing running around like some leather-jacketed DS from the Regional Crime Squad? You fancied yourself stepping into my shoes next year, didn't you? No chance of that now. Not a bloody chance. Why don't you stay behind your desk and do the job you're paid to do?'

Anderson stood his ground, though he was unsteady on his feet. 'I'm paid to catch criminals, sir. That's what I did. You have both the murderers in custody.'

'No, John,' said Parrish, his voice icily quiet now. 'We do not.' He looked at Anderson with annoyance and distaste, as if he suspected him of malingering. 'For Christ's sake sit down before you fall down.' It was a relief to obey. Anderson slumped down onto the slippery plastic chair in the corner of the room. Parrish stood over him, arms angrily folded. 'Now get this straight,' he said. 'I don't care what you say about Andrea Maguire. We are putting together a case against James Maguire for the murder of Francesca Lyons and Stephanie Pinkney. The evidence you gathered all points to that. And he tried to kill a senior police officer. No jury in the country will believe a word he says. He'll go down for both murders without so much as a bubble.'

'Sir,' Anderson said, trying to keep his voice strong and steady, 'the evidence could also point to Andrea as one of the killers. And I heard her –'

'I do not care what you heard. You want to present the CPS with a case based on a few words that you heard a woman say, not long after you had fucked her, for Christ's sake, and when she was in fear of her life?'

Put like that it did sound pretty thin. But Andrea hadn't been hunting desperately for some acceptable lie, she had been pleading for her life, from the heart. 'Sir, she was telling the truth.'

'She was in fear of her life. You were half stunned and presumably pretty anxious about your prospects too. Were you the best witness? And, if I may repeat, you had just fucked the woman. Defence counsel would smear you all over the court.'

He set his jaw and looked up. 'I'm ready for that, sir.'

'Very noble of you,' sneered Parrish. 'Well, I'm not, John. When that much shit starts flying around it sticks to everyone. We'll get a result with James, close both files with convictions, and that's it, all right?'

It wasn't all right. James hadn't killed Stephanie. Anderson wanted to go on fighting, but he knew that he couldn't. He didn't have the energy. And even if he'd been all in one piece, the appalling fact that he had had sex with Andrea would be there, ready for Parrish to use as ammunition against every argument, every principle. There wasn't any point in going on. He couldn't make himself say, 'Yes, sir,' but he lowered his head and covered his face with his hand.

Parrish watched him for a moment as if he wanted to be certain that he had won. Then he said, 'All right, then, John, I'll leave you to recover. They should be letting you home within a few days. And then I'll arrange for you to have a couple of weeks' leave.'

Anderson's head jerked up and he knew that for a second his shock would have shown in his face. Gardening leave! That would signal to everybody that he was in disgrace. 'Sir, I'd rather get back to the office as soon as I'm fit. Next week. I could be back next week.'

Slowly Parrish shook his head. He was enjoying this, the malevolent bastard. 'Two weeks' leave, John. Minimum. Fielding will sort out putting the case against Maguire together. I just want you to take all the time you need.' He turned to the door, seemed to be struck by a thought and turned back. 'Oh, and John.'

'Sir.'

'Next time, keep your prick in your pocket. All right?'

Anderson wasn't going to show Parrish how he felt. He kept his eye contact steady and his voice level. 'Yes, sir.'

Parrish stared at him for a long moment, then turned and

marched out of the room. He didn't bother to close the door.

Anderson slumped back in his chair and closed his eyes. He sat quite still for a couple of minutes, then got up with an effort and walked slowly across to the window. He placed his hands on the windowsill and let his forehead rest against the cool glass. It failed to soothe the pounding in his head.

Less than a week ago he had sat at dinner with Catherine and told her about himself and his work. 'I'm good at my job. I make as few mistakes as possible.'

Well, he had made a bloody big one now, hadn't he?

Whatever had got into him? What had he been trying to prove? That Catherine wasn't the only woman that found him attractive? That he was a better lover than James Maguire, whom he detested? A mistake like that, just because he was on the rebound. God, it was pathetic. Andrea had set herself out to be attractive to him, she had seduced him. He had told Catherine that he didn't like to be used, but Andrea Maguire had used him so successfully that she was going to get away with murder.

He hadn't even kept to his own rules of investigation. How often had he lectured Fielding and McKie: base your theories on the facts, all the facts, not your interpretation of them. Don't come to any conclusion until you're sure you understand everything. And he hadn't understood everything. He hadn't understood why James had killed Stephanie, which of course he hadn't, or how he had coerced Andrea into selling the forged works, which he probably hadn't either.

He moved away from the window and slumped again into the slippery visitor's chair. He wanted to bury his head in his hands, but his left arm was in a sling. His head drooped and he closed his eyes as if he could shut out the world.

For a moment he saw himself disobeying Parrish, arresting Andrea, interrogating her, presenting the case to the CPS, testifying against her in court. And he saw her looking at him from the dock, and saying – what? That he had slept with her to entrap her? That she had made up her confession to arouse him, as part of their sexual games?

It was impossible. He would be a laughing stock. He had

to do as Parrish wanted, he had no choice.

Footsteps in the corridor. They didn't pass the door. A nurse, maybe, wondering why he was out of bed. In a minute she would come in and treat him like a four-year-old, the way nurses always did.

The footsteps came slowly into the room. He didn't lift his head or open his eyes.

Then a warm, hesitant voice said softly, 'John.'

He didn't look up at once. Catherine! And she had seen him like this, bowed, beaten, hopeless. She would pity him. He wouldn't be able to bear it. She would want to know what had happened. She would want him to lay his stupidity bare so that she could commiserate with him.

He lifted his head and saw her flinch. It didn't help to know that he looked repulsive, beaten and bruised and bandaged. He said, 'Catherine.' His voice was harshly controlled. Well, better harsh than shaking.

She was wearing business clothes, a smart dark grey suit, a close-fitting black body, a simple gold necklace. Her professional appearance contrasted with her uncertain stance, her twisting hands. 'John. I heard on the news, I heard you were hurt. I –' She swallowed hard. 'I didn't want to – send you flowers or something, it's so impersonal. So I came to say, I hope you feel better soon.'

Why didn't she just admit that she wanted him and what he could give her just as much as he wanted her? She was exploiting his weakness, while she concealed hers. He looked down at the floor and said, 'Thanks.'

She took a little step to one side. His coldness was upsetting her. Right now he found it hard to care. 'Is it – bad?' she asked hesitantly.

'They're keeping me in for observation. Concussion, two broken ribs, suspected fracture in my left wrist, possible spleen damage,' he said, as if he was talking about someone else. 'I should be out by the end of the week. Then I'll take a couple of weeks off. I think I'll go up to my place in Scotland and really relax.'

He met her eyes, his face neutral, revealing nothing. She seemed to hunt for words, then said, 'Well, I hope –They said on the news that a man was helping the police. I hope that means that you –'

'Got a result?' He couldn't keep the bitterness from his voice. 'Yes. I think you could say that.'

'John –' Her voice, her face showed that he had hurt her. For a moment he thought that she would say so. If she would open up to him, then perhaps he could tell her how he really felt. But she twisted her hands together and jerked up her head and said in a bright businesslike voice, 'Well, I hope you feel better very soon.' She smiled, a travesty of the warm, generous smile he knew. ''Bye, then.'

He said, 'Goodbye.'

She looked into his face, then dropped her eyes and turned away.

All he had to do was speak her name. One word, and she would come back to him.

But his failure choked him, and he couldn't speak.

## CRIME & PASSION

# DEADLY AFFAIRS
by
Juliet Hastings
ISBN: 0 7535 0029 9
Publication date: 17 April 1997

Eddie Drax is a playboy businessman with a short fuse and taste for blondes. A lot of people don't like him: ex-girlfriends, business rivals, even his colleagues. He's not an easy man to like. When Eddie is found asphyxiated at the wheel of his car, DCI John Anderson delves beneath the golf-clubbing, tree-lined respectability of suburban Surrey and uncovers the secret – and often complex – sex-lives of Drax's colleagues and associates.

He soon finds that Drax was murdered – and there are more killings to come. In the course of his investigations, Anderson becomes personally involved in Drax's circle of passionate women, jealous husbands and people who can't be trusted. He also has plenty of opportunities to find out more about his own sexual nature.

**This is the first in the series of John Anderson mysteries.**

## CRIME & PASSION

## A MOMENT OF MADNESS
by
Pan Pantziarka
ISBN: 0 7535 0024 8
Publication date: 17 April 1997

Tom Ryder is the charismatic head of the Ryder Forum – an organisation teaching slick management techniques to business people. Sarah Fairfax is investigating current management theories for a television programme called *Insight* and is attending a course at the Ryder Hall. All the women on the course think Ryder is dynamic, powerful and extremely attractive. Sarah agrees, but this doesn't mean that she's won over by his evangelical spiel; in fact, she's rather cynical about the whole thing.

When one of the course attendees – a high-ranking civil servant – is found dead in his room from a drugs overdose, Detective Chief Inspector Anthony Vallance is called in to investigate. Everyone has something to hide, except for Sarah Fairfax who is also keen to find out the truth about this suspicious death. As the mystery deepens and another death occurs, Fairfax and Vallance compete to unearth the truth. They discover dark, erotic secrets, lethal dangers and, to their mutual irritation, each other.

**This is the first in a series of Fairfax and Vallance mysteries.**

## CRIME & PASSION

# INTIMATE ENEMIES
by
Juliet Hastings
ISBN: 0 7535 0155 4
Publication date: 15 May 1997

Francesca Lyons is found dead in her art gallery. The cause of
death isn't obvious but her bound hands suggest foul play.
The previous evening she had an argument with her husband,
she had sex with someone, and two men left messages on the
gallery's answering machine. Detective Chief Inspector
Anderson has plenty of suspects but can't find anyone with a
motive.

When Stephanie Pinkney, an art researcher, is found dead in
similar circumstances, Anderson's colleagues are sure the culprit
is a serial killer. But Anderson is convinced that the murders
are connected with something else entirely. Unravelling the
threads leads him to Andrea Maguire, a vulnerable, sensuous art
dealer with a quick-tempered husband and unsatisfied desires.
Anderson can prove Andrea isn't the killer and finds himself
strongly attracted to her. Is he making an untypical and
dangerous mistake?

*Intimate Enemies* **is the second in the series
of John Anderson mysteries.**

## CRIME & PASSION

# A TANGLED WEB
by
Pan Pantziarka
ISBN: 0 7535 0156 2
Publication date: 19 June 1997

Michael Cunliffe was ordinary. He was an accountant for a
small charity. He had a pretty wife and an executive home in a
leafy estate. Now he's been found dead: shot in the back of the
head at close range. The murder bears the hallmark of a
gangland execution.

DCI Vallance soon discovers Cunliffe wasn't ordinary at all. The
police investigation lifts the veneer of suburban respectability
to reveal blackmail, extortion, embezzlement, and a network of
sexual intrigue. One of Cunliffe's businesses has been the
subject to an investigation by the television programme, *Insight*,
which means that Vallance has an excuse to get in touch again
with Sarah Fairfax. Soon they're getting on each other's nerves
and in each other's way, but they cannot help working well
together.

**A Tangled Web is the second in the series
of Fairfax and Vallance mysteries.**

# HOW TO ORDER BOOKS

Please send orders to: **Cash Sales Department, Virgin Publishing Ltd, 332 Ladbroke Grove, London W10 5AH**.

Be sure to include with your order the title, ISBN number, author and price of the book(s) of your choice. With the order, please enclose payment (remembering to include postage and packing) in the form of a cheque or postal order, made payable to **Virgin Publishing Ltd**.

POSTAGE AND PACKING CHARGES

UK and BFPO: £4.99 paperbacks: £1.00 for the first book, 50p for each additional book.
Overseas (including Republic of Ireland): £2.00 for the first book, £1.00 each subsequent book.

You can pay by VISA or ACCESS/MASTERCARD: please write your card number and the expiry date of your card on your order.

*Please don't forget to include your **name, address and daytime telephone number**, so that we can contact you if there is a query with the order. And don't forget to enclose your payment or your credit card details.*

Please allow up to 28 days for delivery.

# A Blakes Cottage for Only £5* per person, per night when you buy any two Crime & Passion books

### Offer is open to UK residents aged 18 and over. Offer closes 12th December 1997.

Booking your Blakes Cottage is easy. Just follow the step-by-step instructions listed below:

1. To book your Blakes Cottage for only £5* per person, per night, simply call 01282 445056, quote the Crime & Passion £5 per person, per night offer and reference MPJ702.

2. The Blakes Holiday Adviser will ask you for the following:
   - the number of adults and children in the party
   - your preferred holiday dates (the duration must be a minimum of one week)
   - you preferred holiday area

3. You will then be offered a choice of selected properties and provided with details of price, location, facilities and accommodation.

4. To confirm the booking you will be asked for full payment by credit card or cheque.

5. Send the completed application form show below, together with two Blakes Cottages/Crime & Passion tokens and a till receipt highlighting your purchase to: Blakes Cottages, The Crime & Passion Offer, Stoney Bank, Earby, Colne, Lancs BB8 6PR.

## Application Form

Title   Mr/Mrs/Ms ...............................................

First Name(s) ...............................................

Surname ...............................................

Address ...............................................

...............................................

...............................................

Postcode ...............................................

Telephone Number ...............................................

```
C & P

One Token

Intimate
Enemies
```

If you do not wish to receive further information and special offers from Virgin Publishing or Blakes Cottages you should write to Blakes Cottages, Dept. DPA, Stoney Bank Road, Earby, Colne, Lancs, BB8 6PR

## Terms and Conditions

1. Each property must be booked at maximum occupancy (i.e. four people cannot occupy a property which sleeps seven).

2. Holidays must start and finish between the following dates: 5 April–23 May; 13 September–17 October; 1 November–19 December 1997 inclusive.

3. All holidays and properties are subject to availability.

4. * Blakes Cottages standard booking terms and conditions apply. These are published in the Blakes Cottages Brochure and are available on request. This offer applies to new bookings only. Blakes Cottages, the name of which is used under licence from Blakes Holidays Limited, is a trading division of Holiday Cottages Group Limited.

   Prices do not include Blakes' compulsory cancellation protection insurance cover (£17 for a family of 4 staying in a £5 per person, per night property). There are additional charges for pets, linen, credit cards payments and additional insurance if required. Details of the relevant amounts are given in Blakes Cottages Brochure or at the time of booking.

5. No cash alternative is available.

6. Closing date for bookings is 12 December 1997.

7. The offer is available only to people over 18 and resident in within the UK. The offer is not open to employees or their families or agents of Holiday Cottages Group Ltd or Virgin Publishing Ltd. All holidays are subject to Blakes Cottages standard Booking Conditions. These are published in the Blakes Cottages Brochure which is available upon request from Blakes Cottages or through any travel agent. Properties are available throughout England, Scotland and Wales.

Blakes Cottages, the name of which is used under licence from Blakes Holidays Limited, is a trading division of Holiday Cottages Group Limited.

Promoters: Virgin Publishing Ltd., 332 Ladbroke Grove, London W10 5AH; TLC Ltd., 48 Harley Street, London W1N 1AD and Blakes Cottages, Stoney Bank Road, Earby, Colne, Lancs BB8 6PR